A Home Subscription! It's the easiest and most convenient way to get every one of the exciting Coventry Romance Novels! ...And you get 4 of them FREE!

You pay nothing extra for this convenience: there are no additional charges...you don't even pay for postage! Fill out and send us the handy coupon now, and we'll send you 4 exciting Coventry Romance novels absolutely FREE!

SEND NO MONEY, GET THESE
FOUR BOOKS
FREE!

CO881

MAIL THIS COUPON TODAY TO:
**COVENTRY HOME
SUBSCRIPTION SERVICE
6 COMMERCIAL STREET
HICKSVILLE, NEW YORK 11801**

YES, please start a Coventry Romance Home Subscription in my name, and send me FREE and without obligation to buy, my 4 Coventry Romances. If you do not hear from me after I have examined my 4 FREE books, please send me the 6 new Coventry Romances each month as soon as they come off the presses. I understand that I will be billed only $9.00 for all 6 books. There are no shipping and handling nor any other hidden charges. There is no minimum number of monthly purchases that I have to make. In fact, I can cancel my subscription at any time. The first 4 FREE books are mine to keep as a gift, even if I do not buy any additional books.

For added convenience, your monthly subscription may be charged automatically to your credit card.

☐ Master Charge   ☐ Visa
      42101   **42101**

Credit Card # _____

Expiration Date _____

Name _____
(Please Print)

Address _____

City _____ State _____ Zip _____

Signature _____

☐ Bill Me Direct Each Month **40105**

Prices subject to change without notice.
Publisher reserves the right to substitute alternate FREE books. Sales tax collected where required by law. Offer valid for new members only.

Lord Brandsley's Bride

by

Claire Lorel

FAWCETT COVENTRY • NEW YORK

LORD BRANDSLEY'S BRIDE

Published by Fawcett Coventry Books, a unit of CBS Publications, the Consumer Publishing Division of CBS Inc.

ISBN: 0-449-50200-7

Printed in the United States of America

First Fawcett Coventry printing: August 1981

10 9 8 7 6 5 4 3 2 1

Lord Brandsley's Bride

chapter one

The Marquess of Brandsley, head of the ancient and honorable house of Despard, narrowed his eyes against the sun and leaned on the pitchfork in his hands, watching a chaise and four bowling at a smart pace along the road to his home, Louth Hall. The soft, annoyed exclamation that left his lips caused his bailiff, standing beside him, to hide a smile. His lordship's gray glance caught it, and was first wrathful and then rueful. He put down the pitchfork—something Mr. Hopley was vastly relieved to see. Although it was gratifying to work for a member of the aristocracy who took a real interest in his estate, and his lordship's agricultural innovations had won his bailiff's first reluctant and then admiring approval, to see the marquess taking part in the laboring tasks of that estate offended every notion of what was due to his consequence.

"It seems my Aunt Crawley is honoring me with an unexpected visit," his lordship said. Impatiently he pushed back sweat-dampened dark hair from his tanned brow, and added, "I had better go and make my apologies for not being at the Hall to receive her."

Since the countess had neglected to give notice of her visit, it might have been supposed that his apologies would be received with a good grace. But when the marquess, correctly attired in Hessian boots, and an impeccable superfine coat over quiet-colored pantaloons and immaculate linen, joined her in one of the salons a bare half-hour after her arrival, her frosty look scarcely thawed under his polite excuses.

Fixing him with a look of disapproval bordering on horror, she inquired, "*Was* that you, Brandsley, that I saw just now along the road, working like a common laborer, and in your *shirtsleeves*?"

"I am afraid it was, my good aunt," the marquess answered imperturbably. "As I have said, your arrival was unexpected."

Lady Crawley's ample bosom swelled and subsided under the influence of some perceptibly strong emotion. "*Really*, Grenville, I knew that you had become absurdly rusticated here, scarcely visiting London for a week at a time, and quite doting on your farms and your new methods of agriculture, but I was not aware that you had become *eccentric!*"

"No, have I?" A grin lightened his strong features. "I was not aware—"

"Eccentrics never are, I believe," said her ladyship crushingly. "But what else do you call wielding a pitchfork in company with your own tenantry's farm labor—"

"I call it capital exercise," her nephew informed her, his voice faintly bored, his lids dropping over his eyes slightly, hiding their expression. "Perhaps you would find it less objectionable if I was to wield a pitchfork on some other landlord's estate?"

"Now you are being ridiculous!" Lady Crawley snapped. "You know very well that is not at all what I meant. If you want exercise, I should think you could find enough in horseriding and hunting, not to mention shooting your own game. Your acres are extensive enough, heaven knows!"

"They are not fulltime occupations," the marquess reminded her.

"Well, you could show your face in town for the season!"

His smile a little less charming than the spontaneous grin that had gone before, he replied, "And get my exercise dancing with insipid society misses at Almacks, and guiding my horse at a sedate trot through a throng of fashionable show-offs in Hyde Park? I thank you, but the prospect does not appeal. I'm grown too old for it."

"Stuff! You are barely five and thirty, Grenville. Not at all too old—you could still marry, if you chose—"

"What—and cut out young Lindo? Much you'd thank me for *that,* ma'am!"

His aunt flushed a little with vexation. "I have never counted on my son's succeeding to your dignities, Brandsley," she said stiffly. "Though if you are going to turn yourself into a *recluse—*"

"An *eccentric* recluse," murmured the marquess. "It has a ring about it, don't you think?"

"If you are going to be a recluse," her ladyship repeated ruthlessly, "you can hardly expect to meet—let alone attach—an eligible lady. And Lindo *is,* after all, your legal heir, which is why I have come to you. For although Crawley loves Lindo as if he were his own son instead of your poor departed uncle's, I *cannot* persuade him to see the necessity of persuading Lindo to be sensible—"

Aware that the point of her visit was on the verge of being revealed, his lordship said lazily, "Possibly Lord Crawley has given up hope of ever seeing Lindo sensible. Since he came of age, the young cawker has indulged in every folly young men commonly engage in who have too much time, too much money and not enough responsibility. Your husband has been an indulgent stepfather—a little *too* kind, perhaps, but my uncle, if he had lived, might have given the same advice. Lindo may be a little foolish, but he is not vicious, and will probably come about of his own accord."

"Vicious! Certainly not!" her ladyship cried, bridling at the aspersion on her firstborn. "He is only too good-natured—" Here she was obliged to break off and fumble in her reticule for a small phial of lavender water to which she had recourse, while the marquess watched, frowning a little.

"Are you quite well, ma'am?" he inquired quietly, as she opened her eyes and raised her head, restoring the phial to its place.

"Thank you," she said faintly, "I shall do. It is only that I am so anxious."

His voice softened a little; Grenville said, "I wish you will tell me what troubles you so. Is Lindo in debt—or in bad company, perhaps? Or—he is a good-looking boy—is it women?"

"It is—a *woman!*" his aunt said tragically.

Preserving a grave countenance with a little difficulty, her nephew said soothingly, "Well, that is not so very bad, you know." He wondered how to question her tactfully as to whether the boy had given some light-skirt a slip on the shoulder, or set one up as his regular mistress, and decided that if he said nothing the whole story would no doubt be poured into his ears.

He was right. It came in fits and starts and was less than a connected tale, but he gathered after ten minutes of patient listening and questioning that Lindo was dangling after a widow, years older than himself, and had hinted to his mother and stepfather that he had met the love of his life, who alone could make him happy.

"But surely, ma'am—I'm persuaded you are upsetting yourself for nothing at all. The boy is obviously in his calf love, and no sensible woman of quality will take him seriously. Depend on it, even if he should be foolish enough to propose, she will decline the match."

"But she is *not* a woman of quality!" wailed the afflicted mother. "She is a *nobody* who got some doting old baronet to marry her when she was yet in her teens, and now that he is dead, she hopes to marry into the peerage. To such a woman as *that*, what does it matter that her husband is ten years younger? It is enough that he is a viscount!"

"Are you sure of your information, ma'am?" asked Grenville slowly.

"It is common knowledge!" she told him. "And it is known that her first husband was wheedled into providing her with *masses* of jewels until she became so greedy that he complained of her almost beggaring him. They lived in the country, but she barely wore her blacks the year, before she put off her mourning and arrived in London and made herself the talk of the town."

"You make her sound like a vulgar harpy." He frowned. "Surely Lindo would not be deceived—"

"Oh, she is not precisely *vulgar,*" her ladyship conceded with angry reluctance. "She has a ladylike air and is received everywhere! She is said to be a beauty, and even has vouchers for Almacks—it is my belief that one of her flirts persuaded Lady Jersey to provide them. But everyone knows she has *no* connections other than those provided by her marriage, and her husband was only a countrified baronet, after all. And why should she come to London and set herself up in a town house, and gain entry to all the *ton* parties unless she is on the catch for a husband? Why, it is perfectly obvious what she is about, and although the gentlemen positively *flock* about her, her husband could have left her no more than comfortably off."

"So she is unlikely to be snapped up by one of the gazetted fortune hunters," Grenville said. "Still—an accredited beauty, even a widow, might well be the choice of some titled widower if she should attach such a man—surely a more attractive catch than a green boy."

Lady Crawley stiffened, her head coming up, the feathers that adorned her satin beehive bonnet trembling alarmingly. "As *I* did?" she inquired in a mortified voice. "I believe the case to have been quite different, however. I did not marry Crawley until five years after your uncle's untimely death, and I assure you, Brandsley, that the welfare of my little son was always uppermost in my mind. At nine years old he needed a father's hand, and Crawley has been, indeed, *more* than a father to him, although in this instance he has—alas!—failed me!"

Deciding to ignore the latter part of this speech, the marquess assured her, with barely hidden impatience in his voice, that he quite realized the cases were entirely different, and that nothing had been further from his mind than any implied criticism of her marrying again after being widowed young, and with the future of her infant son to think of. He kept to himself his opinion of the nature of the Earl of Crawley's affection for his stepson, which from the first had taken the form of indulging him in everything that money could provide for his comfort and entertainment, while skillfully avoiding on every possible occasion both his prolonged company and any necessity to correct his manners, curb his youthful mischief or form his developing character. He was not at all surprised that the earl had refused to bestir himself to the unpleasant task of trying to dampen the boy's infatuation for a handsome older woman.

"Are you sure you are not exaggerating the seriousness of the attachment, ma'am?" he suggested, trying to sound reassuring.

"He thinks, I'm sure, of marriage!" she said. "I believe it is only *my* feelings which have so far prevented him. He is—the dear boy—always tender of them, but he says although it pains him that I cannot approve, his mind is set, and he is sure that when I meet this—creature!—then I must be reconciled."

"One presumes he did not describe her in quite those terms," murmured Grenville.

"He described her in such extravagant terms that I was quite out of patience with him!" the countess said snappishly.

"And refused to meet her, I take it?"

"Certainly I did."

"Was that wise, do you think?" asked Grenville mildly.

"I refuse to give him any reason to suppose that I might be brought to countenance such a *mésalliance*."

"My good aunt, has it not occurred to you that too determined opposition might serve only to make Lindo stubbornly adhere to his infatuation, and possibly lead to a hasty and disastrous conclusion—where an appearance of complaisance, or at least a certain open-mindedness, on your part, might lead him to be a little less headstrong? If the affair can be slowed down a little, his feelings may well burn themselves out in time, with no harm done."

His aunt frowned, her lips compressed. Then, a look of dawning respect on her face, she said, "Brandsley—there are times when you talk a great deal of good sense."

"I thank you. Was it to obtain my advice that you came to visit me?"

"Not precisely. I came to persuade you that it is your duty to speak to Lindo on this matter."

"I hope I have persuaded *you*, that nothing could be more disastrous. Besides, I collect you were not able to persuade Lindo to accompany you?"

"I meant that you should come to London and see him there," Lady Crawley explained impatiently.

"You know I never go to London except when the utmost necessity calls me there."

"I should have thought," the countess said indignantly, "that your cousin's future is of sufficient importance—"

"No, should you?" The marquess was amused.

"Pray do not take that stupidly funning tone with *me*, Grenville!" his aunt snapped, sorely tried.

His eyes glinting a little, her nephew replied, "And I should be obliged if you refrain from using *that* tone to me, ma'am. I will take it from none, I assure you!"

Her color high, she glared back at him, and he relented, smiling faintly. "Come, shall we both forget what has just passed, and agree we are far too high in the instep to apologize to each other? Cox tells me he has directed your baggage to be carried to the Green Room. You know the way, of course, but I shall send Mrs. Bingham to attend you in case there is anything at all you need."

His pull on the bell rope brought his butler in with an alacrity that implied he had been hovering in the hall. Cox had lost the apprehensive look with which he had greeted the marquess on his return from the fields, with the news that as her ladyship had indicated her intention of staying overnight, he had taken the liberty of assigning the Green Room to her use, and carrying some refreshment in to her. He received the news that her ladyship was ready to be conducted to her room, there to be waited on by the housekeeper, with more equanimity than the countesss, who shot a speaking look at her noble nephew as she swept by him and out of the room.

The deference of Mrs. Bingham, saying everything that was proper, supervising the making up of the bed with properly aired, lavender-scented sheets, and personally directing the housemaids, promising that a warming pan should be provided directly, soothed her outraged nerves considerably. After the ministrations of her own maid, Poulett, had been carried out, she felt quite a new woman. Travel-creased garments removed and replaced with a quite new dinner gown of blue sarcenet with a Gothic trim, and a silk turban carefully arranged on newly crimped hair, she sailed down to dine, with her confidence in her ability to bring her nephew about to her own view that his presence in London was urgently necessary, quite restored.

That she failed entirely was not at all her fault. She ran the gamut of wheedling, imperiousness, appeals to duty and family feeling and even resorted again to bravely suppressed tears and lavender water, but nothing availed to move her nephew. He had suggested to her the only course of action which he felt might serve, and was convinced that no good could come of his own counsel added to hers.

At the last she castigated him for an unfeeling, selfish and cold-hearted brute, and became the more angry when he laughed and begged her to have another helping of the excellent veal cutlets provided by his cook.

At length she lapsed into a sulking semisilence, to be coaxed out of it less by her companion's determined efforts to maintain a decent civility than by her own reflection that all the Despards, including her own late first husband, the first Viscount Edgely, were notoriously strong-minded, and that the way to win her point was through guile rather than goading.

She came about again later when tea was served in the drawing room, with a sentimental recital of all that he had meant to his younger cousin from the time Lindo was in short coats. Various incidents were recalled as proof of the affection the cousins had always felt for each other—Lindo's rescue from a watery grave when at the age of five he had fallen into the ornamental lake in the park at Louth Hall ("Hardly," murmured the marquess. "The water at that edge is only inches deep, and he was more muddy than wet.")—Grenville teaching his cousin to shoot at a somewhat later age—Lindo's frequently expressed admiration of his tall, strong, older cousin. "For he always says," the countess said, with an arch little laugh, "that Cousin Brandsley is a *great gun!*"

"I should think the cub must have outgrown the hero-worship stage by now," Grenville said, concealing irritation with amusement. That Lindo should now have passed to an infatuation with some charmer of the female sex, he found not at all surprising and scarcely alarming.

But his aunt, every other weapon exhausted, decided on a last and possibly rash resort. Gathering her forces, she said with great dignity, "I had not thought, Brandsley, that *you* would be blind to the dangers of *such* an attachment. When I think of the *worry* your poor dear mother was in when you announced your intention of marrying that *unsuitable* girl—and what a *relief* must she have felt when the chit ran off with Hawsbridge! Which *must* have proved to you that she was nothing more than a cheap little adventuress—!"

Under the impact of her nephew's arrested but suddenly arctically cold eyes, her tone sharpened into waspishness. "Well, you must know what a narrow escape you had!" she went on. "I should have thought the least you could do would be to make some push to save poor Lindo from falling into the same folly!"

Softly he said, "But I did not fall into any folly, my dear aunt. I must confess I was not aware that my mother had confided in you my youthful scrapes."

From his face it was obvious that he regarded the news without relish. Trying to make a recovery, for it seemed she had succeeded only in arousing his quite formidable hostility, Lady Crawley said tartly, "Of course she did! Dear Lavinia and I were the greatest of friends. And when you became involved with that cit's daughter, she naturally confided her anxieties to me. And if she were alive today, I *know* she would adjure you to do your utmost for my poor Lindo!" An affecting catch in her voice, her ladyship raised a hand to her eyes. "For her sake, indeed, if not for mine—"

"For God's sake, ma'am—!" Grenville exclaimed, driven almost beyond endurance.

"Grenville!"

"I beg pardon," he said in clipped tones. "If it will satisfy you, Aunt, I shall engage to come to London if, after meeting the lady in question, you still feel there is cause for alarm. I should advise you to take note of her manner with young Lindo, and if she treats him with marked favor I promise to obey directly should you send me a summons to come."

With that she was obliged to be satisfied. It did not content her entirely, but was so much more than he had at first been willing to concede that she left the following morning tolerably pleased with her mission. It was perhaps unfortunate that tact deserted her again as he handed her into the chaise for her return journey, and led her to add to her anxious reminder of his promise, the rider that a sojourn in London would do him a great deal of good in any case. "For I'm sure I never thought to see the Marquess of Brandsley in his *shirt-sleeves* and laboring like a common farmer. I know you took over the estate when your father died, and it was that which you made the excuse for leaving London and retiring to the country, but plenty of gentlemen manage their properties without spending the entire year on them—why, you scarcely even appear in the House. I can tell you, we looked for you to come to London for the season, at least, in the first year or two after your father died, if only to find a wife."

His smile was satirical. "I'll be bound all the mammas with marriageable daughters were bitterly disappointed when I did not appear," he said. "It was precisely what I did *not* want, and I'm heartily glad to have avoided the matchmakers."

"All these years!" his aunt exclaimed, exasperated. "Well, let me tell you, you would do well to find an eligible girl before you become too old to attract anyone except a girl who would marry *anyone* for a title and money. You may still be good-looking enough to amuse yourself with the local peasantry, but once a man reaches his forties, even the commonest girl will look elsewhere, and *they* cannot give you a legitimate heir."

Looking faintly startled, he regarded her steadily nevertheless. "You're very generous, considering if I don't marry, Lindo remains my heir. But let me assure you, ma'am, I'm not in the habit of 'amusing' myself with the daughters of my tenants, nor of scattering my bastards about the countryside," he concluded, matching her outspokenness. "Let me assure you that I shall be quite happy for Lindo to carry on the family name and title, in the event that I never marry. And although I'm not in my dotage yet, as you have pointed out, the prospect becomes less likely with time."

"Lavinia was right!" her ladyship said unexpectedly, making him frown. "She *said* that girl had a lot to answer for—how *very* right she was!"

The blankness in his face changed to ironic comprehension. "Perhaps," he acknowledged. "But you are speaking of past history, I think, ma'am. That is nothing to the point now, I assure you."

He stepped back, bowed and closed the door on her, spoke to the postilions and watched as the chaise bowled away. His mouth had assumed a grim little smile. The picture his aunt evidently cherished of himself as a broken-hearted lover was distasteful to him, and even more so the nagging thought that his mother's confidence was not certainly safe from repetition. He had thought that only his parents had been aware that he had asked Catriona Bankes to marry him, and that she had accepted his suit, before she ran off unexpectedly with a man old enough to be her father, but reputed to be quite fabulously wealthy. At twenty-four he had been his father's heir and in receipt of a gen-

17

erous allowance, but Catriona had obviously preferred a presently wealthy bird in the hand to one whose future depended on a father who at forty-nine had appeared at the peak of health. That only a few months after she had united her future to Sir Walter Hawsbridge's, the fourth marquess was carried off by an untimely chill which turned to pneumonia, was a trick of fate which at the time Grenville had savagely hoped would sting her as her defection had stung him.

His only faint comfort at the time was that although his pursuit of the pretty Miss Bankes had hardly been secret, the humiliation of being actually, though privately, betrothed to her before she flew to her elderly lover's arms was not known to one and all. Now he must wonder how many others had been told—in the strictest confidence, of course—by his Aunt Crawley. The idea of being laughed at by the *ton* was decidedly unpleasant, although the thought of Miss Bankes herself—whose face he had not called to mind for years—caused him nothing more than a faint disgust, etched with sincere relief that he had not had time to commit the ultimate idiocy of marrying her.

He looked at the ancient stones of his home, the high towers that had been built in the time of the Normans, the later wings with leaded windows looking out over the moat, and thought how glad he was that he had not made Catriona its mistress. Blinded by infatuation, he had thought her hoydenish ways delightfully natural and high-spirited; now he looked back and thought them vulgar. Her taste for bright colors and fashionable gimcrack, which had seemed symbols of a gay and happy disposition, now appeared as plain bad taste, and he shuddered as he pictured her replacing the ancient tapestries and gracious hangings with machine woven materials in garish colors, and filling the gracious old rooms with gilded tables and Egyptian sofas piled with tasseled cushions.

It was a long time since his heart had ached for her. That no other lady had so touched it, he admitted was his misfortune. There had occasionally been women who pleased him for a time, but he fancied his aunt was right, and he would not find a wife in the country.

There were single ladies residing in the parish, but those of a suitable age were not only plain; they bored him. And the younger ones, he admitted to himself, bored him even more. He was, he supposed, a great deal too nice in his notions. The idea of casting his eyes over the current crop of hopeful young ladies during the marriage mart of the London season had slightly repelled him even in his greentime—as one of the more eligible young bachelors from the time of his coming-of-age he had been a target for several years before he had met Catriona.

There had been some girls he liked, and several that he was briefly but mildly in love with—mostly those with whom it was the fashion that season to be in love. But with Catriona Bankes he was head over ears. Until then, the life of a young man about town had been infinitely preferable to the shackles of the married state. Hunting and shooting in season, racing against other young bloods, a bit of sparring for fun and fitness, and a certain amount of gambling in gentlemen's clubs in company with congenial friends had seemed a pleasantly full life. He would have liked to have gone into the army, but as his father's only son he had to admit the force of the arguments the older man produced against buying him a commission.

Now his estate occupied his time and his mind almost exclusively. His father had left it in good heart, but times were expensive, and old-fashioned ways no longer sufficient to keep up healthy revenues from the land. He could wish that his father had been more willing to allow him to take part in the administration of the lands before he succeeded to the title and the estates, but it had been the previous marquess's nature to be the only master, and he had brusquely brushed off any suggestion of delegating any estate matters to his son, merely growling that "The lad's turn will come, and soon enough. Let him enjoy his youth while he can."

Grenville did not entirely share his sire's views. In his own case his father's relatively early demise had enabled him to take up the reins at about the time he had become thoroughly bored and disillusioned with a life of unlimited pleasures. His young cousin Lindo, succeeding to his father's estates and dignities too early to be capable of managing them, had been provided by his stepfather's influence and the estate's revenues with an excellent agent whom he was still content to leave in charge of Greatstones. Grenville had little doubt that he would eventually settle there for most of the year and administer the place himself, finding it a satisfying occupation.

He hoped so. He most fervently hoped that Lindo's mother would not find it necessary to summon his cousin from Norfolk to assist her in her efforts to prevent him from contracting a disastrous marriage. Grenville strongly suspected that the countess's alarm was mere female flummery, for she had always been an overprotective mother and very prone to flying into unnecessary fusses.

But only a few days later a letter arrived at the Hall which made it necessary for him to redeem his promise, and made him wonder if perhaps he had been too sanguine. The countess, it seemed, was seriously alarmed, and there was "No time to be Lost." Lindo was talking of "Making an Offer for The Creature's hand." The woman herself had boldly hinted to Lady Crawley that Lindo's mother might look to have her for a daughter-in-law.

Frowning, Grenville prepared himself for a journey to London.

chapter two

"*Damaris, dear!*" Mrs. Newington said in faintly scandalized tones. "Are you certain it will stay *up?* So very *daring—*"

Before her niece could answer, the dressmaker, twitching the tiny sleeves of the dress into place, barely on the smooth shoulders of her lovely client, sniffed, "But of course, it will, *madame*. The cut will insure it— and Lady Waring, if I may venture to say so, has just the figure for it. It is perfection!"

Damaris surveyed herself critically in the long mirror, her unusual, golden brown eyes sweeping over the fashionable cut and curl of her glossy, mahogany-colored hair, a straight nose and a firmly pretty mouth to a nicely rounded chin, a slim neck and the high firm bosom which the champagne silk of the snugly fitting bodice scarcely covered. Her slim waist needed no boned stays beneath the straight fall of the high-waisted skirt, and her legs were long enough to wear the fashion to advantage. She did briefly put her hand over the fair skin exposed by the low neck of the gown, in an access of modesty. But the remembered sting of a carelessly loud comment on her evident rustical notions of fashion, overheard when she had first come to London from Somerset, overcame her own scruples. She hastened to reassure her aunt. "It is the fashion," she said lightly to Mrs. Newington, removing her hand and shrugging her shoulders to test the truth of the dressmaker's assurances. The material was firm and did not slip in spite of its precarious-looking position, and she laughed and said, "I assure you, Aunt Tabby, I shall not be in the least out of the way—I daresay no one will look twice at me!"

"As to that, my lady," the dressmaker said, "I beg to differ. Your ladyship will allow me to say that in this dress you will turn many heads! Not—" she added hastily, seeing an I-told-you-so expression on the older lady's rounded face, "not that it is in the least improper—it is only a perfect foil for your ladyship's beauty."

Damaris turned off the compliment with a small laugh, aware that the dressmaker's livelihood depended on flattery of various sorts. But her aunt, although her watery blue eyes softened in fond agreement, said with all the tartness of which her soft, fading voice was capable, "Yes, well, that's as may be, but when I was your age, Damaris, we didn't wear dresses such as are worn these days—so flimsy, and often with not a petticoat or even a shift for the sake of decency—I can't help feeling it's a little shocking, even though I know Lady Waterford was wearing one at *least* as daring the other night at her own rout party—and it's true you *do* have the figure for it, for *she* looked far less elegant than you do, my love! Being a trifle plump—"

Damaris smiled at her affectionately. "Well, at least I don't *damp* my gowns, dearest Aunt."

"I should hope not, indeed. Why, apart from being shockingly immodest, it must be a very unhealthy practice! I wish you would not even think of it, for I'm convinced that is why that vulgar Letty Lonsdale sickened so—and they say she is in a decline."

"I don't think of it," Damaris reassured her. "This one, at least, is very elegant just as it is." She smiled at the gratified dressmaker and turned for the tiny buttons at the back to be undone. "It will do very well for Mrs. Brassington's ball."

As the modiste's fingers worked on the buttons, Mrs. Newington said, "I must say, my love, you don't look in the least like the *Dowager* Lady Waring in that dress!"

A tiny frown of anxiety appeared between fine winged eyebrows. "Is it too young for me?" Damaris asked.

"No, no!" Her aunt hastened to disclaim that notion. "Good gracious, I didn't mean *that!* Only that you look far too young for the title. If anything, the dress is too—too elegantly *mature* for one who is still only a girl!"

A faint shadow in her eyes, Damaris said, "But I am *not* a girl—I'm more than five and twenty, and a widow, Aunt. I cannot dress in frilled white muslin and love knots, you know."

"I suppose not," her aunt sighed. "But I wish you would not talk as though you were not quite young. Five and twenty is no great age, after all. And I'm sure I know at least a dozen young men who would agree with me that to be thinking of yourself as past your youth is ridiculous. Mr. Woodfall, Mr. Aslett, Viscount Edgely—"

"Please, Aunt Tabby, do stop!" Damaris cried, her cheeks flushed with embarrassment at this catalogue of her conquests pouring into the dressmaker's ears. She could only hope that the woman's next client would not be regaled with a recital of them.

Mrs. Brassington was a notable hostess, her private ball an occasion for a very creditable squeeze of fashionable persons to exchange views on the décor, the dancing and the entertainment and food provided. The decorations, featuring card cutouts of gilded angels, were pronounced original; the dancing, which included the waltz and a quadrille, daring; and the soprano soloist very fine. Mr. Brummell himself set the seal on the evening by arriving just in time to partake of a mouthful of duckling and an Italian salad at suppertime.

Grenville arrived at the ball with his cousin. It was years since he had attended such an affair, and his ears rang first with the noise of the horses and carriages that thronged Mayfair as they conveyed their rich and fashionable owners to all the *ton* parties, and then with the loud hum of extravagant conversations that filled the rooms in which a blaze of candles struck sparks from the jewels worn by the women and illuminated the fashionably startling waistcoats of the men. His own evening dress was quietly colored but well cut. In knee breeches and silk stockings with a coat the color of his cloud gray eyes, he felt a little odd, for at Louth he seldom bothered with formality.

Lindo was eagerly scanning the ballroom. Thank God, Grenville thought, the boy had got over his first fit of sullens which had quickly followed the initial pleasure of welcoming the head of his family. No fool, Lindo. No sooner did he hear that Grenville had not determined the duration of his stay in town, and had come straight to his cousin and aunt on his arrival, than the clear blue eyes darkened in suspicion.

"Mamma has sent for you, hasn't she?" he blurted out, his fair head thrown defiantly back. "Well, I may as well tell you, Brandsley, it's of no use trying to persuade me, for my mind's made up!"

"In the first place," his older cousin drawled, "you should know that I have no intention of *persuading* you to anything, for a more bullheaded whelp I've yet to meet, and I'm well aware I would be wasting my breath. And in the second place, perhaps you would care to enlighten me as to what particular corkbrained action you have in that *made-up* mind of yours, now?"

His belligerent air melting a trifle, Lindo said uncertainly, "Well, if you *don't* mean to—Not but what I'm sure she *did* send for you, for I know she went to Louth—and it is not corkbrained! I mean to marry Lady Waring."

"Who is Lady Waring?"

Suspiciously, Lindo regarded him. "Surely Mamma told you—"

"I have never heard the lady's name in my life," Grenville said truthfully, forbearing to inform the viscount of the other information his anxious parent had imparted. "Who is she?" he repeated.

"She is—oh, Grenville, she is a goddess!" Seeing the smile, compounded of amusement, affection and cynicism, which touched his cousin's mouth, the young man flushed. "Well, I am not the only one to think so!" he said defensively. "She is a widow—why, she must have been married from the cradle!" he exclaimed indignantly. "And her husband's name is perfectly respectable!" he finished.

Grenville's eyebrows rose just a fraction. "Do I take it her own connections are less so?" he inquired.

"No! That is, I am not perfectly sure—one doesn't *ask*, of course—"

"Of course!"

"But her manners are faultless, and her aunt—she has an aunt who lives with her—a very proper female. And in any case, it don't signify!"

"Of course not," Grenville said soothingly. "I collect the size of her fortune is—insignificant, as well?"

"I don't *care* for that!" Lindo said fiercely. "My own is enough for us both."

"I see. I collect felicitations are in order?"

"Well—as to that—not quite yet," Lindo said unhappily.

Grenville was silent.

"The thing is," Lindo said, "I have not precisely asked her yet. She is—I think she looks on me with—with favor, but there are so many other cursed fellows always about her, and even when I visit her, if she is not *surrounded* by them, her aunt is by, and—Lord, Grenville, how does one get a gently bred female alone? I can't propose to her in the midst of 'em, can I?"

Grenville, torn between sympathy and laughter, did not tell his young cousin that in his place he would have simply demanded a private interview. He said gently, "I think one waits for the lady to indicate that she would—welcome being alone with you. If *she*

25

wishes it, a hint will be enough to procure you the privacy that you desire."

"I *have* hinted!" the young man said in despair.

"Then perhaps the lady is not yet ready to receive your addresses," Grenville suggested mildly.

Suspicion hovered over Lindo's face. "If that is meant to be a put-off—"

"It is meant to be very good advice. Nothing will be gained by rushing your fences, and if she is unsure of her feelings, you risk a rebuff—which will make it hard for you to come about and attempt her again. How long have you known her?"

"Two months. If that is not long enough for me to know my mind, let me tell you—"

"Long enough for *you* perhaps," Grenville interrupted. "But a woman's heart is not often so quickly won. If she smiles on you—"

"She does! More so than on any other man, I swear!"

Grenville's eyes narrowed a trifle as he surveyed the eager young face and slight, youthful form of his cousin. But he said merely, "Then I imagine a short period of patience is called for. It is polite in these affairs, you know, to let the lady set the pace."

When he left the viscount he was tolerably satisfied with his morning's work, for he thought that Lindo was disposed to be thoughtful, and would give some heed to his advice. But the boy's own account of the lovely widow's behavior had given the marquess himself food for thought. Her evasion of Lindo's hints argued an unwillingness to receive the proposals which she must have guessed he meant to make. And yet his conviction that she favored him above her other flirts indicated that she certainly did not mean to lose him. Even if the preference was mainly in his own bemused imagination, Lindo was not obtuse, and it was evident that she at least encouraged him enough to keep him dangling after her. An accomplished flirt might do so simply to demonstrate her pretty power and minister to her own vanity. An adventuress might be keeping him in reserve in case she failed to bring some better matrimonial prospect up to scratch.

He had not yet seen his aunt, who had been out when

he called at Lord Crawley's London house. Lindo had not yet set up his own establishment or installed himself in lodgings, possibly because his mother would have raised tearful objections. He was her only child, two daughters of her second marriage having died in infancy, and Grenville was aware that although her solicitude chafed Lindo, he was too goodnatured to hurt his mother unnecessarily. Which made his determination to offer for the unsuitable Lady Waring the more serious.

When the marquess did see his aunt the following day, he was perhaps more receptive to her increased concern. She came to his house in Cavendish Square when he had barely eaten his breakfast, and poured the tale of her meeting with Lady Waring into his resigned ears.

"She called Lindo her *most particular friend!*" she told him tragically. "And said she knew very well to whom she owed the honor of my visiting her—you can imagine with what a knowing look! And when I brought up the subject of the Princess Charlotte's engagement, she was most *pointed* in her opinion that young people should not be—as she said—*at the mercy of their parents* when it comes to matrimony. When I ventured to hint that I hoped *my* son would never marry to disoblige his family, and that I was confident his affection for me would prevent it, she looked me boldly in the face and said she fancied he would marry whom he chose, and it *would be wise* in me not to strain his affection by showing my disapproval. For if I did, I might lose it altogether. It was a *threat,* I know it! The particular way she looked—such a stubborn, angry air—! And when I said that *nothing* would prevail on me to accept an alliance with a young woman of no fortune and no family, with nothing to recommend her, and that Lindo would be guided by my advice and his family's, she laughed in a hard, vulgar way, and said, 'Well, ma'am, we shall just have to see, shan't we, which of us is right?' I tell you, Grenville, she means to have him, I know it! And the poor boy is in her clutches—he will not hear a word against her."

Grenville refrained from adding to her distress by

recounting the details of his own interview with Lindo. That the matter was more serious than he had at first supposed, he could not now doubt. It appeared the lady was so sure of her youthful swain's devotion that she had not scrupled to antagonize his mother. Thoughtfully, he said, "If the boy is so besotted, I should advise you to take pains not to criticize, Aunt. Try, if you can, to assume an air of perhaps somewhat reluctant complaisance—and leave the rest to me."

"If you think *you* can influence him where I have failed—" the countess said, somewhat illogically, since it was precisely what she had tried to persuade him to do.

"I shan't try," the marquess said, a smile hovering about his mouth which gave her a sudden twinge of unease, his eyes narrowed and looking away from her. "I fancy there is another way of going about the business which will answer far better. If Lindo is determined to remain fixed in his intention, the thing to do is obviously—divert the lady. I think I shall remain fixed in town for some time."

Mrs. Brassington's ballroom held enough people to be sure of earning her ball the accolade of being one of the celebrated squeezes of the season, but Lindo's eyes soon lit on the one face above all others that he wished to see.

"There she is!" he said almost reverently, grasping his cousin's arm. "Talking to Aslett and—" his face darkened a little with annoyance, "—and Haines, by God!"

"What has poor Haines done to earn your displeasure?" Grenville inquired curiously.

"You must know the fellow is nothing but a damned rake, Gren," Lindo said. "The thing is *she* is so innocent, she don't know it, and I hate to see him about her."

"Does she not?" murmured Grenville, his eyes on the lady as she smiled and inclined her head to Lord Alfred Haines, who was leaning over to speak in her ear. She looked a handsome young woman with a beautifully proportioned figure shown to advantage by the low-necked gown that seemed in danger of slipping from her shoulders.

As Lindo urged him over to her side, he expected to find the lovely face at close quarters carefully overlaid by powder and rouge to preserve the illusion of youth, but as she turned to his cousin's greeting, he realized with a shock that Lady Crawley had exaggerated the difference in age. Her complexion was not the milk white of fashion, but only the most jealous of tabbies could have labeled it sallow. And its clear, healthy sheen, the palest golden cream in color, owed nothing to artifice. Her quick smile, certainly more warm and natural than the one she had recently bestowed on Haines, when turned on Lindo showed white and even teeth, and the eyes which looked curiously into Grenville's when Lindo begged leave to introduce him, were clear and bright, and a most unusual shade of sherry brown. She could not be more than four or five years older than Lindo, at most.

He had no need to feign admiration of her looks as he bowed over her hand, but when he raised his head he saw that her smile had become fixed, and there was a wary look in her eyes. When she made to withdraw her hand, he retained it for a moment in tightened fingers, and saw a quick flash of anger in the sherry-colored depths before he released her.

The orchestra striking up, Haines claimed her hand and led her off to dance, and Grenville, a tiny frown between his brows, answered absent-minded agreement to Lindo's demands to know if he did not feel obliged to admit that Lady Waring was undoubtedly the loveliest woman in the room.

Later he solicited her hand for a waltz, and she accepted after a hesitation that was brief but pointed. She danced lightly in his very correct embrace, but his eyes on her face found it averted, her own eyes cast down. He had seen her animated, dancing with others, and determined if he could to discover the reason for her reserve with him.

"You have known my cousin long, Lady Waring?" he asked politely.

Her eyes fleetingly met his. "Only since the beginning of the year," she answered coolly. "Before that I was—living in the country."

"This is not, surely, your first visit to London?"

"Yes, it is," she said. "My husband was not fond of society."

"You were widowed quite recently, I believe?"

"It is over a year, Lord Brandsley." Her tone was steady, but his hand on her waist felt the slight stiffening of her body, and he fancied that her cheeks flushed slightly with something other than the exertion of the dance.

He murmured proper words of condolence, and she accepted them with a brief word and a slight nod.

Trying again, he said, "Are you enjoying your stay in town?"

"Very much. We—my aunt and I have taken a house in Harley Street, and from the first we have found London very congenial. We visited the British Museum and saw the Parthenon marbles exhibited, and have been to Somerset House to view the paintings in the Exhibition Room. And in January we were fortunate to see Mr. Kean as Shylock at the Drury Lane theater."

He wondered if she was trying to impress him with the seriousness of her tastes, and decided to attempt a more direct approach. "I would not have taken you for a bluestocking," he said, and waited for her reaction.

She flashed him a look that held uncertain laughter, and said, "No, sir, why should you?"

"I shan't, if you tell me you have also visited Astley's for the circus, and seen Mr. Bullock's museum in Piccadilly, and gawped—I beg your pardon—*gazed* at the Crown Jewels in the Tower."

A reluctant smile curved the corner of her mouth that he could see. As he whirled her into a turn at one end of the room, she said, "The Tower, sir, is a repository of history; we found it extremely edifying." She ventured a glance at him and seeing his raised eyebrow let the smile turn to a brief, attractive laugh. "And Mr. Astley's circus is very diverting. As for Bullock's Museum—it is—it is most interesting. I have heard it described as 'one of the most refined, rational and interesting exhibitions the metropolis has ever witnessed.'"

"Did you find it so?" he demanded, recalling the crowded rooms filled with a jumble of antiquities, stuffed African animals and exotic birds, and ancient armor that he had once visited with Lindo.

"I found it fascinating," she said, with unmistakable candor. "I have never seen a stuffed elephant before— *nor* a rhinoceros, or zebra. And my aunt was quite frightened by a snake climbing up one of the palm trees round the enclosure. It looked almost uncomfortably realistic!"

Grenville began to perceive how his cousin had been able to call the lady an innocent. Her initial constraint had vanished, and remembered enjoyment animated her face so that she had the appearance of a young girl enjoying her first season.

"Did you not see the Royal Menagerie when you visited the Tower?" he asked her.

"Why, no. There was a great crowd of people, and my aunt became very tired, so we were obliged to return home after seeing the Crown Jewels. But I hope to return there another time."

"You are fixed in London for the present, then?"

"For the present, yes."

There seemed a hint of uncertainty in her voice, but he was given no time to assess its cause. The smile had vanished and her eyes, raised to his, held them with a particular expression that he could not interpret. "And you, Lord Brandsley," she inquired. "Shall you be in London for long?"

Promptly he replied, "I have this moment decided, Lady Waring, to remain for an indefinite stay, if you will allow me the pleasure of calling on you and your aunt in Harley Street tomorrow."

Her foot missed a step, and he steadied her within his arm. She murmured, "We should be honored, of course," but her face lost its animation, her eyes remaining downcast, and her mouth firmly closed for the remainder of the dance, except when his determined efforts to maintain a conversation forced a polite reply from her.

Ruefully he wondered if his plans had suffered a setback already, since the lady appeared to have taken him in dislike. The possibility that she was shy he confidently discarded, since her manner to every other gentleman she danced and spoke with was too obviously unaffectedly easy, and sometimes bordered on flirtatious. Her smile was bewitching, her laughter frequent although not vulgarly loud, and her conversation animated enough to keep a small crowd of young and more mature men amused in the intervals between dances.

Lindo might have said something to prejudice her, but he doubted if the boy's initial suspicion of his presence in London had lasted long enough for him to have done so.

He was not unaware of the good looks which enhanced the attraction of his name, rank and fortune, for he had seldom suffered a rebuff, and he knew that he had sufficient address to please most women. His reputation was honorable, and his temper, though formidable when roused, was not so touchy that he had earned a name for its quickness. Not deigning to join the little court that was gathered about Lady Waring, he stood a small distance off and watched her as her swains vied for her attention. At one point she looked up. He did not withdraw his glance, and she lifted her chin for a moment, her eyes coolly blank, and turned away with a haughtiness worthy of a duchess, covering the pretty bosom, on which his eyes had been resting appreciatively, with an ivory-sticked painted fan.

Lindo was hovering by her side, and she turned to him, touching his sleeve and smiling with that special sweetness that Grenville had noted earlier, as she spoke to the boy.

A slight sense of pique which Grenville had experienced at her coldness to himself turned to a slow, calculating anger. Already determined to make the lady aware of the attractions of his own superior rank and fortune over Lindo's, for his cousin's sake, he was now more set than ever in his purpose, and for a more personal reason. He disliked the unaccustomed sensation of being slighted by a woman—and a woman who had nothing to recommend her but her looks and a coquettish manner. His lips curled in a slight, hard smile, Grenville turned away. Lady Waring, in the not very distant future, would pay for that indifferent, haughty glance. Before, he had thought that to dangle his title and his money before her mercenary eyes would suffice to prevent her accepting Lindo, at least until the boy outgrew his infatuation. He had not thought of touching her heart. Now, nothing would suffice but that she would love him, so far as that mercenary organ would allow. And she would love unrequited.

It did not occur to him that it was an extravagant revenge for a minor transgression against his pride, nor that she had wakened long-dormant vengeful feelings which properly should have been directed at another woman. He did not think of Catriona, but only of Damaris, Lady Waring, who was going to regret slighting a Despard, and a Marquess of Brandsley.

chapter three

When the marquess made his promised call in Harley Street the following day, Damaris was entertaining other guests, Lord Alfred Haines among them. When the Marquess of Brandsley was announced, and this gentleman murmured something about taking his leave, Damaris said in a low, urgent voice, "Please don't go!" before turning to greet the newcomer.

He bowed over her hand with great propriety, and acknowledged the introduction of her other guests, Mrs. Rathbone and her unmarried daughter, with considerable charm, nodding a greeting to Haines.

As she begged him to be seated he looked about inquiringly and said, "Your aunt—?"

"She is fetching a receipt that Mrs. Rathbone requested from her, for a physic to cure chilblains."

He turned to Mrs. Rathbone, politely expressing the hope that she was not the sufferer.

"No, indeed!" the lady replied. "But in the winter poor Charlotte suffered dreadfully—did you not, my dear?"

Charlotte, blushing painfully, acknowledged the severity of her sufferings, and the marquess said sympathetically that it had been a remarkably cold winter, and asked if she had been in town for it.

Emboldened by the sympathy, Miss Rathbone ventured to say that they had been in London since Christmas, and that although the weather had been cold, they had had the greatest fun at a skating party, and at the frost fair that had been held on the Thames. "For you must know," she added breathlessly, "that it was quite frozen over, from Blackfriars to London Bridge!"

The marquess smiled kindly and said he had heard that it was so, and he was glad that there had been some compensation for the pain of her chilblains.

Damaris, attending with half an ear to the compliments that Lord Alfred was whispering into it, saw the smile and wondered at it. It was in marked contrast to the smile she had glimpsed on his lips last night as she had, with vast relief, at last seen him turn away from his contemplation of herself.

Her aunt entered the room at that moment, and when the introductions were completed entered into a comfortable conversation with Mrs. Rathbone. But Lord Brandsley took advantage of having risen at Mrs. Newington's entrance, to take a chair nearer to his hostess and ask her if she, too, had attended the frost fair. Meeting his eyes, she saw a teasing smile in them, and knew he meant her to recall their light conversation of last night when he had quizzed her about her supposed bluestocking tastes. The tug of attraction which had momentarily lowered her guard last night brought an involuntary smile to her lips, and she said, "Yes—Mrs. Rathbone was kind enough to include us in her party. We enjoyed it immensely."

"As much as the paintings at Somerset House?" he asked smoothly.

"One can hardly compare the two, sir. Appreciation of the arts is surely a quite different kind of enjoyment from savoring the delights of a fair."

"But you do have an appreciation of the arts."

"Why—certainly!" she answered with spirit. "It is one of the chief attractions of London, that one's tastes may be indulged in so many directions."

"I wonder if you have seen Sir Simon Clarke's private collection?"

"No. I don't have the honor of Sir Simon's acquaintance."

"I do. I shall be delighted to arrange a viewing for you and your aunt, Lady Waring."

Her dismayed protest was smilingly overridden with the blandest courtesy, the marquess promising himself the pleasure of escorting the ladies when he should have arranged a date with Sir Simon. He then returned to his seat beside Miss Rathbone and appeared well amused with trying to overcome her shyness, for the next twenty minutes, at the end of which he took his leave.

Lord Alfred following suit shortly afterwards, the ladies were left to enjoy a feminine coze on Lord Brandsley's address, his conversation and his air of breeding.

"So condescending—" Mrs. Newington said flutteringly, recalling his graceful bow, his almost deferent manner, his solicitous way of handing her into her chair.

"Not a bit toplofty," Mrs. Rathbone agreed approvingly.

"So very kind and friendly—" Charlotte said. "Don't you think he is quite like his cousin, Damaris?"

"Like Viscount Edgely?" Damaris queried, amazed. "Good heavens, Charlotte, I should be hard put to it to find anyone *less* like, I should think!"

"Not in *looks*," Charlotte said hastily. "But in their manners they are both so—gentlemanly."

Damaris was saved from having to reply to this by her aunt's breaking in with eager agreement, adding her grateful surprise at his offer to procure them a viewing of Sir Simon's art collection. Damaris, who had been wondering how she could decline the invitation on the plea of another engagement when Lord Brandsley had set a day, resigned herself to enduring it for Mrs. Newington's sake.

Lord Brandsley's manners might be all that Charlotte said they were, but Damaris distrusted him. When she had first seen him last night he had been looking across the room at her, inspecting her gown with a critical air that made her almost expect him to produce a quizzing glass at any moment. By the time his gaze reached her face, she had turned to Lord Alfred Haines as he bent to whisper in her ear some flattering comment on her attire, and as Viscount Edgely and the newcomer moved towards them, Haines had looked up and laughed softly, saying, "Good Lord! I thought Brandsley had given up bearleading his cousin years ago. Lady Crawley must have more influence with him than I thought!"

And to her puzzled request to know what he meant, her companion laughed and said, "You will enjoy the joke, Lady Waring. My mother and Lady Crawley are bosom-bows, you know, so I happen to know that Lady Crawley has recently been into Norfolk for the express purpose of requesting Brandsley, as the head of the family, to exert his influence with Viscount Edgely on a certain—delicate matter of the heart—"

Because it was expected of her, she gave a little laugh, but she found the joke much less funny than Lord Alfred seemed to expect. She had not enjoyed her sole interview with Lady Crawley, and the news that her ladyship had asked Lord Brandsley to intervene in his cousin's affairs resurrected some of the indignation she had felt on that occasion.

When she saw the faint flicker of surprise on Brandsley's face before he bowed over her hand and held it a fraction longer than courtesy allowed, the indignation flared into a brief anger. He had, she was certain, expected her to present the air of a vulgar adventuress.

The admiration that succeeded the surprise was a balm, but she was not so vain that she accepted it at face value. That he had deliberately set out to charm her during their dance together, she was aware, but of his motives she was still suspicious. When he had announced his intention of calling in Harley Street, she wondered if he meant to attempt a less blatant warning-off than his aunt had subjected her to, and although she had almost begun to like him for a few minutes, caution returned. She thought that he had probably hoped to be able to speak to her privately in order to carry out his aunt's wishes, and that the invitation to view Sir Simon's art collection was probably another attempt to procure a *tête à tête*.

Two days later a note was brought to Harley Street setting two alternative dates for the viewing, and requesting her to inform him which would suit. She sent a civil reply, and was duly informed that his carriage would call for her and her aunt on the appointed day. The distance was so short that Damaris felt a carriage was not in the least necessary, but to send *another* message refusing it seemed absurd. Although she had dreaded receiving another visit from him, she now began to feel irritated that he had not conveyed the arrangements in person to herself and her aunt.

There was one advantage in that the brevity of the drive to Gloucester Place precluded any conversation other than the merest commonplaces.

Sir Simon himself greeted them and gave Mrs. Newington his arm as they strolled about the picture gallery, pointing out his particular favorites and expounding on their origins, their merits and the artists who had painted them. "The Regent himself offered twice what I paid for this one," he said proudly, pausing before the portrait of an opulent lady posed in a gloomy interior. "But I refused to part with it."

Lord Brandsley had offered his own arm to Damaris so pointedly she could not have refused without gross discourtesy, and she was aware that he was deliberately loitering behind the other two, her efforts to keep up being blandly foiled by his polite remarks on the paintings and requests for her opinion.

Her replies were brief because she wished to hurry on, but had the opposite effect from that she wished. He stopped and looked down at her, his gray eyes questioning. "I have the feeling," he said, "that you would have preferred to visit Madame Tussaud's waxwork museum."

Mortified to think her manners had been at fault, she took a deep breath, to stop a blush rising to her cheeks, and said, "Why, not at all, sir. It is only that I am overwhelmed by so much—so much wonderful art, and—and the honor of being allowed to see it quite privately."

She knew from the sardonic gleam in his eyes that he did not believe her, but he bowed his head a little in acknowledgement and turned her attention to a bloodthirsty representation of Saint Sebastian pierced by myriad arrows, which made her shudder and desire him to walk on.

"You surprise me, Lady Waring," he said. *"You* shaft arrows at the hearts of men without a qualm."

She stiffened, casting him a glance that made his brows draw together in faint puzzlement. "You are wrong, sir, I have never deliberately wounded any man. I am sure that those who claim some injury to their heart, show a remarkable power of recovery in that organ."

A burst of spontaneous laughter came from him, and she stopped and looked up at him, her teeth on her lower lip. His mirth subsided quickly, however, and he said soberly, "I think that my cousin Edgely's may be still young enough to be tender."

"Oh, but he is—different!" she exclaimed.

His suddenly narrowed eyes almost made her quail, the silky note in his voice starting a shiver up her spine. *"Is* he?" the marquess said. "He is more eligible, perhaps, than the others. Does that make him less liable to having his heart broken?"

She looked at him steadily. "At my hands, at any rate," she said, "he is perfectly safe."

She saw at once that he had misunderstood her meaning. The gray eyes were flint-hard, his mouth taut with sudden anger.

He mastered his expression in an instant, schooling his mouth to a smile and his eyes to blankness as he said, "You relieve my mind greatly, Lady Waring. I am particularly fond of my young cousin."

She was fond of him herself, but this hardly seemed a propitious moment to say so. She wondered how the marquess would receive it if she told him that she had no intention of marrying the viscount, and decided that he would no more believe her than he had her Banbury story about being overawed by the art collection.

She sighed a little, and he said, "Are you tired?"

Tempted to say yes and bring the visit to a speedy end, she changed her mind on the thought that the marquess wished to cut it short also. Her feelings smarting from his evident opinion of her, she resolved instead to punish him by forcing him to carry out to the hilt his obligations as her escort. She dawdled, and exclaimed and asked questions, and generally showed as keen an interest in the collection as any solicitous host could have wished. And had the doubtful pleasure of watching Lord Brandsley determinedly hide his growing impatience behind a stiff, polite mask.

When at last he returned them to Harley Street he refused to come into the house but expressed the hope of seeing them both at Mrs. Rathbone's rout party, to which that lady had been kind enough to send him an invitation.

Hiding dismay, Damaris listened to her aunt's assurances that they would be there the following evening.

Tempted to cry off from the party, Damaris instead dressed for it with great care, in oyster crêpe which set off her eyes and hair to perfection, adorned with a velvet ribbon tied beneath the bust, its ends trailing to the hem of her gown. She carried a tortoiseshell fan, and wore a sparkling necklace and earring set of topaz. Mrs. Newington pronounced her to be looking in great bloom.

Mrs. Rathbone was a cousin of her late husband, and had earned her gratitude by her kindness. While others of Sir Walter's relatives had treated her with barely concealed dislike and contempt, Mrs. Rathbone had taken pity on a young girl tied to a man old enough to have fathered her, and when he died had urged Damaris to take a London house, and had taken her under her own wing to launch her into society. Damaris was well aware that with a daughter of her own who had been out for two seasons without attracting a single offer, her cousin by marriage was being singularly generous in sponsoring her own *entrée*.

Charlotte herself shared her mother's temperament, although her sweetness of nature was hidden by a burden of shyness which she found impossible to overcome. Her features were not precisely plain, but in company such a woodenness overcame her expression that she was apt to be passed over, or dismissed as a dab of a girl with no countenance and little to recommend her. Before she was *out* this quietness was regarded as a virtue, but a young lady having made her début was expected to be able to hold light conversation, at least, with some appearance of ease.

Knowing that Charlotte found it hard to assume such an appearance, Damaris was surprised to see her laughing unaffectedly with Lord Brandsley at her mother's party. She noticed Viscount Edgely join them and glance curiously at Charlotte as though he, too, was surprised to see her looking so unusually animated.

After a few minutes Lord Brandsley strolled away, leaving the two young people together, and Damaris was pleased to see that Charlotte continued to talk to Lord Edgely with shy friendliness. Since both of them were frquent visitors in Harley Street, and had the same set of acquaintances and friends, they had met a number of times. Damaris hoped that Charlotte felt she now knew the viscount sufficiently well to treat him as a friend rather than a frightening stranger.

Indeed, there was nothing at all frightening about Lord Edgely. His older cousin, Damaris felt, was a different kettle of fish altogether. In vain she told herself she had no need to fear him. He had made her nervous from the first moment she saw him, looking her over with a coldly calculating air. And the brief glimpse of his temper she had seen before he mastered it the day before, had confirmed her fear. Not all the suave courtesy of his subsequent manner to her could erase that memory from her mind. She knew him for her enemy, and although common sense told her he could not possibly be a danger, the very sight of him caused a tremor of apprehension to prickle over her skin. She was sure he was not a man who would give up easily anything he set out to do. He had misinterpreted her hint yesterday, and would doubtless try to find some other way of separating her from his cousin.

She felt herself at a standstill. Every feeling shrank from the bold impropriety of informing the marquess outright that she had no intention of marrying Viscount Edgely, especially since the viscount had not even offered for her. And even if she nerved herself to do so, she had no cause to revise her opinion of yesterday that the marquess would not believe her.

Not for the first time, she wished she had kept a tighter rein on her own temper when Lady Crawley had visited her. At first she had been amused and a little incredulous that the countess took her son's regard for Damaris so seriously, for it was obvious from her pointed remarks that anxiety over his association with Lady Waring was the cause of her visit. But amusement gave way to annoyance as the countess became more supercilious and more offensive in her hints, scarcely bothering to disguise the disdain she felt for a nobody who she believed had dared to aspire to marriage with her son. The climax came when she dared to snub poor Mrs. Newington. Damaris ceased trying for a tactful way of reassuring the countess and instead decided it would be her just desert if she was led to believe that her concern had some ground in fact. Lady Crawley, she thought, was a bully and a fool, not at all like her son, of whom Damaris was genuinely fond.

Had she been aware of Lord Brandsley's activities since he had left her yesterday, both her trepidation and her anger would have increased. Strolling to a club of which he had long been a member, although infrequently making use of its facilities, he had spent a pleasant and profitable few hours renewing old acquaintances and demanding to be brought up to date with the latest *on-dits*.

An ex-army major who prided himself on having private and reliable sources of information regaled him with the news of the latest developments in the war with France. Napoleon's brilliant recovery after Orthez, he averred, was the last desperate throes of a dying monster. His army was decimated and riddled with desertion, the allies overwhelmingly outnumbered his remaining forces. The allied armies were advancing on Paris and could not be stopped.

After twenty years of war, the major's optimism was received with hope but not certain acceptance. Grenville gave a brief, rueful thought to his early ambition to join the army, and expressed the sincere hope that his informant was correct in his predictions.

Beau Brummell was still out of favor with the Regent, someone told him, and not likely to regain it, after his calculated insolence at Lord Alvanley's select Dandy Ball where the Prince cut him dead and Brummell asked loudly, "Who is your fat friend, Alvanley?" Prinny would accept meekly George's strictures on his colored coats and follow his dictates as to the fall of his cravat, and might even in time have forgiven the Beau's tactless remarks about his beloved Mrs. Fitzherbert, but the grossness of his figure in portly middle age was a tender point with him, and no forgiveness was now possible. Brummell still reigned over the world of fashion as arrogantly as ever, but there were those who said his star was on the wane. Royalty, even fat, peevish and unpopular royalty, must be a better investment, thought some hostesses, than the clever, witty, audacious, but quite untitled son of a valet.

At last the conversation turned to the reigning beauties of the season, and Grenville's interest quickened. When Lady Waring's name was mentioned he said idly, "I have met the lady. A beauty, certainly—a veritable diamond. But who is she—her family?"

"A lawyer's daughter, I think," someone said. "Before she married Waring. But Ibster is your man—he comes from that part of the country, and knew her husband."

Ibster, when applied to, proved a mine of information. A handsome man of forty or so summers, he confessed to having felt sorry for the late Sir Walter, who had succumbed to a middle-aged fancy for a pretty, scheming miss and lived to regret it. Besotted at first, he had given his new bride every trinket she fancied, and run through a tidy sum providing her with expensive jewelry. And the lady, apparently, from the despondent hints her spouse had dropped when in his cups, had become cold when her bridegroom ceased to shower her with baubles. "I have seen tears in his eyes when he spoke of the change in her," Ibster said. "From a fond, grateful little thing to a cold, contemptuous wife who refused him an heir—"

"*Refused him?*" Grenville asked, his voice quiet but cold and sharp as an icicle. Overcoming his distaste for this kind of gossip, he said, "Did he tell you so?"

Slightly discomfited, Mr. Ibster shrugged. "It was the great regret of his life that his marriage did not bring him an heir, and although I never heard him say so outright, no one who knew them doubted the reason. Why, I myself have seen her turn her shoulder to him in public, when he only spoke to her."

Grenville said carefully, "I take it he had no other reason to reproach her?"

The other man grinned slyly, and Grenville suppressed a twinge of shame, reminding himself that this was for Lindo's sake. Ibster said, "She had too much care for her reputation to risk a scandal. In the class of society she came from, respectability is all, you know." He spoke sneeringly, and Grenville decided that he definitely did not like Mr. Ibster. But that was unfortunately no reason to discount his evidence, for it was, after all, firsthand. "There was Sir Walter's chaplain," the man went on. "Quite a young fellow, who had certainly a *tendre* for her, which I sometimes suspected she returned. There was a certain partiality in her manner—but they were discreet—oh, very. They were dependents of Sir Walter, after all, both of them."

The sour taint of that conversation lingered with Grenville still as he strolled in on Mrs. Rathbone's party. After meeting Lady Waring he had wondered if his aunt might have exaggerated in other directions as well as about her probable age, but yesterday her quick riposte when he had mentioned her effect on his cousin's heart had confirmed Lady Crawley's account of her brashness. She had as good as told him that Lindo's love would not go unrewarded, that she would not refuse his suit. He had been sorely tempted to give her a tongue-lashing then and there, only he recalled in time that to antagonize her could only drive her into Lindo's arms and make her more than ever determined on marriage.

Her patently feigned interest in the art works after that exchange had been intended, he knew, to provoke him. The tiny smile that etched her lips when they took their leave of Sir Simon indicated that she knew, too, that she had succeeded, and that irked him.

When he saw her that evening he felt a savage disgust, but to his chagrin it was impossible to resist the simultaneous thrust of sheer pleasure at her beauty. Jewels glittered at her throat and in her ears, enhancing the healthy glow of perfect skin, her dark eyes shone softly in the candlelight, and when she moved across the floor he could not but be conscious of the lightness and grace of the figure outlined by the flowing of the soft stuff of her dress.

His cousin was here, too, and he watched narrowly from a distance as she greeted Lindo, smiling bewitchingly with that special softness that she seemed to reserve for him, allowing him to lead her away from a half-dozen disappointed admirers to the table where cool lemonade drinks and champagne were offered to the guests.

He made his way over to them, pausing now and then to exchange brief greetings with friends but not allowing himself to be detained. Lindo looked up and his smile widened in greeting. He saw the lady's fractional hesitation before she turned, too, and acknowledged his bow with a cool little smile.

"Lindo," he said, "Bournehall was looking for you. I promised I would send you to him. Something about messages for your mother, I believe."

Mr. Bournehall had, in fact, been interrupted by the marquess in a recital of the civil messages he wished conveyed to her ladyship, by Grenville's intimation that her son was present, and would make a far more satisfactory messenger than himself. Mr. Bournehall was an elderly, boring and rather sycophantic gentleman, and in Lindo's place Grenville would have had no compunction in ignoring his desire to send civil and unnecessary messages to Lady Crawley. But Lindo had been brought up with a strongly formed notion of the deference due to his elders, if not betters, and he groaned and said he would seek out Mr. Bournehall when he had procured a seat for Lady Waring.

"I will take care of Lady Waring," Grenville told him easily. "You have monopolized her long enough, in any event. I'm surprised no one has challenged your right to do so before this moment."

"Well, I should not give up so easily to anyone but you, Gren," Lindo grinned. "Pray excuse me, Lady Waring—Mr. Bournehall is an old friend of my mother's. Although it's my belief that Brandsley put the idea into his head, merely to give *himself* the chance to monopolize you!"

"Not at all!" Grenville replied promptly. "In fact, he was intent on burdening *me* with all manner of good wishes for your mamma, until I informed him you were here. Then nothing would do but that I should send you to him. You will find him in the other room, through the archway over there."

Lindo laughed and moved off, and Grenville took the empty glass from Lady Waring's hand, asking if she wished him to procure another drink for her.

Being answered with a negative, he gave her his arm and proceeded to make a way for them through the crowded room into a spacious conservatory where couples strolled arm in arm between the plants, or sat on vaguely rustic, though cushioned seats.

He handed her into one of these, saying, "You will find it cooler here," and seating himself beside her.

"Lindo is quite right, of course," he said, half-turning so that he could study her profile. "I did want to have you to myself."

She stiffened and flicked open the fan she held in her fingers. "Did you have something particular to say to me, sir?"

He took the fan from her, ignoring the slight resistance she made, and began plying it gently near her cheek.

"I have several particular things to say to you," he said. "I suppose you have already been told that you are without doubt the most beautiful woman here to-night."

She flashed him a searching look, then glanced away and said, "Not by you, Lord Brandsley."

"Are you waiting to hear it from me?" Not giving her a chance to answer, he said, "But I don't like to be behindhand, and I'm sure you have heard it from a dozen others. I shall tell you instead that you disappoint me."

This time she did not look at him, but her chin lifted a fraction. "In what way, sir?"

"You have never yet smiled at me as you do at my cousin."

That brought her eyes to his in a wide, startled glance. He smiled himself, at her evident surprise, his eyes resting on her slightly parted lips, until she turned away again.

He snapped the fan shut and placed the tortoiseshell sticks under her chin, turning her face again toward his. "Will you not smile for me?" he asked softly.

She put up her hand to take the fan, and rose to her feet in the same instant. He followed, and she took an involuntary step backwards.

Amused, he said, "Now, what have I said to frighten you?"

"I'm not frightened!" she said, a flash of anger in her eyes. "Merely, I think it is time we returned to the salon."

"Already? I protest at surrendering you so soon, Lady Waring. I have not said half of the *particular things* that I wished to."

She turned away, but not in the direction of the door, for he was blocking it. "If they are in the same vein, sir, I wish that you will not!"

"Do you object to receiving compliments?"

"You have not paid me any!"

"Ah—then you object to *not* receiving them. If I promise to remedy the omission—?"

"You know that is not what I meant!"

"Then I confess that I am at a loss to know what you did mean. Shall we stroll and admire the plants in silence while I apply my poor intellect to divining your meaning?"

He possessed himself of her hand and tucked it into his arm so that she was obliged to walk with him. Her teeth bit into her lower lip for a moment, but she was unable to prevent the escape of a brief, pretty laugh.

He glanced down at her and said, "Now that is even better than a smile. Why don't you wish me to pay you compliments? I'm sure Lindo has done so often enough?"

"*His* are sincerely meant, sir."

They had reached the end of the conservatory, and he stopped and looked down at her averted face. "You doubt my sincerity?" he asked.

"I think that you underestimate my intellect as much as you pretend to underestimate your own," she said, raising her eyes to his. "You think that if you flatter me I shall be amenable to persuasion—"

"You suspect me of being a seducer, Lady Waring?" he asked, his eyes alight with sardonic humor.

Her eyes flashed. "For all that I know, you may be!" she retorted. "But it was not of *that* I was speaking, as well you know." She took a breath and went on, "I know what you want of me, Lord Brandsley—"

"Do you indeed?" he murmured, allowing himself one suggestively comprehensive glance over her slender person, and a jeering smile at her heightened color and indignant eyes.

"Let me tell you that *nothing* that you or Lady Crawley has to say will make me change my—sentiments in any way," she said. "*You* may be more circumspect in your approach, but the fact is that both of you are on the wrong tack, with your hints and suggestions. You would have done very much better to have told me frankly what was in your minds, instead of wrapping it up so!"

"Would we, indeed? Then if it's plain speaking you want, tell me how much you want, in return for not marrying my cousin Edgely?"

She paled suddenly, and the fingers that held the closed fan tightened dangerously on its slender sticks. Then she said in a low, trembling voice, "How—*dare* you!" And turned and left him, walking swiftly towards the door.

chapter four

Fortunately most of the people in the conservatory were too occupied with their own partners to notice Lady Waring's abrupt departure from her escort. Grenville met one curious stare and returned it with a coldly aristocratic one of his own, whereupon it was hastily withdrawn.

Outwardly unperturbed, he was inwardly cursing himself for a cowhanded fool. Of course he had known it was useless to offer the little jade money. She would be a fool to settle for that instead of a lifetime of comfort as the Viscountess Edgely. The thing was she had succeeded in making him angry again, and he had sufficiently lost his temper to deliberately insult her. The candidness of her eyes, the unexpected, delicious laughter he had surprised from her, had for a few moments disarmed him, but when her temper flashed, it had roused his own, and her stubborn avowal of her purpose fanned it to a sudden fury.

His strategy had been shot to pieces, he realized. But not entirely—she had not divined the full extent of his plan. If he was less careless he might yet come about and carry the day.

The first thing he noticed on reentering the salon was Lady Waring, smiling into Lindo's face, her hand resting on his arm. For the first time, it occurred to him that she might have some genuine feeling for the boy, quite apart from his title and fortune. He was, after all, a handsome lad, and with a great measure of youthful but genuine charm. And she certainly treated him with marked partiality.

Or did she? Grenville frowned as Mr. Woodfall joined the couple he was watching, and the lady instantly transferred her smile to him. Woodfall was rather older than Lindo, and a good deal more adept at games of dalliance. He soon detached Lady Waring from the viscount's side, and bore her off in triumph. She showed little reluctance, saying something laughingly over her shoulder to Lindo as she went.

He watched her flirting with Woodfall, and later with another gentleman he had never seen before. If she was in love with Lindo, he thought, she had a very odd way of showing it. When he casually inquired of an acquaintance the identity of the gentleman who was now the recipient of her wayward favors, and learned the size of the fortune enjoyed by him, his mouth curled cynically. Woodfall would probably not come to the post, having evaded matrimony for almost as many years as Grenville, but the newcomer might prove an adequate second string to Lady Waring's bow. He dismissed his doubts and began to plan a recovery from the setback he had brought on himself tonight. He would have to recover his position before planning another sortie.

When her butler announced the Marquess of Brandsley and Viscount Edgely the following afternoon, Damaris first thought to deny them, then hesitated, partly from an unwillingness to hurt the viscount, and partly because her aunt was already making little exclamations of pleasure. If the marquess had been alone the rebuff would have been administered regardless of the fact that she had other visitors whose presence was well advertised by their voices floating out of the drawing room door, and who would have been agog to hear her inform her butler that she was not at home to one of the most eligible men in England.

She rose reluctantly to greet the two men as they entered the room, her eyes finding first a pair of cool gray ones with an ironical smile in them that acknowledged the hostility in hers. She gave the marquess a stiff nod and turned to offer her hand to his cousin, who shot a puzzled glance at them both before bowing over it. "You remember my Cousin Brandsley, of course, Lady Waring?" he said awkwardly.

"Of course," she said, her smile just skimming the top button of the marquess's waistcoat, and turned to introduce her other guests, and invite the new arrivals to sit down.

Taking pity on the viscount's unease, she engaged him in a sparkling conversation about the ball and other balls which they had both attended, and even allowed him to enroll his cousin's opinion, listening with a polite smile affixed to her lips as Lord Brandsley agreed lazily that everything had been very fine, very amusing and very enjoyable.

But his replies lacked the right amount of enthusiasm for the viscount's satisfaction. "Oh, come, Grenville," he rallied the older man. "You must agree that everything was of the first stare!"

"I thought I *had* agreed to it," Brandsley retorted with tolerance. "You must excuse me for not going into raptures—*you* may find London parties the epitome of excitement, I'm well past that stage. The season's entertainments palled for me some years ago."

"Then what keeps you in town this year?" Damaris challenged him directly.

"Yes," Viscount Edgely said laughingly. "Why do you stay so long, when you told me that you were here only on a matter of business?"

"But Lady Waring knows why," said the marquess,

his eyes meeting hers. She stiffened, but he went on smoothly, "*You* introduced me to her, Lindo—do you wonder at it that I cannot tear myself away from London, now?"

The viscount's smile became a little set, and Damaris got to her feet. "Lord Brandsley makes pretty speeches," she said to the younger man. "If he is not careful his tongue will get him into trouble one day."

She went to sit by one of the other visitors, a young woman who had called with her husband and two single gentlemen, one of them her brother, who had, she said, demanded an introduction to Lady Waring. Damaris had accepted the introduction to a plump, moustached Mr. Stenhouse, whose skintight inexpressibles made her hold her breath as he bowed excessively low over her extended hand, with what she hoped was civility; she did not, however, desire to pursue the acquaintance. Mr. Stenhouse wheezed slightly when he spoke, and she suspected that he was wearing a tight corset under his wasp waisted coat. But even without the wheezing, his conversation would have been intolerably boring. It consisted mainly of remarks on the weather and an interminable and complicated recital of his family history. It transpired that the point of this labored exercise was the proof of his quite remote relationship to a certain duchess whose acquaintance, he claimed, Lady Waring must have made. Since Damaris could not recall ever having met the duchess, this conversational gambit failed.

Damaris looked to the gentleman's sister, hoping to extricate herself, but Mrs. Webster had engaged in conversation with Lord Edgely, while her husband and the other gentleman had strolled to the window together and were looking out at the street.

She caught the eyes of the marquess resting on her with a certain cold interest, and turned to Mr. Stenhouse again with a show of animation that concealed her boredom and her irritation. She saw Lord Brandsley rise, and hoped he would take his leave, for she was sure the company was below his touch, but instead he strolled over to sit near her, and give a creditable impression of taking part in her conversation with the plump young gentleman. He soon drew Mrs. Webster and the viscount, seated nearby, into it, and skillfully managed to withdraw from the conversation himself and turn to Damaris to say in a low voice, under cover of a spirited discussion on horseflesh, "You have been more charitable to me than I expected, today."

"For your cousin's sake, sir," she said. "Had you come alone, I must tell you that you would not have been received."

"I don't doubt it. Why do you imagine I took care to come in his company?"

The faintest smile touched her mouth. She had to admit it had been masterly strategy. And bold.

He was speaking again. "I have to tell you that I most sincerely regret certain words I spoke to you last night—words that you quite naturally must have deeply resented. My only excuse is that I lost my temper."

She looked at him searchingly. She supposed this was an apology, but could see no sign of contrition in his face. He looked aloof and hard and there was a faint twist of distaste at the corner of his mouth.

"I did resent them," she said. "I do. The implication was one which—which—"

"Which no man of honor would make to a lady of quality," he said. "I freely admit it."

She supposed the distaste might be because the Marquess of Brandsley was unused to having to apologize for his actions—or words.

"Are you asking me to forgive you?" she murmured.

There was a tiny pause before he said, "Do you find it unforgivable? Perhaps I should get Lindo to plead for me."

"Did you tell him...?"

"No." He did not ask her not to mention his insolent offer to the viscount.

"Why did you lose your temper?" she asked warily. "Is it a frequent occurrence with you?"

"Not especially," he said, a faint, appreciative smile touching his lips. "Cannot you guess the reason?" The smile reached his eyes, but behind the appreciation there was also a hint of cynicism he was unable to hide.

She stared at him, her teeth just touching her lower lip, her eyes wary. "If you mean that you are jealous," she answered uncertainly, "I think that you credit me with a great deal more vanity and less sense than I possess. I find *that* implication almost as insulting as the other. Why, we had scarcely met—and I don't believe that *you* are as susceptible as—as some younger gentlemen may be to—to a new face."

"*You* underestimate yourself," he replied. "I may be past the age of falling head over ears on first seeing a lovely face, but believe me, yours is exceptional enough to induce any man to linger in town—and your style of deportment and conversation is an added attraction. I am not in love with you, Lady Waring, but I find myself very much drawn to you—your face, your figure, your manner, are as pleasing to me as to my young cousin—or nearly. And I am not accustomed to having my interest in a woman referred to as an *insult*."

That had stung him a little, she realized, and was not sorry. He spoke so dispassionately that she was almost inclined to believe what he told her, even though a note of wryness tempered the sincerity in his voice. But even as she stared up into his hard, handsome face, trying to gauge the truth of his feelings, her attention was called by Mrs. Webster.

The subject under discussion was still horses, and to the other woman's query as to whether she rode in London, Damaris answered a negative. "I have no horse here," she said.

"For shame!" her friend cried. "I recall that at Lord Beresford's house party, you were accounted a distinguished horsewoman. I was sure I should see you in the park one morning."

Damaris laughed regretfully and shook her head.

The marquess asked, "Did you ride often in Somerset?"

"Yes, often," she answered, the reserve in her voice failing to hide the wistfulness behind it. "It would not be the same in Hyde Park, in any case."

Lord Edgely broke into the conversation at this point. "No, for a good gallop one must go to Richmond. It is by far more congenial, in my view!"

Damaris turned to smile at him. "Yes, you would prefer it!" she said. "I know you prefer an out-and-out gallop to a tame trot."

"Well, do not you?" he demanded. "*Anyone* who truly enjoys riding must do so!"

Damaris laughed at him, but said, "I have to admit, I do agree. It was my chief pleasure in the country to let my mare have her head across the dales. But *that* is not possible in London."

"Is that why you prefer not to ride here?" the viscount asked.

Her hesitation and faint flush were barely noticeable. Then she answered, "Partly," and turned to address a remark to Mrs. Webster.

Shortly afterwards the lady and her party made a move to leave, and when they had done so, Grenville caught his cousin's eye and they also took their departure.

Mrs. Newington was not to be seen today, and as Lindo preceded him Grenville made an inquiry after her the excuse to linger a few moments with their hostess. She was, it seemed, in good health and spirits, having merely stepped out to Bond Street to purchase some ribbon, but had doubtless found other delectable merchandise to catch her eye and detain her.

When his cousin was safely out of earshot, Grenville said in a low voice, "Dare I hope that if I call alone, I will be received next time, Lady Waring?"

Her candid eyes on his face, she said steadily, "It occurs to me, Lord Brandsley, that you might have many reasons for regretting what you said to me—and also that in saying so, you did not ask me to forgive you. Should I offer a forgiveness that has not been requested?"

"May a man not hope for more than he deserves?" he murmured. But he knew she had called his bluff. If he begged her pardon now, she would probably extend it. He would not do it.

He saw the confirmation of her suspicion in her face as she watched him. She gave an odd little laugh, and said, "I see you *are* a man of honor, sir. Such a one does not lie, does he?"

Torn between a reluctant admiration for her perception, and annoyance that she had perfectly understood the hidden insolence of his apparent apology, he began to perceive that the lady might be an opponent worthy of his steel. He acknowledged it with a small, stiff bow, and was surprised when she gave another brief, vexed laugh and said, "So long as you enjoy the protection of your cousin, Lord Brandsley, I shall receive you."

She was entitled to tilt at his pride, he supposed, but all the same she would answer for that one day. And neither his cousin nor anyone should protect her then, he thought with secret fury.

Aloud he said merely, "Thank you." He took her hand and bowed over it, although she had not offered it. "I have not lied to you, Lady Waring," he said deliberately, and was satisfied with the faint flush in her cheeks and the slightly startled look in her eyes as she took his meaning.

He smiled at the evidence of a slight confusion in her, and left tolerably satisfied. He had not, indeed, lied to her about his feelings, although he had withheld some of them. He was unwillingly attracted to her, so strongly that he could have liked her very much if his knowledge of her character had not intervened. Had he been younger and less experienced he might have been as besotted as Lindo. But he felt himself in no danger of allowing the lady's beauty and charm to override the angry disgust he felt when he reminded himself of what she really was.

It was some time before the marquess called again in Harley Street, but he was frequently a guest at the balls and parties that Damaris attended with her aunt. She tried hard to treat him with an indifferent civility, which appeared to amuse him. That annoyed her, and he would set himself out then to make her laugh, succeeding with a frequency that made Damaris wonder at herself. He was a man who had insulted her beyond bearing, whose opinion of her character set her smoldering with indignation, who she was very sure had made her acquaintance only in order to insure that she did not become connected with his odiously toplofty, aristocratic family. And yet when he set himself out to be charming to her she was incapable of resisting him.

So she talked with him, danced with him, laughed with him, and admitted ruefully to herself that although she distrusted him entirely, the Marquess of Brandsley was exceedingly good company, and any gathering at which he did not appear seemed to her to be sadly flat. It was a vexatious state of affairs, and she would by far rather have disliked him intensely; it was really too bad that she found herself unable to do so.

She never flirted with him, turning off his occasional compliments with a cool smile, and discouraging any hint of gallantry. Defiantly, she gave her warmest smiles in his presence to his young cousin, and if the young Viscount Edgely was said to be exceedingly particular in his attentions to the Beautiful Widow, it was equally said that she was showing a marked partiality for him. A few gossips speculated that Brandsley had entered the lists against his cousin, but it was generally agreed that nothing would come of *that*. *He* would be unlikely to look for anything other than a mild flirtation with a woman of no family or fortune, and *she* was undoubtedly much more inclined to favor the younger man, as anyone could plainly see when they were all three present at some fashionable gathering.

One or two perspicacious souls wondered what Brandsley was up to, and one old friend dared to ask him point blank if he was bent on spiking Edgely's guns. To which the marquess replied, blandly smiling, "Why, certainly not. Whatever made you think that?"

"Haven't seen you in town this age," the friend said bluntly. "Got a notion you're here to see Edgely don't make a fool of himself."

"I find that country life palls occasionally," the marquess replied calmly. "And Lindo is of age. And not a fool, I believe."

"Any man can be made a fool of by a clever beauty—at any age."

"*Any* man?" queried the marquess softly, his gray eyes glinting suddenly.

"Lord, Gren, the Widow had a middle-aged husband before she was twenty. What's to stop her snaring a pup like Edgely if she wants him?"

"I wonder," murmured the marquess, his gaze keen and thoughtful.

"Wonder what?"

"What would stop her wanting a pup like Edgely?" the marquess suggested.

"Why, nothing but a bigger fish in her net, I should think!" the other gentleman said without thinking.

"How very clever of you!" said the marquess gently. "I congratulate you on your acumen."

The other man stared, then said, "Good God! Is that what you're up to?"

"I've no idea what you mean," Brandsley told him. But his friend eyed the slight curve at the corner of his mouth and the amused glimmer in the gray eyes and said frankly, "Yes, you have. You play a deep game, Brandsley. Mind you don't get your fingers burned."

"Unlikely."

His friend grinned. "Once bitten, eh?"

The frosty stare this brought forth made him hurriedly stumble into speech again. "Might as well tell you, the betting in the clubs is in favor of the Widow, though."

"Indeed?"

"Tell you what, though, I'm going to bet against the marriage coming off, after all. Shouldn't wonder at it if you turn the trick, Gren. In fact, I think I see Caseby now—I'll just go and have a word with him."

Grenville smiled and watched him move off, with a pang of wry compunction. He rarely snubbed his friends, but the sudden confirmation that he had been right in suspecting that his Aunt Crawley had made his youthful humiliation public property had stung. Damn it, he seemed to have become remarkably quick to take offense of late, he reflected. He had no hesitation in laying the blame at Lady Waring's door. He spent so much time and effort trying to win her confidence and allay her suspicion of him, and controlling a frequent strong desire to wring her pretty neck when he saw her hanging on Lindo's arm and giving him that special smile, that his temper was uncertain with others. It was another thing she should answer for some day, he promised himself grimly. That, and her determined indifference to himself while she flirted with Woodfall and Aslett and a dozen others, and flaunted her preference for Lindo in front of him at every opportunity—

These reflections led the marquess, a short time later, to present himself at the house in Harley Street, walking past the butler with the information that he would announce himself, and striding into the drawing room where Damaris was helping Mrs. Newington to retrim a bonnet.

He gave Mrs. Newington his most charming smile, and met the other lady's indignant stare with a smiling challenge in his eyes.

"Forgive my informality," he said. "I was impatient to see you, and quite outstrode your butler—I fancy the fellow is getting on in years—an old family retainer, perhaps? Anyway, he is too slow for me on the stairs. How delightful to find you without company!"

The butler was not an old family retainer, as Damaris suspected his lordship knew very well. He was a little elderly, and because a position in a respectable household was difficult to obtain at his age was willing to accept the meager wage that Damaris was able to pay.

Mrs. Newington threw her niece a meaningful glance which Damaris ignored, her mouth stubbornly set, while their guest patently waited to be invited to sit down. Mrs. Newington remedied the omission in a fluttering voice, adding, "I was just saying to Damaris that we have been thin of company these few days, really quite dull for us! She suggested going for a walk—but there! If we had, we must have missed Lord Brandsley," she said, turning to her niece.

"Yes indeed! So we should," Damaris murmured, her eyes expressing emotions that her aunt had not perceived, but which seemed to afford the marquess some quiet enjoyment. "But it is a lovely day, Aunt. I believe we should have been very well employed taking the air." She allowed herself a wistful glance at the window, as though their visitor had disrupted a favorite plan.

The corner of Lord Brandsley's mouth twitched a little in appreciation. "But I've not told you why I called," he said. "I have my curricle outside, and hoped to persuade you to take a turn beside me, Lady Waring—it being such a fine day, and, as you say, far too pleasant to stay indoors."

"Thank you, sir," she answered promptly. "But I shall not leave my aunt—"

"Nonsense, child!" her aunt interposed. "When Lord Brandsley is offering precisely what you just told me you have longed for, and has been kind enough to call specially to invite you—"

"I daresay he was passing, Aunt."

"Not at all," the marquess said coolly.

Mrs. Newington said, "There! Of course you must go. I shall be quite comfortable here trimming my bonnet, as I told you when you said you would go out walking."

"You will want to change," said the marquess. "And meantime I shall keep Mrs. Newington company."

She kept him waiting for more than half an hour, although fifteen minutes had sufficed to discard her morning gown in favor of a walking dress and cape in a shade exactly matching her eyes, and a small velvet hat adorned with a curling ostrich feather.

He did not seem to find the wait tedious, and even lingered a few more minutes talking to her aunt after she had appeared in the drawing room to join him.

He handed her into the carriage and sprang lightly up beside her as the groom let go of the horses' heads.

Lord Brandsley drove four-in-hand, and Damaris could not help a faint sigh of admiration as she surveyed the sleek bays with their proud heads.

The marquess turned his head and glanced at her curiously.

"They are beautiful horses," she said. "And splendidly matched."

He smiled and did not answer at once, expertly urging the team to a smart trot as they turned towards Cavendish Square. When he did speak it was to say, "You are a judge of horseflesh, Lady Waring?"

"I was not pretending to that," she said stiffly.

"You mistake me. *I* was not pretending to criticize your judgement. I know that you are fond of riding. I've been wondering if you would allow me to provide you with a mount while you are in town."

Surprise held her silent for a moment, and he added, "By way of atonement."

"Thank you, but I cannot accept," she said briefly.

"Cannot?"

"You must know it is impossible for me to allow—"

"You mean it is improper."

"Yes."

"Even as a loan, merely, not a gift?"

"I could not accept it from *any* gentleman," she said finally.

After a moment he said, "Thank you, at any rate, for that."

She looked away as they skirted the circle of iron railings protecting the green in the middle of the square. He drove into one of the narrow streets leading from it into Oxford Street, not even checking as they passed a gig with an inch to spare. Her quick glance at his face showed her that it was quite unruffled.

They did not speak again until they reached Hyde Park. Here the fine day had brought out many of the Quality, and Damaris could not help a wistful glance or two at some of the ladies who were fortunate enough to be riding fine horses. Watching her eyes follow one of these, Lord Brandsley said softly, "Have you reconsidered, perhaps?"

She shook her head. "No. I am firm, but please be so obliging as not to tempt me any more, sir!"

He said nothing, but his smile and his glance brought a faint glow to her cheeks. She saw Lord Alfred Haines riding slowly on the back of a showy black, and bowed a greeting. Her companion nodded to the other man but did not slow, as Haines returned the salutation and looked after them curiously.

Seeing him reminded her of the first time she had met Lord Brandsley, and the brief flash of warm gratitude she had experienced at the offer of a horse suddenly dissipated.

He looked down at her bleak expression and frowned a little. "Are you offended?" he asked.

"No, of course not!" she answered with some constraint. It had occurred to her to wonder what his motives were. "I was merely trying to guess what prompted your generosity."

"Believe me, it arose from a simple desire to please you. Do you look for hidden motives when Lindo—or Haines—offers you a gift?"

For a moment she said nothing. Then she spoke in a low voice. "I have offended *you*. I'm sorry if I seemed ungracious."

He looked as if he would reply, but an acquaintance hailed him from the footpath, and the merest courtesy obliged him to stop and talk. When they drove on he turned the conversation to other channels and she was content to follow his lead.

When he helped her from the curricle at her doorstep later, she thanked him with genuine warmth, for she had enjoyed the drive.

He looked enigmatic, and carried her fingers briefly to his lips before he left her. He held her hand for a little longer, looking down at her face with a curious expression in his eyes.

She looked questioningly at him, and he smiled. "You were angry with me when I came," he said. "Am I forgiven?"

"For coming up unannounced?" Resignedly she said, "It would be decidedly uncivil in me to say *no,* after so enjoyable an outing."

"Decidedly!" he agreed, with a smile in his eyes, as she firmly withdrew her hand. "Almost as uncivil as if you were to instruct your butler to refuse admittance to me the next time I call upon you."

His eyes challenged her, and she gazed back at him, torn between chagrin and an unwilling appreciation of his methods. He had trapped her, giving her a choice between accepting his visits or appearing both petty and ridiculous.

Briefly she hesitated, then said reluctantly, "You will not be refused."

He bowed again, and left her. She went into the house and up the stairs, stripping off her gloves with impatient movements as she wondered how it was that Lord Brandsley always managed somehow to get his own way.

chapter five

Having made one concession, Damaris was determined not to make any other. At Almacks she stood up twice with Lord Edgely, but Brandsley had to be content with one dance. He accepted her refusal of another with apparent equanimity, and instead led out a blond and sparking beauty whose smile of triumph as she took her place in the set beside Damaris made her wish that she could inform the young lady that his first choice had been herself.

When he called in Harley Street, Lord Brandsley found his hostess distantly gracious, but much taken up with other guests, and even an invitation to take another turn in his carriage met with polite excuses. She turned off his attempts at gallantry with a cool smile and an indifferent shrug of her shoulder, and because she saw that it annoyed him, was especially charming to Lindo in his presence.

Then at the beginning of April news reached London of the surrender of Paris. The city rejoiced with dancing in the streets, and the houses were decorated with laurel wreaths and colored transparencies of victories in battle, and everyone, it seemed, had lighted candles in their windows.

The long shadow of twenty years at war was at last lifting, and by Easter Day, the tenth of the month, it was known that Napoleon was finally beaten and abandoned, and the Bourbons recalled to France by the Senate. Walter Scott might be moved to pity the "poor Devil," and Lord Byron call him Prometheus Chained, but to most the occasion was one calling for unmitigated rejoicing.

The weather was warm and balmy and the general air of thaw and euphoria may have been responsible for Damaris allowing Lord Brandsley to take her off guard one day and procure her promise to drive with him as far as Richmond Park. The expedition proved so congenial that when he claimed her hand for a waltz two days afterwards in a fashionable ballroom, she accepted with unconcealed alacrity, causing him to exclaim, "Now, *that* is what I have been waiting for these past many weeks!"

"To dance with me?"

"For you to smile at me in that particular way."

"I'm sure I have smiled at you before, Lord Brandsley."

"Not as I would have wished, however."

"I don't know why you should wish it," she said. "When I consider your opinion of me!"

"Might I not have revised my opinion?" he asked softly.

She searched his face, finding it softer than usual, but not easy to read.

"Have you?" she demanded.

He did not answer at once, but continued to study her. Then he said rather slowly, "To a considerable degree—yes."

Almost in a spirit of mischief, she said, "Then you would not object, after all, to my marrying your cousin?"

Unexpectedly his fingers tightened on hers until his grip became painful. "On the contrary," he said, his eyes suddenly alight with anger, "I should have very strong objections!"

So he had not really changed his mind about her at all, she thought. With his hateful penchant for sarcasm and double meanings, he had probably meant that his view of her character was now a good deal worse than it had been, when he said he had revised it.

Recklessly, she said, "That is a pity, Lord Brandsley, because I must tell you that I mean to have him."

He stopped himself from saying what was in his mind—*Over my dead body, you vulgar little harpy!* But she saw the snap of his fine teeth as he bit back the words, and the deep spark of a frightening fury in his eyes. To the sharp hurt within her was added a quick spasm of fear.

His smile was hardly more friendly. She had the impression that his lips moved over clenched teeth. "Do you," he said. "Why?"

Refusing to be intimidated, she gave an artificial little laugh and said, "Why? Because I like him, of course! Why should I not?"

"*Like* him, do you?" he muttered in a furious undervoice. "How much would you have liked him had he possessed no title and no fortune, I wonder? Can you answer that, madam?"

"No," she said coldly. "I never answer stupid questions."

He gave a crack of derisive laughter. "It *was* a stupid question, was it not? But tell me, since my cousin has neglected to inform me of his approaching nuptials, when is the happy day to be?"

"I—it is not certain," she stammered, suddenly disconcerted. She glanced about the room and discovered Lord Edgely dancing with Charlotte Rathbone, who was looking up at him with a shy smile as he talked to her. Supposing Lord Brandsley was to speak to him about her foolish claim! She said, "I must ask you to say nothing—it is not as yet known—Lady Crawley—"

"Lady Crawley would be infuriated," he said. "But

67

even Edgely might be a little surprised. When do you mean to tell him?"

"What do you mean?"

His smile held an ironic tilt that she disliked. "Oh, I don't doubt that you can have him whenever you want," he drawled. "But the fact is you've not accepted him—yet. I'm in his confidence, apart from knowing him very well, and I'm perfectly certain that he has no hope of an early marriage."

"I didn't say that I had accepted him," she argued feebly.

"No, and if you take my advice, you won't," he said forcefully. "Good God, girl, don't you realize how you will be talked of? A penniless widow, and several years older, entering into marriage with a youngster like Edgely?"

"I am not penniless!" she protested angrily.

"Your husband left you barely enough to live on. You had no fortune of your own..."

"How can you know that?" she exclaimed.

"It isn't difficult to find out these things," he replied. "You have spent more than you can well afford to come to London and sell yourself on the marriage mart."

She paled and cast him a glance of mingled anger and pain. "That isn't true! I never intended—"

"Spare me your excuses!" he interrupted brusquely. In a slightly softer tone he added, "I don't blame you for that, in any case. For a woman in your position there can be little other choice than to enter into an advantageous marriage, I suppose, and you are fortunate in being still young and personable enough to expect to do so."

"Thank you!" she said in a stifled voice. "But I collect that in hoping to attach *your cousin*, you think I am flying too high."

"Not at all." She looked up and was nonplussed by the sneering smile that accompanied his words. "Has it not occurred to you, you little fool," he said almost detachedly, "that you might have looked a good deal higher?"

Her foot missed a step, and momentarily his arm about her waist tightened as he steadied her.

Breathlessly she said, "I don't know what you mean!"

He said deliberately, "*My* fortune is larger than Edgely's, my estates greater; my title is superior and older; I have no anxious mother to make you uncomfortable, and neither is my age such as to make you appear the least ridiculous in the eyes of the *ton*. Had it not occurred to you that you might well try to attach *me?*"

"*You!*" she said, so stunned that she stopped dancing altogether.

Impatiently, he swept aside a curtain nearby and pushed her almost roughly into the small anteroom beyond it.

She turned to face him, staring into a face that was almost frightening in its rigidity, the mouth uncomfortably firm, the eyes glittering with an emotion she could not fathom.

"Why not me?" he demanded softly. "Am I so much less attractive to you than a whelp like Edgely, than that rake Haines, or a coxcomb like Aslett? Why look so surprised? You must know it has been an object with me these past six weeks to win only a smile from you."

"Yes," she said, recovering some of her composure. "It *has* been an object with you—to make me like you. At first I thought that it was because you hoped to persuade me to rebuff your cousin. But lately—" she lifted her chin, her eyes meeting his. "Lately I have wondered if I wounded your pride a little, and for that reason you were determined I should like you after all."

A faint smile touched his mouth and lit the narrowed eyes regarding her. "So far, you were right," he admitted. "But I told you once before, you underestimate yourself."

Her lips parted a little, and she moistened them with the tip of her tongue. "You are not in love with me!" she said uncertainly.

His eyes, which had been disconcertingly on her mouth, shifted to hers again. "Perhaps not," he said. "I have a very strong desire to make love to you, however."

Startled and angry, she stiffened, her eyes flashing. "If you mean to insult me, sir—!"

"Certainly not. I'm not offering you a *carte blanche*. I believe you to be virtuous, at least—"

"Thank you!"

"Neither am I offering you marriage," he added quite coolly. "As yet."

Before she could assure him that she would not accept him if he did, he went on, "You have kept me kicking my heels in town for two months, Lady Waring, the first woman to do so in ten years or more. Without making the least push to do so, you have intrigued me, enchanted me. Don't you wonder how I might react if you set yourself out to do so? Already I cannot tear myself from your side. Doesn't it tempt you to see if you can bring me to your feet?"

"What are you saying?" she said blankly, trying to understand what he was suggesting. "Are you challenging me to—to make you fall in love with me?"

"To bring me to the point of proposing to you, anyway," he told her. "You might, of course, run the risk of losing Lindo's affections, if he thinks I mean to cut him out. But you would gain a bigger prize, if you succeed."

"That is what you mean, by this—this *outrageous* suggestion, isn't it?" she demanded. "You are still bent on—*rescuing* your cousin from my *clutches*. You think that if I imagine I might bring *you* to—to offer for me, that I will have to let your cousin go. And you have no intention of offering me marriage at all. It is nothing but a despicable scheme to get what you want!"

"You don't believe you could bring me to the point?" he taunted.

"Please take me back to the ballroom," she said, unsteadily.

"Chicken-hearted, Lady Waring? I never thought *that* of you."

"This is a ridiculous conversation!" She turned to leave him, but he caught at her wrist, turning her to face him.

Her indignant eyes flew to his face, and the protest on her lips died as she saw his expression. It wore a teasing, taunting smile, but in his eyes there was something else that constricted her throat and made her heart thump alarmingly. Softly he said, "You could do it, you know—if I could only believe those eyes are as candid as they appear, if your lips are as sweet as they promise..."

Even as she made a move to free her wrist, he suddenly pulled her close, his other hand on her waist holding her against him, and his mouth pressed briefly, hard and warm, on hers before she wrenched away from him.

He laughed, adding to her confused sense of anger and humiliation and shame. "So you refuse my challenge?" he said. "A pity—I promise you, honey was never as sweet."

About to annihilate him with her opinion of his challenge, his character and his manners, she paused to give herself breath, and was struck by a thought that made her catch her lip in her teeth to stop the sudden exclamation that rose in her throat. Supposing, her thoughts ran, she *could* bring him to ask for her hand. What sweet revenge—and vindication—it would be to *refuse* him. She was quite sure he had never meant to propose, but she was sure, too, that his admiration of her looks, although reluctant, was genuine, and that he was not lying when he said he wanted to make love to her. Gentlemen were able to feel that way about women they neither loved nor respected, which was very odd in them, but quite well known. She knew that in spite of the attraction he admitted freely, he held her in contempt and dislike, but suddenly the picture of Lord Brandsley's pride humbled and his conviction shaken, that she was bent on selling herself to the highest and most noble bidder, was before her. Perhaps, she thought, with stirring excitement, it *was* possible.

She took a quick breath and said clearly, "But I have not refused your challenge, Lord Brandsley." She saw the sudden narrowing of his eyes, the tautened muscles of his cheeks, and wondered fleetingly if she was quite mad. She took another breath to steady her voice and said with all the calm that she could muster, "Shall we return to the ballroom?"

* * *

The music was just drawing to a close as they reentered the room, and Lindo, looking across Charlotte Rathbone's neat head, frowned as he saw the tight, oddly dangerous expression on his cousin's face, and the flushed cheeks and brilliant dark eyes of his partner.

He had stopped dancing automatically, but remained on the floor staring until a gentle tug at his sleeve recalled him to his duties to his own partner.

"I beg your pardon, Miss Rathbone—I was—thinking."

Charlotte smiled wistfully, but with a hint of mischief that surprised him in so quiet a girl. "Damaris is very beautiful, isn't she?" she said, as he led her from the floor.

"Yes," he said simply. Then, it occurring to him that he was possibly being untactful, he added, "But *you* too—I mean, beauty is not anything without true goodness of heart, which I am persuaded *you*—"

He was stopped by a small, chuckling laugh. "Oh, pray *don't!*" she said. "You cannot be persuaded of anything of the kind, for you don't know me well enough! You are being kind because I'm not even *pretty*, as I well know—but you have no need to, indeed. I *could* not be jealous of Damaris, you know, for besides being quite shatteringly lovely, she *does* have *true goodness of heart*, and we are the greatest friends!"

"But that isn't true!" Lindo exclaimed. "That you are not pretty!" he explained as she raised startled eyes to his. "You are not a showy beauty, but when you forget to be shy, and your countenance is animated by laughter, you are very pretty indeed!"

Quite a taking little thing! was the phrase that sprang to his mind, as he watched her reception of his compliment.

Charlotte, unable to doubt the sincerity in his voice, was regarding him with her soft mouth slightly parted in a small, startled "o," and a rosy flush in her cheeks. This reaction produced in him a surprisingly agreeable sensation of amused tenderness, and he found himself wishing he could kiss the temptingly pursed lips and watch how she reacted to *that*.

Since that was clearly impossible in the circumstances, he contented himself with a warm look and said softly as they reached her mamma's side, "You have quite overset me, you know!"

Her glance was puzzled and almost shocked, and he reflected that hazel eyes were remarkably expressive. Taking pity, he said, "I quite thought that you and I were friends—we are forever meeting at parties, and have had, I thought, some enjoyable conversations—but now you say I don't know you well enough to judge your kindness of heart—"

A more experienced lady would have laughed at the consciously hurt look he assumed, but Charlotte looked positively stricken. "Oh, Lord Edgely!" she exclaimed. "I didn't mean—I didn't mean to offend you! I too have enjoyed—*very* much enjoyed our conversations. You have always been so kind—so very polite, even when I could see you were *longing* to speak to Lady Waring—"

Lindo's jaw tightened at this, and a sudden wave of color stained his own cheekbones. His teasing had rebounded on himself, and he did not relish the picture she drew, precisely because he recognized its truth. It *was* politeness and a natural kindness which had led him punctiliously to chat with Miss Rathbone many times when his heart longed only to be near Lady Waring. That he had allowed his true wishes to show so clearly shamed him, and Charlotte did not realize that the anger she saw in his face was directed at himself, for what he considerd a shocking lapse of manners. Her voice faltered into a stammering whisper as she tried to assure him she was *honored* to be his friend, if that was how he truly thought of her, and that she most sincerely begged his pardon for suggesting otherwise, for she had always known him to be truly kind—

Unable to bear these coals of fire, he cut her off abruptly. "If you please, Miss Rathbone! Say no more. The fault has been entirely mine, and I shan't tease you any longer. Forgive me!"

He bowed to her stiffly and excused himself, leaving her dismayed and very conscious of having said the wrong thing.

Some time later, when he had recovered his own

equilibrium and was leading another young lady into a country dance, he noticed her sitting out and she briefly raised her eyes to his. He had seen that she was wearing her wooden expression, but the misery in her eyes that he glimpsed before she hastily lowered them, startled him.

He felt with a sense of deep compunction that he was the cause of it, and although he had no opportunity during the rest of the evening for private speech with her, he presented himself the next day at as early an hour as could be reconciled with good manners, at her home.

He found the ladies both at home, and Charlotte's father also sitting with them, reading aloud from the *Times* an account of the French king's triumphant emergence from his exile. He had been cheered all the way from his temporary home at Hartwell in Buckinghamshire to Stanmore, where the Prince Regent had met him with great cordiality, and escorted him along the Edgeware Road in a procession of seven carriages escorted by a troop of Life Guards, for a state entry into Piccadilly. He was installed in Grillon's Hotel in Albemarle Street, awaiting transport to Dover where he would shortly embark for France. In the meantime the Regent had invested the monarch with the Order of the Garter and honored him with a magnificent dinner at Carlton House.

Louis and the Regent, the paper declared sententiously, had done their duty, and merited and obtained the Applause of Mankind.

"The applause of the rabble, more like," Mr. Rathbone snorted, casting the paper aside. "I could scarcely move through Piccadilly in my carriage yesterday for the crowds gathered to stare at the King."

"I should like to have seen him," Charlotte said quietly.

Glad of an opportunity to open a conversation with her, Lindo said, "You might have been sadly disappointed, Miss Rathbone. I've heard he's as fat as a flawn."

She was looking down at some embroidery in her hands, but the needle in her fingers was not being plied.

74

For a moment he thought she was not going to answer him. Then she seemed to take a deep breath. Her eyes, with an anxious look in them, met his, and she said, "He *could* not be fatter than the Regent, surely!"

Lindo smiled at her. "Why, sadly, yes!" he said.

Her mother said pensively, "The Regent was a very handsome man in his youth. And *much* admired."

"He's gone to rack and ruin since," her consort growled. "In more ways than one!"

"Quite so, my love!" Mrs. Rathbone agreed, casting a warning glance at Charlotte.

Lindo did not suppose for a moment that even the most carefully reared girl could be entirely ignorant of the Regent's well-publicized peccadilloes among certain ladies of his realm. Nor could she have escaped some knowledge of the scandalous proceedings in Parliament, repeated only the previous year, against the Princess of Wales on charges of adultery. But he was ready to join in the fiction that gently nurtured young ladies were entirely ignorant of such matters, and hastened to introduce another subject by praising the ball they had enjoyed the night before.

Unfortunately this had the effect of inducing Charlotte to pretend a great interest in her embroidery, from which she could be diverted only to give the briefest replies civility allowed, and only when he spoke to her directly. Her mother was obliged to sustain the major part of the conversation, aided by an occasional remark from her husband.

The advent of another set of visitors was welcome to all of them, and when Lady Waring and Mrs. Newington were announced Lindo barely greeted them before making their presence an excuse to sit himself closer to Charlotte where he could speak to her privately.

She had returned to her sewing, and he watched her for a few moments before he said, "Have I offended you, Miss Rathbone?"

She cast him a fleeting glance and said in a low, agitated voice, "Of course not! Indeed, it was *I* who— I thought that you were angry with me!"

"With you! How could I be?"

"I'm afraid I said something—you seemed put out—!"

"If I was annoyed it was with myself for being such a clodpole—Forgive me!"

"Oh, no! There is nothing to forgive. You are always so kind—so polite." She looked across to where Lady Waring was chatting with her mother. "Please, you must not feel obliged to entertain *me,* when I'm sure you would liefer—you have scarcely spoken with Lady Waring."

He glanced up, his color a little heightened, and said, "Lady Waring is perfectly happy talking to your mother—as *I* am talking to you. You know, if you mean to fob me off on some other lady every time I manage to snatch a few private words with you, I *shall* become offended—and angry, too! I was hoping you would feel obliged to entertain *me!*"

This speech threw her into such confusion that she blushed again and stammered out something about there being no feeling of obligation, only the greatest pleasure! That it was very goodnatured in him, and she had not meant to make him angry, but he was only funning, wasn't he?

Lindo looked into the anxious eyes that seemed too large and luminous for the small, becomingly flushed countenance before him, and smilingly reassured her. But the power of throwing a young lady into such a pretty turmoil was a novel delight to him, and one which he determined to repeat. It behooved him *now* to soothe her agitation with commonplace remarks to which she was soon able to reply with equanimity, and it was not long before he had her chatting to him in the unconscious, friendly fashion that had lately marked their conversations. Dash it, he thought as he took his leave later, she *was* a pretty little thing if one only took the trouble to draw her out a little, and in her own way had a quiet and unexpected sense of mischief that was positively charming.

She would never turn off a pretty compliment with a tolerant laugh that made a fellow feel like a schoolboy aping his elders, or encourage a flock of useless fellows to flirt with her at every party, or treat him like a rather dear but very much younger brother....

He recalled how she had stared at him last night with her lovely eyes searching his face, and her mouth so sweetly and unconsciously inviting, and again the delicious amused tenderness invaded him. He smiled to himself as he planned how he might induce her to look at him like that again. Preferably when they were alone and he might hope to snatch a kiss....

chapter six

On April 24th, Louis XVIII sailed for France to the sound of cheering led by the English Regent in person. Already the Prince was planning elaborate victory celebrations for the month of June, when the rulers of the Allied states had been invited to be present. In the meantime hostesses vied with one another to startle the world of fashion with the originality, the *éclat* and the expense of their various parties. Never had London known such a season! There were breakfast parties at which champagne was served, picnics on barges that sailed up and down the Thames, levées, soirées and balls by the dozen, and, as the army began to trickle back into the country, it became an object with the ladies who led society to include as many personable officers as they could find on their invitation lists.

Dining privately with his cousin one evening, Lindo

remarked a little bitterly that he wished *he* had had the luck to wear a pair of colors.

Grenville looked at him with a sympathetic gleam in his eyes. "I had the same ambition, once," he admitted. "You have never confessed yours to me, however."

"I never had such an ambition, until now," Lindo grinned. "It's only that whenever one asks a lady to dance, these days, it's ten to one some fellow in a peacocky uniform has already engaged her. And the talk is all of battles and regiments, wherever one goes!"

Grenville laughed aloud. "So you have discovered that a *peacocky* uniform outweighs a title, have you? Females are notoriously fickle beings, Lindo. Never mind—I have an excellent Madeira with which we can console ourselves."

He glanced sharply at the flicker that crossed the young man's face, and thought with some rancor himself of the handsome and romantically wounded major who had lately attached himself to the small court that surrounded Lady Waring. Lindo was still very much a member of it also, and the marquess wondered with some misgiving how the young man would react if he knew of the developing relationship between Lady Waring and himself. The advent of the major, with his arm encased in a sling, and his faintly melancholic adoration of the Beautiful Widow had evidently drawn Lindo's attention from the lady's increasing acceptance of the attentions of the Marquess of Brandsley, but the viscount was not stupid, and Grenville lived in daily expectation of being brought to book, or at least looked at askance.

There had been one or two occasions when he had wondered if the boy had suspicions he did not wish to entertain. It would be like him, Grenville thought with a faintly vexed compunction, to be generous in doubt.

"So, you didn't want to be a soldier?" Grenville said meditatively as they sat over their wine after the covers had been removed from the table.

"No. Oh, at one time I thought of the navy, but my mother, you know—"

"Yes. I know." Lindo's father had been in the diplomatic service of his country when the ship in which he traveled was engaged by the enemy and sunk. "So," Grenville said. "Are you going to leave the management of your estates in your bailiff's hands, now that you're of age?"

"I have been down to Greatstones, you know," Lindo said defensively.

"I know. And stayed a few days each time. Doesn't it interest you?"

"Well, of course it interests me. But the thing is, Sandwoods has everything in train, and has been used to having a free hand. *I* know precious little about rents and cropping, and the maintenance of the park, and as for the financial side, I have no head for figures! Sandwoods was quite painstaking in showing me all, but dash it, Gren, I felt a fool! The fellow might be as deferential as you please, but I could tell he thought me hopelessly stupid."

"Sack him," Grenville advised briefly.

"What?"

"Turn him off," the marquess told him. "And find a man who won't make you feel a fool. And learn to run the place yourself."

Half laughing, Lindo protested. "I couldn't! The fellow has been in charge there almost since I was breeched—my stepfather swears there's no more honest agent in the country."

"Are you fond of him?"

"Fond? Good Lord, no! I scarcely know him. But I *cannot* turn him off. What a reward for so many years of faithful service!"

Grenville looked at him over his glass, a smiling gleam in his eyes. "Then make it clear to him you're not a fool and won't be treated like one, deferentially or no."

Lindo chuckled. "Yes, *you* would do it easily enough, if anyone dared try such tricks with you!"

His cousin's glance was enigmatic. "You think me ruthless, do you?" he asked.

"Yes, when you like to be. But more than that, you have a way of looking, if something don't please you, that would freeze a pot of boiling water at ten paces."

"Indeed?" Grenville raised his brows. "Have I ever looked at *you* in that way?"

"Not often," Lindo grinned. "I've taken good care that I shouldn't incur your wrath."

"Brat!" his cousin admonished him affectionately.

"You think I *should* spend more time at Greatstones, don't you?" Lindo asked.

"Should you hate it?"

"Good Lord, no!" He sipped his wine and said, "To tell the truth, I've become heartily sick of town life at times. I spent some time with my friend Sefton last winter at his seat. He and his wife gave us the greatest time—myself and a few others."

"And a taste for country life?"

"Well, yes! But it's different if a fellow is married, you know!"

"Perhaps I should not say so," murmured the marquess reflectively. "But I think that I do know—what you mean, that is."

Laughing, Lindo went on, "Mind you, I think I should like to come to London for the season. All one's friends are here, you know!"

"You have a great many friends in town?"

"Yes—" Lindo looked sharply up and added, "If you are trying to discover if I still go about with Heathcote's ramshackle crowd, the answer is *no*. And I've not been to a hell in *months!*"

A steely glint entered the gray eyes that surveyed him over the refilled wine glass. "If I wanted to know that, I should have asked you, my fine young pup. However, I'm pleased to hear that you heeded the advice I gave you."

"Well, I didn't," Lindo admitted, a faint flush on his cheeks. "The fact is—I was still dipping fairly deeply until not long before you came to town."

Grenville was regarding him intently, saying nothing.

"Well—" Lindo said. "When you made me that loan, you didn't make it a *condition* that I give up gambling—or my friends."

"I never make *conditions* when I help a friend or relative," Grenville said coldly. "But I confess I did hope you would have the sense to see the road you were traveling. And I don't recall suggesting you gave up gambling altogether—only that you gamed in respectable clubs and used some discretion."

"Yes, well, I do—now!"

"So—if it was not my well-meant advice that brought about your reformation, what was it?"

"Actually—it was Lady Waring. Some fellow teased me in her presence about being a noted gamester, and she—well, I don't precisely know what it was she said. But somehow, I felt the foolishness of it as I never had before. And I realized that I should never dream of introducing Heathcote to her—which made me see what a shabby fellow he really was..."

A frown darkened Grenville's eyes. "Lady Waring..." he repeated thoughtfully. "She appears to have your interests at heart."

"She has been all kindness to me!"

"Really?" The marquess shot an enquiring glance at the viscount's face. "I have thought sometimes that her kindness to other men must have hurt you."

Lindo looked uncomfortable. "Well, as to that—yes. But *that* kind of hurt, I suppose, cannot be avoided if a man—a man tries to fix the affections of an accredited beauty! She is so lovely that any man who wants to win her must reconcile himself to always finding a bevy of admirers about her."

"*Could* you reconcile yourself to it?" Grenville asked curiously.

Lindo was silent, looking at his cousin with a slightly flushed face, his expression difficult to read. "Gren," he said abruptly. "When you first came to town, I told you how I felt about Lady Waring—I have had no reason to change my opinion of her. She is not only beautiful, she's truly kind-hearted and although she may flirt a little, and some of the tabbies have criticized her for it, *I* see no harm in it. She never goes beyond the line—"

"The lady's virtue is not in question," Grenville said gravely. Then, coming to an abrupt decision, he added, "You also told me, when I came to London, that she favored you above her other flirts. I should tell you, my young cousin, that I intend to alter that."

"What do you mean?"

"I mean," the marquess said steadily, his eyes on his cousin's face, "that I have the fixed intention of cutting you out."

Lindo's glass descended to the table with a small thud. "With—with Lady Waring?" he asked.

"Yes."

"Do you mean that *you* are in love with her?" Lindo asked.

Grenville's face, which had been carefully expressionless, became, if anything, more masklike. "At any rate, I mean to have her," he said.

Lindo's eyes narrowed a trifle, so that for a moment he looked remarkably like Grenville himself in one of his less pleasant moods. "To have her?" he repeated. "Let us be plain if you please, Brandsley. Are you thinking of marriage?"

The mask lifted a little, a spark of derision showed in Grenville's eyes. "What else should I mean?" he inquired frostily.

Lindo searched his face, and then relaxed a trifle. "Nothing," he replied, a little shamefaced. "I beg your pardon. You have surprised me—although I should have guessed, of course."

"I'm sure it was only a matter of time before you did. Hence my decision to tell you. I need hardly add that this conversation is not to go beyond yourself and me."

"What do you take me for, Gren?" Lindo demanded indignantly.

"A greenhead, to be sure," his elder scoffed gently. "But I congratulate you on taking the news so calmly."

A little stung by the mild reminder of his youth and inexperience, Lindo replied, "Did you expect me to fly up into the boughs? Well—I can tell you—"

"Yes?" prompted Brandsley.

A faint grin pulled at the corners of Lindo's mouth, as a thought evidently struck him. "I can tell you that you won't have it all your own way," he said. "*I* may be a greenhead, but Haines ain't, by God! And you've the major to contend with, you know. *He* learned his strategy in the Peninsula, and so far he has outmaneuvered all of the others. Aslett is quite in despair!"

A slight, sympathetic smile etched Grenville's mouth. "Jealous, cousin?" he asked gently.

Lindo hesitated a fraction of a second, then said, "Are *you*?"

Grenville laughed. "Cry pax!" he said. "I don't parade my emotions for you or anyone. Here—have some more wine. We'll talk of something else."

During the rest of the evening, he cast one or two hidden glances at the younger man, trying to gauge the effect of his stated intention, but Lindo seemed to have put the conversation out of his mind, and to be in perfectly good spirits.

If he had been privileged to see his guest's demeanor after he left the house, he might have been more concerned. Two members of the watch on patrol of the streets met the young man walking with a jaunty step, and as they passed, perceived the grin that seemed directed at empty space before him. A moment later an audible chuckle caused them to turn and look after the gentleman. Several yards away, he stopped, put out his hand to clutch at a lamp standard, and laughed aloud.

"Foxed," one of the men said, *sotto voce*. "Shot the cat."

"Should we take him up for the constable?" his companion ventured, not very enthusiastically.

"Don't be daft! He's Quality, *he* is!" The new gas lighting had not yet reached this part of the city, but the fitful light of the lamp showed snow white linen, a faultlessly tied cravat, and a coat that only the best of tailors could have provided, fitting its wearer to perfection. "Take him up?" the watchman repeated derisively. "Yah, and have his pa come down in the morning with a fancy lawyer jawing away and making out wot *we* was at fault for taking up a gentleman about his lawful pursoots! Like to lose yer job, would yer?"

His companion hastily disclaiming any such desire, the two moved rapidly away, glancing back only to see that Lindo had composed himself and was walking in the opposite direction with remarkable steadiness for one who had evidently been imbibing far too freely.

* * *

Attending a musical party at Mrs. Brassington's, Damaris was surprised to see Lord Brandsley among the guests. She first noticed hin standing against one of the gold-tasseled velvet curtains that adorned the windows, its rich crimson setting off his dark distinction to advantage, and she could not help an involuntary shock of pleasure when he turned his glance from the young lady at present amusing the company with an interminable sonata, to give her a smile and a brief bow.

When at last the sonata ended and the blushing young lady retired to yield her place to another, Damaris found Brandsley beside her chair, asking, "Are we to be favored with a glimpse of your talents, also, Lady Waring?"

"No, indeed!" she disclaimed. "You must know that displaying musical accomplishment is the province of single young ladies, Lord Brandsley."

"Now that you mention it," he remarked, "it is rare to see a married lady exhibiting her skill at the pianoforte or harp. Does a lady's talent die on marriage, or once she has attained that happy state, is her object in displaying her musical ability accomplished? Is that young woman who is about to entertain us, in fact a Circe, and when she has snared her Ulysses, is her song to be stilled forever?"

Since the lady in question was undeniably plump and pudding faced, with protuberant blue eyes and a nose which in the candlelight tended to shine pinkly, Damaris was obliged to bite hard on her lip to prevent a laugh escaping into the hush which had fallen on the audience, politely waiting for the start of another musical treat.

She cast a glance of indignant reproach at Lord Brandsley, only to find him giving her an unrepentant grin, with a lurking something in his eyes that caused her to ply her small ivory fan a little more vigorously.

"Do you *know* the effect that trick has on a man?" he asked quietly, under cover of the crashing opening bars of the piece the ambitious Circe had decided to play.

Turning a puzzled glance to him, she whispered, "What trick?"

"That way you have of biting on your bottom lip."

She turned away, coloring faintly, and tried to concentrate on the music.

That should not have been difficult, since the musician was attacking the pianoforte with a strength of execution that suggested a pastrycook kneading loaves of bread. But Damaris was only dimly aware of the reverberating chords. Not for the first time, Lord Brandsley had upset her composure with a few low-spoken words.

From the time that she had tacitly accepted his outrageous challenge to her, she had been in a fret of alarm, shame and uncertainty whenever she thought of that extraordinary interview. She had told herself that evening that she would exert herself to bring him to her feet, but when it came to the point, she found herself unable to assume the airs of a coquette.

The truth was that she was a novice at the art of flirtation, and had never in her life consciously tried to attach a man's affections. She had been flattered by the attention of the men who had been drawn by her beauty, and enjoyed their admiration—as what woman would not? The extravagant and practiced compliments of Lord Alfred Haines and his like, she accepted with a grain of salt, and intrigued them the more by showing them a hint of skepticism. Lindo she treated more gently, but until he should have got over his touching infatuation with her, she tried to discourage his gallantries without wounding his feelings, by adopting an air of friendly tolerance. It had taken a great deal of patient ingenuity to prevent him from making a declaration which would have forced her to wound his young heart, and a certain amount of skill to keep unobtrusively throwing in his way a succession of suitably younger and attractive ladies.

Lord Brandsley, of course, was quite in ignorance of her care for his cousin, and she sometimes wondered if it would be possible to tell him of it. But when once or twice she had ventured to put out feelers, and speak of Viscount Edgely, such a look of cold discouragement came into his face, and such a note of biting sarcasm into his voice that she almost quailed, only hiding the apprehension he aroused in her by whipping herself into anger, and quarreling with him.

That had the effect of banishing the chilly look, but since it was replaced by a very provoking expression of cynical amusement, she had found these essays more than unsatisfactory, and decided with obscure logic that if he was so determined not to give her the opportunity of explaining the real relationship between herself and his cousin, he would be well served if he never learned it.

And deep down was an unacknowledged feeling of relief, for she still half believed that his interest in herself would wane if he realized that she had none whatsoever, except of a vaguely sisterly nature, in his cousin.

In the meantime, she accepted his invitations and his company with a pleasure she had no need to feign, although she was frequently thrown into confusion by such remarks as he had just made. Fortunately she was no longer a green girl, and made push to hide her feelings to some extent. Still, she had seen a look of puzzlement in his eyes once or twice when she had felt herself at a loss to reply adequately to one of his quizzical sallies.

For his part, Grenville had indeed found himself sincerely puzzled on occasions by her manner. He was beginning to be aware that in spite of the admirers that gathered about her, and the tongue-clucking of one or two matrons, Lady Waring used none of the tricks of the experienced coquette. She accepted a compliment with sincere pleasure or a faintly skeptical smile, and her speech was direct and intelligent rather than titillating or teasing. Her gaze was frank and open and all the more devastating for that, for her eyes were beautiful, clear and expressive. She gave no sidelong, inviting glances, and she used her fan, though gracefully, to cool herself rather than to draw attention to her eyes, or her lips, as some women did.

In fact, he noted with amusement, she did sometimes bring it into use in a curiously modest fashion, by opening it in such a way that the low décolletage of her gown was hidden, as some amorous spark bent to solicit her hand for a dance or whisper his compliments into her ear.

It was true that she did nothing to discourage the attentions of the gentlemen who vied for her smiles, but no one had ever accused her of overstepping the bounds of propriety.

Grenville had discovered in himself an at first reluctant and now almost eager suspicion that his opinion of Lady Waring had been mistaken.

Unfortunately he was unable to put this novel theory to the test immediately. The energetic pianoforte player having earned her round of polite applause, a short interval was allowed, and Lord Alfred Haines descended on Damaris and monopolized her attention until the advent of the next performer, a girl as thin as the last had been plump, who drooped romantically against an enormous harp placed in the center of the room by a couple of perspiring footmen.

Grenville was accosted by his hostess and borne off to make the acquaintance of the willowy harpist immediately after the harp was removed from the floor, and it was some time before he was able to return to Lady Waring's side.

Meantime, Lord Alfred had not wasted his opportunities. It had occurred to him some time ago that Brandsley was taking an unusual interest in the lady, and lately it had seemed to him that she was not indifferent. He thought it was time something was done about it. Edgely was a negligible rival; Aslett and the rest, even the dashing major, easily dealt with, he confidently believed. But Brandsley was a danger. His consequence was better than Haines's, for his father had conveniently died at a reasonable age, while Haines was a younger son whose father held only a courtesy title, while the old duke, his grandfather, bade fair to live out his centenary. Nor was the marquess lacking in charm.

What Brandsley wanted, Haines was not sure. It seemed unlikely that he thought of marriage, but if the lady thought she could bring it off, it would obviously be foolish of her to settle for something less. Lord Haines, who had hoped to induce her to settle for a good deal less on his own behalf, and was planning a discreet but very enjoyable affair, when he had persuaded the lady that the path of virtue was not the only road to follow, found the advent of Lord Brandsley a very unwelcome complication. He had seen the effect the marquess had produced tonight with a few quiet words. Clearly it was time to do what he could to queer his lordship's pitch.

Lord Alfred was a man of some honor, and any man who accused him of lying would have found himself looking down the barrel of a pistol at twenty paces some misty morning. But fortunately he was in possession of some information which he felt would serve his purpose very well.

In the course of a recital of the latest *on-dits* suitable for a lady's ears, he said abruptly, "I'm surprised, Lady Waring, to see you so friendly with Lord Brandsley."

"Why?" she asked candidly. "Should I not be friendly?"

Haines contrived to look conscious, uneasily failing to meet her eyes. "You know I must disapprove of your being kind to any other man," he said lightly.

Brushing that aside, she said, "But you expressed *surprise*, just now—not disapproval."

Haines gave an embarrassed laugh. "Take no notice—it was merely that—but of course you can have no knowledge—"

"Of what?" she asked. "I wish you would explain what you mean."

Looking vexed, he said, "Forgive me for a gabbing fool, Lady Waring. I should not have mentioned it. And yet—"

He hesitated, looking troubled.

Damaris, her eyes fixed on his face, said quietly, "And yet—what? I collect that you have heard something about *me* which you hesitate to repeat."

"No!" he hastened to assure her, too quickly. "Nothing that reflects on you, at least. Rather, it is to Lord Brandsley's detriment, that he should have allowed himself to boast in public of an intention that no man of breeding—"

"Tell me!" she commanded, her face a little pale, her chin firm.

"I should not!" Haines said, apparently conscience stricken. "And yet, it would be infamous in me not to warn you..."

"Then you had better do so," Damaris said firmly. "Warn me of what?"

"There is talk of a bet," Haines said uncomfortably. "Of odds being taken that Brandsley will cut out his cousin by dangling his own fortune and consequence as a counterweight for your—for your favor. Caseby told me that Brandsley admitted the whole at his club, among friends, which made the betting swing in his favor."

His anxious look as he finished this recital was not feigned, for he thought that she looked devilish pale, and was afraid she might faint. "I should not have mentioned it," he muttered, with something approaching genuine remorse.

Her eyes as they met his looked oddly blind, but to his relief a hint of color was returning to her face. "No," she said. "You were quite right. As it happens, the warning is unnecessary. I am—I have been aware for some time of the nature of Lord Brandsley's attentions. But I did not know that he had seen fit to make me the subject of—of a *wager* with his *gentlemen* friends. Thank you for telling me. It is unpleasant, but—but I'm glad to know of it." She took a quick, gasping breath and said hurriedly, "I wonder, Lord Alfred, if you could procure for me a glass of wine?"

He rose with alacrity to do so, and she used the few minutes that he took to bring her the glass to regain a semblance of composure. She told herself that there was no reason to feel so overset. As she had told Lord Alfred, she had not been unaware of the marquess's intention, for he had been brutally frank with her about it himself. Nothing had really changed.

Only the thought of him boasting in his club of what he meant to do, of allowing, even *encouraging,* his friends to lay bets on the outcome, of bandying her name in those surroundings in a way in which, as Haines had said, no man of breeding would mention the name of any woman whom he held in the slightest respect....

Yes, the thought of it made her feel sick with disgust and humiliation. What a fool she had been, imagining that of late the marquess had begun to genuinely like her, that the glow in his eyes sometimes held more than mere sensual appreciation. He had not become softer at all, but was only playing a cruel game with great skill and refinement.

Haines, a distinguished player of games of love, himself, watched until he saw a faint spark of anger replace the shock in her eyes, and was satisfied. When Brandsley rejoined them, he was quite amenable to taking himself off and leaving Lady Waring with his rival. He hardly thought the marquess would advance far in the lady's affections tonight.

Damaris greeted the marquess with a brilliant and brittle smile. No good, she decided, would come of her challenging him with what she knew. She could not, in any case, trust herself to speak of it without betraying her feelings, and she wanted above all to hide the fact that his lack of ordinary decent respect for her name had deeply hurt her. That he had the power to wound her, he should *never* know.

So she hid her emotion beneath a light, provocative manner and seized the first opportunity that offered of leaving his company, for she found she could not bear to be near him.

But he sought her out again, later, and she felt a quick spurt of anger that he should do so. Apparently she failed to conceal it.

"What have I done?" he asked, his eyebrows raised in surprise.

Tempted to rip up at him, she curbed the words on her tongue and said colorlessly, "Done, Lord Brandsley? I'm sure I don't know what you mean."

"I have annoyed you in some way," he said. "That much is evident. I wish you would tell me in what way."

Bitterly she said, "You set yourself out to insult and annoy me almost from the moment that we met. I have tried to accord you the civility that good manners demand, in spite of it, but there are times when the mem-

91

ory of your insolence, your arrogance and your monstrously improper conduct towards me, becomes too much to bear. I have been obliged twice tonight to endure your company—a third conversation with you is asking too much of my forbearance!"

For a second or two she saw a murderous light replace the surprise in his eyes, before he bowed to her with steely correctness and said, "I beg your pardon for inflicting my presence on you yet again. You have not, lately, shown such reluctance for my company. And don't tell me again you have merely tried to be civil. I apologize for the insolence, deny the arrogance, and if the *improper conduct* you speak of is by way of saying I should not have kissed you, I freely admit it. But for *that* I refuse to express regret. I found it exceedingly pleasant."

The anger in his eyes was dying, to be mingled with a familiar, teasing challenge. But this time she refused to be coaxed into charity with him. His charm was potent, and too many times she had allowed him to beguile her into forgetting the ruthlessness that underlay it.

"*I* did not!" she informed him coldly. "And I don't wish to be reminded of it."

He looked for a moment as though he would challenge her on that, too, and her heart gave a little bump of trepidation. The extraordinary thing was that deep down she knew she had lied. And she was very much afraid that he might know it.

But he said, "And you don't wish to tell me why you are angry with me, either, so let us talk of something else. I have been speaking with my cousin."

Since he did not seem to have any intention of taking her hint and leaving her, she reconciled herself to enduring his company. "Not an unusual occurrence, surely, sir?" she inquired satirically.

"We spoke of you."

"Indeed?" she said frostily. "Where was this—at your club?"

He frowned. "No," he said shortly. "At my home. He dined with me—alone. He spoke of you with the greatest admiration and—"

"And respect?" she asked with a hint of irony.

Apparently struck by her tone, he said, "To my knowledge he has never spoken of you in any other manner."

Her face softened slightly. "No, I'm certain Viscount Edgely would not speak otherwise of me."

His own expression, conversely, hardened a trifle. "He told me something that I have to admit surprised me considerably. That, in fact, *you* were the reason he stopped making a fool of himself in certain unsavory gaming establishments. I had, perhaps *arrogantly*— must I admit that also, now?—thought the credit was mine for persuading him away from the road to ruin. But it seems my warnings were of small account. It was your strictures that affected him."

"Not strictures!" she protested.

"Then what? Tell me how a woman's wiles succeeded where my sound advice failed."

Damaris almost smiled. Had it pricked his pride, she wondered, that a mere woman had succeeded where he had not?

She shrugged. "I merely hinted," she said, "that of course the rumors I had heard could not be true, since only the greenest of green boys are foolish enough to allow themselves to be fleeced in disreputable gaming haunts. Sophisticated men of the world, of course, will indulge in a little mild gaming at gentlemen's clubs or private parties, but only a complete sapskull would endanger his inheritance at the tables. I'm glad he took the hint."

"So am I. I have wondered why—" He was looking at her with an air of appraisal.

Sudden bitterness rose in her. He had wondered, and no doubt come to his own quite erroneous conclusions. Her hand made a sudden, swiftly checked movement. She saw his eyes drop to it, and deliberately loosened her clenched fingers, following his gaze to her slim wrist, adorned by a pretty diamond-set bracelet.

She did not know that Grenville was hesitating on the brink of telling her that he believed he might have been mistaken in her character, of making her a genuine apology for his suspicions. Stemming a sudden urge to weep, she gave him instead a glittering smile and said, "But I'm sure you know why, Lord Brandsley. It is my fixed belief that young men should not waste their money at the tables. I can think of so many *much* more satisfactory uses for it—don't you agree?" And she lifted her wrist, transferring her smile to the glitter of the jewels that encircled it, then raised her over-bright eyes again to his.

Her bravado shivered to pieces under the impact of the narrowed gray gaze that met hers, for it was piercing and furiously angry. She was devoutly thankful that their hostess interrupted them at that moment in the course of her social duties, and when, shortly afterwards, the first of the guests took their leave, she lost no time in finding her aunt and hastening her to their carriage.

She had only a confused idea of what had prompted her to behave so outrageously. Now she must have confirmed every discreditable notion that he had of her. To the tormented question *why?* that beat in her tortured mind with the same insistent rhythm as the horses' feet ringing on the cobbles, she could only answer despairingly, *I don't know!* But it had seemed at the time that the only alternatives were to break down in tears in Mrs. Brassington's overfull drawing room, or to cause a scandal by striking the Marquess of Brandsley in front of all the company gathered there.

chapter seven

Lord Brandsley was obliged to leave town for a week in order to attend to business on his estate, and Damaris tried to pretend she did not miss his company. When Lord Alfred Haines expertly detached her from a party visiting the Vauxhall Gardens, lured her to one of the grottoes dotted about the grounds and attempted to make love to her, she rebuffed his advances with repugnance. But she was less shocked by the importunities of Haines, than by the realization that if only it had been Lord Brandsley's arms about her, his lips on hers, she might have been tempted to return his improper embrace. Certainly when he had kissed her she had not instinctively shuddered away.

As she awaited his return with a mixture of trepidation and longing, her feelings began to alarm her. She *must* not be so foolish as to develop a tenderness for the marquess. He might once have cynically urged her to see if she could bring him to offer for her, but she knew herself incapable of carrying out her original intention, for she had no idea of the tricks necessary to captivate such a man. She was aware that she attracted him, for he had freely admitted it to her, and he continued to form one of the circle of her admirers, but his disgust of what he believed to be her true nature must have deepened after Mrs. Brassington's party.

The marquess's return in the first week of June coincided with the landing of the Tsar Alexander and the King of Prussia at Dover, accompanied by the Austrian chancellor Metternich, and Blücher, the Prussian commander. The following day the populace of London was in a happy uproar as it greeted the distinguished visitors with a heroes' welcome. Calling in Harley Street, Brandsley was able to describe to the ladies the tall, dark and distinguished appearance of the Tsar, for he had glimpsed him on the balcony of the Pulteney Hotel as he found his way with difficulty through the crowds in Piccadilly.

"I thought he was to stay at the palace?" Damaris said, surprised.

"Yes, and the Regent has been awaiting him at St. James with the Lord Chamberlain and half the officers of state, but it seems the Tsar prefers to stay with his sister. The Grand Duchess Catherine has been fixed at the Pulteney now for weeks."

Lord Alfred Haines, arriving a little later, brought with him the further news that on learning of his guest's determination, the Prince had ordered his carriage, and was even now attempting to wait upon the Tsar and welcome him to England.

"It's my belief he'll never get there," Haines grinned. "The crowd has gone quite wild, alternately hissing and booing, and obstructing the royal carriage, and then hallooing for the Russian to show himself again on the balcony so they can cheer him to the skies!"

"Hissing the Regent!" Mrs. Newington exclaimed. "How shocking!"

"Well, he is very unpopular, you know," Haines said.

"Yes, but—well, I must say I think he has treated the princess quite *shamefully,* and one cannot blame the people for not approving, but a royal prince—so disrespectful!"

"Yes," Brandsley said. "And what is more, the only one of the Allied heads of state who has consistently opposed Napoleon from the very beginning, even though he was never in the field. For that, he does deserve some credit."

"He won't get it," Haines said carelessly. "The Tsar is the Hero of Paris, and the mob have already taken Blücher to their hearts. They took the horses from the shafts of his carriage as it came through the Horse Guards, and knocked over the sentries at Carlton House, pulling it into the palace."

"Good gracious!" Mrs. Newington said faintly.

"If this is the welcome they give to foreign heroes," Brandsley mused, "I wonder how they will react when Wellington comes home!"

A new element now entered into London's fashionable parties. Even more of a feather in a hostess's cap than a British uniform was the acquisition of an exotic Cossack officer, or, even better, one of the tall, blond Prussian princes.

At a ball, Damaris had the honor of standing up with one of the latter, who trod energetically on her slippered toes, clicked his heels with great *élan* as he restored her to Mrs. Newington's side, and visited her next day apparently for the express purpose of declaring in execrable English that he had conceived an undying passion for her.

Not sure whether to be amused or alarmed, Damaris managed to fob him off with half-promises to dance with him again, and had barely recovered her composure when Lord Alfred Haines was announced. He found her alone and, judging the opportunity too good to be missed, attempted a renewal of the importunities he had indulged in at Vauxhall.

Damaris boxed his ears.

Haines, clearly unused to such summary treatment at the hands of ladies he favored with his attentions, grabbed at her wrists and jerked her roughly toward him, just as the butler coughed meaningfully in the doorway, and begged to inform her that the Marquess of Brandsley had called.

Frightened by the ugly look on the face of the man who had dropped his hands as though her arms had been hot coals, but stood facing her with menace in his eyes, she gasped thankfully, "Show him up!"

By this time, the marquess was on the landing, and as he strode in, Haines was bowing stiffly out of the room, casting him a glance of acute dislike as he passed.

The butler withdrew and Brandsley looked frowningly at Damaris, in his face an unexpected concern.

"W-won't you sit down," she said, trying to regulate her quickened breathing, and putting a shaking hand to her hair, which she felt sure must be sadly disheveled.

"In a moment," he said, and took her hands firmly in his. "What has transpired?" he demanded gently. "Tell me!"

Damaris experienced an extraordinary desire to place her head on the broad shoulder before her and weep on his lordship's elegant superfine coat. She curbed it with a little effort and said, trying to move her hands from his grasp, "Why, nothing!"

But her eyes were still full of fright, and her fingers in his trembled. Looking at the distressed flush on her cheeks, he said, "I think I can make a fair guess." His glance fell to her wrists, and he exclaimed, "Good God!"

The pink marks of a rough grasp were fading but unmistakable on her skin, and she made a further agitated effort to move out of his hold. It had no effect, and she saw that his mouth had become a taut and implacable line. "Lord Brandsley," she whispered. *"Please!"*

He released her and said in an odd, rough voice, "Haines—what did he do to you?"

"It was nothing!" she assured him. "Merely—" She met the fierce accusation in his eyes and said, "He kissed me. Nothing more. And when I hit him, he was angry. I'm not hurt."

"So you didn't *want* him to kiss you!"

"Certainly not!"

He paused, looking at her intently. "You seemed

very agitated," he said. "In a young girl it would be understandable, but—forgive me—you have been a married woman. It appeared to me that you were frightened to a degree hardly warranted by one unwelcome kiss. You did not react so strongly when *I* kissed you."

"Please!" she said, moving away from him. "It was nothing more—only that he became so angry that I confess he did frighten me a little. It was foolish of me. Pray, let us speak of something else."

After a moment he said, "As you wish. Where is your aunt?"

"She had a headache, and went to lie down when the prince was here. Not—not the Regent," she explained hastily, and gave him a drastically edited account of her meeting with the scion of the Prussian royal house, and his subsequent visit.

He looked a trifle askance, and though conscious of it, she felt quite unable to explain that her aunt's exaggerated respect for royalty—*any* royalty—had led to her abandoning her niece to a *tête à tête* with the visitor as soon as he had conveyed his desire to be alone with Lady Waring.

After a few minutes, however, the marquess began to look amused. "So you have made another conquest!" he said. "The major will sustain another injury, I fear."

"I—don't know what you mean," she said uncertainly.

"Why, his nose will be sadly out of joint!" he replied gravely. "A Prussian prince quite outranks a mere major!"

She could not help laughing at that, and he allowed a smile to touch his mouth. "Poor Aslett will go into a decline," he said. Then, after a slight pause, he added, "Do you fancy marrying a Continental princeling?"

She said, "That's nonsense. There is no question of *marrying* him. In any case, he seems scarcely older than your—"

She stopped short suddenly in confusion, and Brandsley's eyes on her became keenly interested.

"Yes?" he said sharply. "What were you going to say?"

"Nothing. This—this is a very improper conversation, Lord Brandsley. I'm sure my aunt would be shocked to hear us discussing the prince in this way—"

He stood up, suddenly, and took a step toward her chair. But Mrs. Newington, entering the room on a wave of fluttering apologies and surprise at his presence, prevented him from saying what was in his mind.

He was forced instead to inquire after her headache, which she assured him blushingly was really quite better, for it was amazing how much a little hartshorn in water and a half hour's rest could do to quite restore one!

All solicitousness, he put her into a chair out of the draft from the door and chatted for a few minutes before taking his leave.

As Damaris gave him her hand, he paused with it in his and said, "At Mrs. Brassington's musical evening, Lady Waring, you were wearing a particularly charming diamond bracelet, if you recall? I wonder if you can tell me if it was bought in London. I have been looking for something of the sort as a present for a young relative on her coming out."

"I—I'm afraid I don't recall—" she started to say, but her aunt broke in on the evasion.

"Diamonds? Why, Damaris, my love, it must have been the bracelet that dear Sir Walter gave you to commemorate the anniversary of your marriage—the second—or was it the third? In any case, Lord Brandsley, I think you will find it was not bought in London, for Sir Walter very seldom visited the metropolis."

The marquess released Damaris's hand, but not before she had seen the gleam of confirmation in his eyes. "A pity," he murmured.

Diffidently, Mrs. Newington said, "If I might venture to suggest, Lord Brandsley—?"

Immediately he turned to her, smiling. "Yes?"

"Perhaps you might consult your young relative's mamma before deciding on your present. Diamonds, you know, are not always considered suitable for a girl who is just *out*. Forgive me, you have probably spoken with her already on the matter, and in *your* circles it may be quite acceptable, especially these days...When *I* was a girl, of course, nothing but pearls..."

"Indeed, ma'am, I'm most grateful for your advice, for I fear you may be right, and have saved me from a foolish mistake. I *shall* speak with her mamma."

Damaris, who was perfectly certain that no such young relative existed, and aware that he had laid a trap for her, said sweetly, "I do hope, Lord Brandsley, we shall have the pleasure of meeting your relative, when she has made her *début?*"

"That will not be until next year, Lady Waring—I thought it wise to begin early to look for a suitable gift for the child. But I look forward to presenting her to you when she arrives from—Northumberland!"

"What a very long way away!" she said. "It is to be hoped that when the time comes, she is able to make the journey without mishap!"

"Yes," he said. "There are many dangers in traveling, are there not? Highwaymen might waylay the coach, or some accident befall it on the road—and I believe that part of the journey is over water, too, for her home is in a *very* remote part of the country. And then, there are the hazards of staying at coaching inns along the way, you know. There is always a risk of picking up some infectious disease!"

"Which may well carry one off!" she agreed. "Did you say you intended to speak with the young lady's mamma, before her come-out?"

"*Write* to her!" he replied promptly. "It will be necessary to write."

"Of course!" she said. "Northumberland being so far away." Her eyes innocent, she added, "I wonder you don't advise her not to bring her daughter to London at all, for it is clearly unsafe..."

"I'm persuaded you are quite right, Lady Waring!" he said. "I will lose no time in doing so!"

Here Mrs. Newington, who had been listening in some puzzlement, exclaimed, "Oh, but Damaris! Surely you would not deprive the poor girl—why you, yourself—! I know how disappointing it was that we were unable to bring you out in proper style!"

But Lord Brandsley, with a soothing word to her not to distress herself, had left, and Damaris had collapsed into a chair, with every sign of indulging in a fit of what could only be called giggles.

Doubtfully, Mrs. Newington smiled at her. "You did not mean it?" she ventured.

"No, dear Aunt Tabitha! We were funning!"

"Well, I should not have guessed it," Mrs. Newington said. "But I can see it has thrown you into whoops. Which," she added, "I am *very* pleased to see, for you don't laugh much, and it has lately appeared to me that you are not enjoying your season in London as you ought."

"Of course I am enjoying it!" Damaris assured her. "Why, I have been to parties and assemblies and balls until I have become quite tired of them—I shall soon be one of those tedious creatures who do nothing but complain of the *ennui* of having nothing but a choice of pleasures, day and night! And I have been courted and flattered by so many obliging gentlemen, that my head is quite turned! It is everything you wanted for me, Aunt, everything you told me it would be. How could I not enjoy myself?"

Her aunt smiled a little sadly. "It is too late, of course. You should have had at least one season when you were seventeen."

"Nonsense! I should not have enjoyed it half so much. Why, at seventeen I was such a timid little thing, I should have been so afraid of taking a wrong step in the ballroom, or saying something foolish if a gentleman even glanced my way, that I should probably have been in an agony of embarrassment the whole time! But *now*, although a widow must be careful of her reputation, I am not so hedged about as a young girl in her first season, and have far more freedom to enjoy myself, than I should have had *then*."

"Of course," Mrs. Newington sighed, "it was impossible with your uncle being so ill, for so long a time, for I *could* not leave him, and the medical expenses..."

"I know," Damaris assured her gently. "Believe me, Aunt, I understood perfectly."

"You were so good," her aunt said. "No word of disappointment or reproach—"

"*Reproach!* I should think not indeed! Why, after you

and Uncle taking me in so generously when my parents died in that horrible epidemic, rearing me and loving me quite as your own child, even saving so unselfishly to give me a London season! Of *course* it had to be used to pay the doctor's bill, Aunt. A fine figure I should have looked, dancing away the nights at Almacks, and buying feathers for my presentation at St. James, while my uncle lay ill..."

"It did not save him, anyway," her aunt sighed, brushing away a tear.

Damaris came to sit on the carpet by her chair, taking her hand.

"No, but we were with him until the end, and he had the best of care," she soothed.

"Yes, he did," her aunt agreed. "And Sir Walter was so generous..."

"Indeed, yes," Damaris said in a steady voice.

"He was a very good friend. I have sometimes thought, though—"

Damaris looked up into Mrs. Newington's troubled face and said, "Yes?"

"I have sometimes thought—that he was *not* a good husband."

"My dear aunt, you must not judge every man by my uncle. *His* disposition was exceptionally gentle. If Sir Walter sometimes seemed out of temper with me, well, you must know that is common among married people. And you know how generous he was to me!"

"Yes, indeed! All that jewelry, and even though you *begged* him not to—which you did, Damaris, for I heard you myself, on more than one occasion!"

"Yes, well, that was because I was sure he could not really afford it, and—" *And he always exacted a kind of payment,* her thoughts ran, but she could not voice them.

"And I heard him reproach you, later, for making him spend so much on *bedecking* you with expensive baubles, which was *quite* unfair!" her aunt said. "For it was untrue as well as unjust!"

"Yes, it was, but men are not to be held responsible, you know, for what they say in temper."

"Do you know," her aunt said, "before you married

Sir Walter, and we went to live at the Hall with him, I quite thought he was as gentle a man as your uncle."

"So, too, did I," Damaris said. "He had been so kind to us while Uncle lay so ill, I believe I thought of him as—"

"Oh, Damaris!"

The elder lady looked so stricken that Damaris squeezed her hand, saying firmly, "Now, don't be a peagoose, Aunt! It was quite my own idea to marry Sir Walter, you know, and there is nothing for you to be in the least worried over!" She got to her feet, saying briskly, "Well, now, you know you promised to help me alter the neck of my Indian muslin, and trim the sleeves in the way we saw in the *Repository*. We have to contrive, you know, how we may make it look like a new gown altogether!"

The Indian muslin was worn for a tea party arranged by Mrs. Rathbone at the Yorkshire Stingo pleasure gardens at Lisson Grove. The Prussian prince was not of the party, but Mrs. Rathbone was not wholly cast down, for two military gentlemen escorted the barouche in which the ladies rode. Major Kingston, his arm newly delivered from its sling, and a Captain Sothern of the distinguished 43rd, which had been among those chosen to welcome the Tsar on his arrival, rode in the van, while Vicount Edgely, Lord Brandsley and two other gentlemen brought up the rear with a Miss Potter who had elected to make the trip on horseback. Mr. Rathbone had pleaded off the expedition on the excuse of business which must be attended to, and Mrs. Newington had declined the invitation also. Damaris, riding tamely in the barouche with Charlotte and Mrs. Rathbone and two other ladies, could not resist an envious glance at Miss Potter on her pretty, spirited mare.

Her look was intercepted by Lord Brandsley, with a faint smile and a gleam of understanding. Damaris hastily turned away and began to speak to the young matron beside her whose husband was riding beside Brandsley.

They went along the Edgeware Road with the intention of returning by another route that would take them past the site of the Regent's latest and most ambitious building scheme, a new settlement of aristocrats' houses set in a large park, linked with Carlton House by a broad avenue designed by Mr. Nash.

They left the walls of Hyde Park behind, and as a line of new houses bordering the road stretched before them, Mrs. Rathbone remarked that she remembered well when this was all country, and sighed for the sight of green fields.

The gardens did not offer the vulgar delights of the more extensive grounds of Vauxhall, on the other side of London, but there were some pretty walks to enjoy after their tea, and the party soon broke up into several as they strolled about exploring the paths and groves and admiring some interesting prospects.

Damaris found herself walking on the major's arm behind the marquess and Miss Potter. Charlotte and her young friend, who seemed as lively as Miss Rathbone was quiet, had disappeared down another path, together with the captain and Viscount Edgely, adequately chaperoned by the young matron and her husband, while Mrs. Rathbone rested in one of the cool arbors.

The major, when he could be persuaded to cease filling her ears with fulsome gallantries, was an interesting conversationalist, but today Damaris found it difficult to keep up a semblance of attention, for the snatches of conversation which floated back to her from the two in front were tantalizing to her. The lady was animated, the gentleman smilingly interested and sometimes, Damaris thought, gently teasing, for Miss Potter occasionally laughed a protest.

The path that they were following ended in a small marble edifice vaguely resembling a Greek temple, and after they had admired its fluted columns and the carved vine leaves that adorned it, Damaris found herself walking back they way they had come, on Lord Brandsley's arm. She looked back involuntarily to see the major, with a very good grace, escorting Miss Potter, whose demeanor, if anything, appeared more vivacious than before.

"Are you regretting the major's company, Lady Waring?" Brandsley asked her softly.

"Miss Potter may be regretting yours," she retorted.

"That I take leave to doubt," he said. "As Lindo lately complained to me, a uniform these· days outweighs every other consideration when a lady's favor is at stake."

"Not with me!" she said involuntarily.

He glanced down at her and said, "You relieve my mind—or are you merely being polite?"

She laughed and shook her head, refusing to answer.

"Still," the marquess mused, "I should not have thought Edgely would be so fainthearted. Letting the major rout him without even a skirmish," he explained, as she looked inquiringly at him.

"I don't think your cousin is *fainthearted*," she murmured. "Rather, if he desired to indulge in a *skirmish* with the major, which I doubt, his natural good manners would have prevented him."

"Is that a criticism of *mine?*" he asked mildly.

"You know it was not!" she disclaimed quickly.

He looked down at her with an odd expression in his eyes, then asked abruptly, "What caused you to try and flummery me into believing Lindo had given you that bracelet?"

Caught unawares, she floundered. "I did *not*—! I cannot imagine why you should think so—"

"Yes, you can," he said bluntly, and casting a glance behind them, firmly steered her down a side path, where they were soon hidden by a bend and the greenery that divided it from the main path.

Returning to the attack, he said, "You have no need to tell me that you *said* nothing which could have led me to that conclusion, but you know as well as I that your action, combined with the words you did speak, was calculated to give me a quite false impression. It's useless to deny it."

"Then I shall not attempt it," she said, trying for composure. "At any rate, you are always very sure that you are right, Lord Brandsley."

He paused, his narrowed gaze on her averted face, and said, "In this case, I am. A very few minutes reflection must have convinced me that a woman who would refuse even the *loan* of a horse from me, would not have accepted the gift of an expensive piece of jewelry from any man."

Another party approaching along the path enabled her to turn and forced him to accompany her. As they strolled toward the arbor where they had left Mrs. Rathbone, he said, "Your aunt, Mrs. Newington, is also a widow, I believe?"

"Yes. For some years, now."

"And your own parents?"

"I scarcely remember them. When they died, my aunt and uncle accepted the responsibility for me, and brought me up."

"What manner of man was your uncle?" Brandsley asked. "Your aunt is of a timid and retiring disposition, I think. One has the impression that her husband might have been something of a domestic tyrant."

This assessment of her uncle's character was so wildly wrong that Damaris laughed aloud. When she could control her voice, she said, "Nothing could be further from the truth, Lord Brandsley! My uncle was a most temperate man in everything, his manners almost as retiring as my aunt's, in some ways. Certainly far from being a tyrant!"

"Forgive me," he said. "You once defended the Princess Charlotte's reluctance to marry the man of her father's choice, on the grounds that parents should not be allowed the disposal of their children's lives."

Damaris said, with some reserve, "But not to you, I think, sir. I collect you have been wondering if I was constrained into marriage against my will, but I *cannot* allow you to entertain such thoughts of two people I have always dearly loved, and to whom, besides, I owe a great debt of gratitude. My marriage was not of that order at all, but contracted of my own free will."

He was frowning slightly as they reached Mrs. Rathbone's side, finding the rest of the party disposed nearby, and from time to time she found his gaze resting on her with an odd concentration. She was herself low in spirits, though trying to hide it under an animated manner. Her last encounter with Lord Brandsley had left her lighthearted and strangely hopeful of a better understanding between them. Today he had undoubtedly been attempting to discover an acceptable reason for her marriage to Sir Walter, indicating a softening of his attitude. But the reminder that his information about her came from Lady Crawley had made her wary and uncertain. She could not allow a slander on her foster parents to stand in his mind, and at the same time the consciousness of the indelicacy of pouring into his ears the true reasons for her marriage was strong. But she was miserable in the knowledge that her defense of Mr. and Mrs. Newington, and her declaration that she had contracted marriage of her own free will, must have condemned herself in his eyes; that if he had begun to doubt his assessment of her, all his suspicions must now be returning to his mind.

Mrs. Newington could not fail to notice a lowering of spirits in her niece after this excursion, particularly as it succeeded a short period when Damaris had seemed as lighthearted as on their very first days in London. She rapidly dismissed the thought that the change of mood was caused by Lord Edgely's increasing attention to Miss Rathbone, for she knew that Damaris regarded *that* with marked approval, but she did venture one day to suggest that it seemed an age since Lord Brandsley had favored them with a visit.

"It is only a week, Aunt," Damaris replied tranquilly. "I expect he has many engagements. His cousin told me he was invited to Carlton House to meet the Tsar."

"Then I expect he met the Grand Duchess Catherine, too!"

Damaris laughed. "I expect so, since she insists on accompanying her brother wherever he goes."

"Do you think it is true that she attended the Guildhall Banquet without an invitation?"

"Well, if she was there—which none can doubt—it *must* have been only because she persuaded the Tsar to take her, for ladies are never present, you know, at civic dinners."

"It seems very odd behavior, to be sure!"

"Not so odd as saying that the music made her ill, and forcing the poor Lord Mayor to stop the opera singers from entertaining the company. She must be one of the rudest women who ever lived."

"Well, she is a *royal,* you know, my dear—although I must own it seems as well that she is apparently *not* going to marry into our own royal family!"

"Yes, indeed! Though one cannot help wondering if she behaves so badly because she took all the royal dukes in dislike, or if the fact is that none of them bothered to offer for her!"

"Well, they have certainly none of them seemed anxious, hitherto, to enter the married state. Clarence, however, is supposed to have paid court to her."

"*Is* he? Who told you that, Aunt?"

"Mrs. Rathbone said so. But I believe the duke is very much in debt. He cannot have seemed a very good match."

"I should think not—even if the Grand Duchess could be persuaded to ignore the existence of his mistress and—isn't it *ten?*—little Fitzclarences."

"Damaris!"

Her eyes dancing, Damaris said, "My dear aunt, don't look so shocked. *You* must have known of it, and *I* am past my green girlhood, you know. One cannot go about in society and remain ignorant of such matters."

"Damaris—?"

"Yes, Aunt?"

"Are *you* still fixed in your determination not to marry again?"

Taken by surprise, Damaris flushed and, leaving her chair, went to stand at the window. "Why do you ask?" she said at last. "I quite thought that I had made myself more than clear on that point."

"Yes, but—that was before we came to London. I did think that you might change your mind. Your situation, once we return to Somerset, will not be congenial."

"No," Damaris smiled palely. "Sir Walter's nephew never did like, or approve of me. I must own that last year was one of the most unpleasant of my life."

"Yes, indeed!" Her aunt said. "For he treated you very shabbily, Damaris, as soon as he succeeded to the estate. He even contrived to hint that you were not entitled to the use of the dower house, which is nonsense, if I ever heard it. Sir Walter, indeed, left you less well provided for than one might have expected, but he would not have been so mean as to have deprived you of a roof over your head!"

"No, he would not, and you must not blame him for leaving the bulk of his fortune with the estate, for *I* brought no portion with me, you know, and could hardly expect to be provided with a handsome jointure, since I did not even supply him with an heir."

"*Such* a pity," Mrs. Newington sighed. "For only think, Damaris, we might have been quite comfortable..."

"And we shall be," Damaris said. "We shall have to live carefully, of course, and I'm afraid the dower house must be our home. But now that Sir Charles has had time to settle into his new state he may have mellowed a trifle toward us, and if we should become too dull and miserable, I shall have to sell some more of my jewelry. I do think it was a famous notion to sell the other pieces in order to finance our season in London, for we *have* enjoyed ourselves, haven't we, Aunt?"

"Yes, indeed," her aunt murmured. "And of course, we shall have it to remember, when we are back in Somerset. Only, if some eligible gentleman *were* to offer for you—"

Damaris laughed a little unsteadily, and shook her head. "I shall not marry again, unless the match is one of genuine attachment," she said. "And I'm afraid *that* is unlikely to come my way."

Almost eagerly, her aunt said, "But if you found such an attachment existed—?"

"If—!" Damaris laughed. "Since the only offers I have had have been quite unthinkable, we need not worry our heads thinking of *ifs*, dear Aunt Tabitha!"

It was true that she had determined not to enter the married state again, for although she believed her aunt's marriage to have been happy, her own had proved disastrous, and, to her shame, her chief emotion on the death of her spouse had been one of guilty relief.

She had been barely eighteen when she had married Sir Walter Waring, seventeen when her uncle died and she had seen her aunt go into a panic of fear at the destitution that faced them after his long illness and the debts they had perforce contracted during it. Mrs. Newington, as the saying goes, had married an impecunious country lawyer "to disoblige her family" and although close relatives might have been moved to aid her in her present plight if she had applied to them, there were now none left alive.

Damaris had first thought of becoming a seamstress or a governess to support them both, but her hopes were quickly dashed. Her talent as a needlewoman, like her aunt's, was no more than average, and the profession overcrowded. And her youth and modest education both acted against her obtaining a situation as a governess in a respectable household.

When Sir Walter, to whom they owed many kindnesses during Mr. Newington's illness, suggested that Damaris might become his wife, allowing him to take care of them both, she had seen the quick leap of hope in her aunt's eyes.

To Mrs. Newington's credit, she had not urged the match, had even demurred at the great difference in age, but Damaris could not forget that look, and telling herself sensibly that dreams of handsome young men were foolish and juvenile imaginings that seldom came true for any girl, accepted Sir Walter's suit.

He had been a friend of her uncle's, and in this light she had regarded him. In the few weeks before their very quiet wedding—for she was still in mourning—she bore with his occasional hugs and kisses, and even shyly returned a salute or two against his ruddy cheek when he demanded it, teasing her as he might a little girl, and vaguely thought that marriage to him would entail little more. He seemed to her so old that he must, indeed, be beyond impassioned lovemaking, and in any case, her notion of what the romantic phrase meant was culled from library novels which did nothing to prepare her for the reality that awaited her.

She had come to her aunt after the wedding, her face a frozen mask of shock, to be assured by her that Sir

Walter had not, as she had half-feared, run mad; that the indignities she had suffered and the incredible demands he had made on her were a normal part of a married woman's duties. That in time one became quite used to them, and indeed, her aunt assured her, with a blush, where one enjoyed a genuine fondness for one's husband, these intimacies were not at all repugnant.

Incredulous, but determined to make the best of her lot, Damaris had striven to transform the gratitude she had felt to Sir Walter into love. If he had been a more patient man the marriage might have been a moderate success. But although bluffly generous and not unkind, Sir Walter was quick-tempered in his own home, and not sensitive to the feelings of others. Embroiled in a middle-aged passion for a young girl, the temptation to marry her under the guise of doing her a kindness had been too great, and it was asking too much of altruism to expect him not to lay claim to his marital rights.

His fantasy of initiating a young but loving bride had dissolved under the impact of a revulsion Damaris could not hide. She had been not coy but terrified, and guilt added to his other emotions had turned him into an importunate and callous husband, allaying his conscience with expensive gifts, but unable to stop himself expecting her gratitude to make her more amenable to his advances.

All this Damaris understood dimly now, with a stirring of pity which she had been too frightened and confused to feel at the time. Disappointment, and the fear that he had made a foolish spectacle of himself accounted for much of his ill humor, and the preposterous accusations he had made against her in later years had their roots, she knew, in his need to avoid blaming himself for taking advantage of her youth and her situation.

But she had done him a great disservice by marrying him, and was determined not to repeat the mistake.

chapter eight

Damaris had not seen Haines since the contretemps
Lord Brandsley had interrupted. But one night as she
was enjoying the opera from the Rathbones' box at the
Haymarket Theater, Mr. Rathbone said, with one of
his sudden cracks of laughter, "I see another of your
gallants has his arm hung up in a sling, Lady Waring.
Thinks to outdo the major, perhaps!"

She looked across the floor of the house to find Lord
Alfred bowing stiffly to her, his arm, as Mr. Rathbone
had said, reposing in a sling.

Damaris gave the merest nod in return and looked
away again. She had no intention of receiving his lordship ever again, but she would not tell Mr. Rathbone
so.

Charlotte said, "I had thought he was out of town,
for I don't recall seeing him for some time. I wonder
what accident has befallen him."

Captain Sothern, who was also a member of Mrs. Rathbone's party, made a stifled sound of amusement that caused Charlotte to look at him in some surprise, while Mr. Rathbone fixed him with sudden stare and then said, "Hmm. So that's it!"

Mrs. Rathbone demanded to know what he meant, but her spouse hushed her with a muttered promise to explain later, and significant glances at Damaris and his daughter. And as the curtain drew up at that moment on a scene of pastoral, though painted, splendor, the lady was constrained to obey.

Next day, however, she arrived in Harley Street before Damaris and Mrs. Newington had left the breakfast parlor, and was clearly agog with what she had to tell them.

"Rathbone got the whole from Captain Sothern in one of the intervals," she told them. "And what do you think? Lord Alfred was injured in a duel!"

"A duel!" Mrs. Newington gasped. "Oh, how dreadful!"

"Yes, and the other principal, would you believe, is none other than the Marquess of Brandsley!"

"Brandsley!" Damaris went white with horror.

"Yes, and I know what you are thinking, Damaris, but indeed it is *not* so!"

"He is not injured?"

"Brandsley? Heavens, no! Mr. Rathbone was speaking to him only yesterday at Tattersalls, when he went to see if he could buy a new horse to replace one that has gone lame. And although I know that Lord Alfred has been dangling after you this age, and Brandsley could at least be said to have shown an *interest,* you must not blame yourself, or be afraid that your name will be bandied about in connection with the affair. Rathbone says it was nothing of the kind, but all to do with some game of chance. The captain said the marquess took exception to the way in which Lord Alfred rolled some dice."

Damaris was not quite without some knowledge of the unwritten rules of affairs of honor. Nor did she think for a moment that a man like Haines, however reprehensible his dealing with women, would stoop to cheating in a card game. She recalled the grim set of Lord Brandsley's mouth when he had seen the marks Haines had left on her wrists, and the beating of suspicion in her mind would not abate.

The marquess still did not call, but she was able to speak to his cousin that evening when she accompanied Charlotte, at Mrs. Rathbone's request, to the assembly at Almacks.

Tackled with the story of the duel, he at first professed to know nothing, but when she pressed him, repeated the story of the dice.

With unwonted tartness Damaris said, "Yes, I know all about that, and I don't believe a word of it!"

He smiled with a hint of consciousness, but said, "I can tell you no more, Lady Waring," and it occurred to her that he seemed much more mature these days than when she had first met him, some months ago.

Had she but known it, Charlotte's charming *naïveté* was far more effective in loosening Lindo's tongue than her own skepticism. Having admitted that she had heard about the affair from Captain Sothern, who professed to have no knowledge of the details, Charlotte expressed such confidence in the viscount's superior knowledge that he told her more than he had meant to.

"Do you mean that Lord Alfred Haines *cheated?*" she asked, her eyes wide and shocked.

"No, of course he didn't," Lindo said. "No one thinks that."

"But Lord Brandsley must have—"

Beguiled into showing off his worldly knowledge, Lindo said, "Oh, no. That was to—to keep a certain lady's name out of the affair. Grenville made it a pretext for a challenge, that's all."

"Oh." Charlotte digested that for a moment. Then her eyes flew again to his. "It wasn't—you don't mean Lady Waring?"

"No!" Lindo said hastily. "Certainly not. In fact the lady in question was—well, certainly no one you would know, Miss Rathbone."

Charlotte blinked. Then a spark of the surprising mischief of which she was capable lit her eyes. "Oh!"

she said. "You mean an opera dancer or something of that sort!"

Lindo was startled. "What do *you* know of—Well, the fact is, yes, it—it was something of that sort."

"I expect they were foxed," she said wisely.

"What?"

"Lord Brandsley and Lord Alfred. Gentlemen don't, as a rule, fight over opera dancers, do they? Was he— your cousin—attempting to protect her reputation?"

Lindo grinned, taken off guard, and said, "I don't think Rosie deRoxburgh has a reputation left to protect!"

Since he could have bitten out his tongue the moment this unfelicitous speech left it, it was as well that Charlotte's only answer was, "What a pretty name!"

"I should not have mentioned it to *you,* however," Lindo said in guilt-stricken tones. "You would oblige me, Miss Rathbone, by forgetting that I ever did so."

She smiled up at him with beguiling innocence. "Why certainly, Lord Edgely. I know that it is very disagreeable for any female to know that she is the subject of a duel! I promise I shall not mention it to a soul."

Lindo was reasonably certain that the lady in question would have been in high gig at the prospect of two titled gentlemen aiming pistols at each other in a quarrel over her. Nor would she be under any delusion that either of them was bent on protecting her fair name. He rather thought that Brandsley had carried chivalry too far in defending such a girl at such lengths, but if Brandsley had almost certainly *not* been drunk at the onset of the quarrel, Haines might have been in his cups, and forced it on the marquess.

Rose was as pretty a little ladybird as ever walked, for Lindo had seen her once or twice hanging on Haines's arm, but if Grenville had had a fancy to enliven his stay in London with the company of a lady of easy virtue, he would have been wiser to pick one that Haines was not involved with. He could be an ugly customer when crossed.

Besides, although Lindo told himself that many a man of the world kept a mistress even after marriage, and no one thought the worse of him provided he did not embarrass his wife by being too blatant about it, the thought of Grenville squiring Rosie deRoxburgh after avowing his intention of trying for the hand of Lady Waring, was vaguely repugnant. He had not as yet heard the story of the duel from his cousin's own lips, and was reluctant to seek him out. He knew that the marquess was still in town, but somehow they had not met for over a week.

When they did meet, over a game of macao at Watier's, he found himself borne off to take potluck at Brandsley's house afterwards, and as they sat over their wine, the marquess asked gently, "Now, tell me what I have done to earn your displeasure, bantling."

Caught unaware, Lindo gulped his wine and said in a choked voice, "Why—nothing! Why should you think I'm displeased with you? Do I seem to you cold—unfriendly?"

"No—merely ill at ease and trying hard to hide it with a show of affability."

"Well, I had not seen you for an age. Not since that damned duel of yours—and you might have been killed, you know! Haines is a pretty fair shot, himself."

"Not as fair as I am. If you were concerned about my health, you might have called on me to inquire."

"Well, I had no need to, for I knew you were unharmed."

The marquess regarded him in thoughtful silence, and after a few moments, Lindo burst out, "Well, if you must know, I think it a pretty shabby thing to be dancing attendance on a lightskirt like Rosie deRoxburgh when you have told me you mean to attach Lady Waring! I daresay that marks me as a provincial, and stupidly out of date, but I take leave to tell you, Brandsley, that something about the affair goes against the pluck!"

"On the contrary, it marks you as a man of proper feeling and sensibility. I'm persuaded that *you* would not be tardy in bringing to book a fellow who insulted and manhandled a lady of your acquaintance."

"No, but—" Lindo hesitated. "Well, I suppose if Haines was rough with the girl, you had no choice, but according to the story I heard, you were in company with her at Vauxhall, and surely someone must have told you that Haines has but recently persuaded her away from her last protector—"

"Of course they had—it wasn't difficult to discover the name of his latest ladybird. Nor to persuade her to come to Vauxhall with me."

Lindo stared, beginning to comprehend. "I see," he said slowly, at last. "Rosie was a blind. *She* was not the lady who—" He broke off, his eyes kindling. "You mean Haines dared to—*insulted and manhandled*, you said! By God, Gren, if I had known of it, I would have challenged him myself."

Grenville looked at him with a faint smile. "I don't doubt it. And got yourself killed most likely—now don't pucker up, you know Haines is a better shot. What's more, you hot-tempered young cub, the lady in question might not have relished having her name bandied about as the subject of your quarrel."

"I shouldn't have allowed—"

"My dear boy, you have made her the object of your attention for so long the true case must have been guessed at."

"And *your* attentions?" Lindo asked, flushing a little.

"—have not been so marked, nor so exclusive," Grenville said calmly. "I have not advertised my inclinations as blatantly as you. And I've been careful to keep my distance these last weeks."

"Good Lord, you are the most complete hand, Gren!" Lindo said, startled into admiration. "Still, I might have contrived the business without dragging—the lady's name into it."

"Don't disturb yourself," his cousin advised lazily. "I have saved you the trouble."

Charlotte kept her promise not to mention the name of the wanton Miss deRoxburgh, but could not resist regaling Lady Waring (in the *strictest* confidence, under a promise not to reveal to Charlotte's mamma from whence she had learned it), with the other elements of the story.

"You look surprised," she commented, when she had finished her story. "Of course, it is very shocking that gentlemen consort with that kind of female, but we know they *do*, Damaris, even though, as Mamma says, a well-bred woman contrives to ignore their existence, and if one should chance to meet a gentleman in company with one on the street or at a public function, he will *quite* understand if one cuts him dead—in fact he expects you to pretend not to have seen him. And I do think, don't you, that it was particularly noble of Lord Brandsley to call out Lord Alfred in defense of a girl whose profession is such that few gentlemen would scruple to say she was unworthy of such consideration!"

"That's as may be," Damaris said, her fingers clenched rather fiercely on the forgotten purse she had been netting. "But I take leave to doubt, Charlotte, that Lord Brandsley and Lord Alfred Haines quarreled over the girl's good name. It seems to me more likely that they were fighting over who should have the right to—to enjoy her favors."

"Oh!" Charlotte digested this in silence for a moment, then said, "Like the knights in the old romances, you mean?"

"I do not!" Damaris answered rather sharply. "It is not in the least romantic, it is sordid and disgusting, and I wish you will put it out of your mind. Lord Edgely had no right to repeat the story to you!"

Charlotte chuckled. "You sound exactly like Mamma!" she told her friend. "But you look so young it sits absurdly on you!"

Damaris gave her a slightly strained smile. "Well, I am a good deal older than you—"

"Pooh! A few years only. And don't tell me you have been married for I well know *that* took place when you were barely out of the schoolroom. And *I*, you know, am no schoolroom miss, for I've turned nineteen and have been out, remember, for two seasons now!"

"Why, yes, so you have!" Damaris said lightly. "You will soon be getting quite old-cattish."

But in truth she felt anything but lighthearted, for

Charlotte's story had thrown her into a secret turmoil.

She had bowed to Lord Brandsley at a distance in Hyde Park, and exchanged brief greetings when she had seen him one day strolling in Oxford Street with a friend. They had last week attended the same party and stood up together for one of the country dances, during which it was virtually impossible to conduct a private conversation. She would have been pleased to allow him a waltz, if he had returned to her, but after dancing with one or two other ladies he had retired to the card room and remained there the rest of the evening.

She had thought his behavior puzzling. She could not raise the subject of the duel, thus breaching the pretense that the feminine part of his acquaintance was unaware of what had transpired, and his own conversational gambits had consisted of the merest commonplaces. He had given the impression of a gentleman going through the motions of politeness with faint boredom, and her own spontaneous smiles had soon stiffened on her lips. And she had not seen him since.

When Charlotte left, Damaris cast aside her netting and moodily began pacing about the room. The meaning of Lord Brandsley's behavior was now all too clear. Far from meeting Haines on *her* behalf, as she had too readily assumed, he had been engaged in a disreputable conflict over the fleeting affections of a cheap *demi-monde*.

How humiliating to realize that he thought more, apparently, of such a girl, than he did of herself. And how stupid of her to have imagined that he might have thought *her* honor worth fighting for!

On the contrary, she realized now, he must have seen Charlotte's increasing influence over the affections of Lord Edgely, and decided that there was no further need for him to continue his attempt to draw Damaris off the scent. Here was the real reason for his recent avoidance of her, his indifference to her at the party. His interest in her from the beginning had been for his cousin's sake. Even the attraction he had seemed to reluctantly admit had been assumed—a pose to hoax her away from Edgely. To mortification at his sudden loss of interest in herself, was added the knowledge that he had apparently transferred that interest to a woman who belonged to a profession renowned for its cupidity and easy virtue.

Damaris had always felt a certain sympathy with the barques of frailty whose only means of avoiding the rigors of poverty was to attract the attention of a wealthy protector—for she was aware that her own marriage had been a transaction not overwhelmingly different in principle—but her tolerance was in this instance sadly strained. She pictured the unknown fair as an unprincipled harpy who rejoiced in the spectacle of two men bidding fair to kill each other for a smile—and a good deal more, Damaris supposed resentfully—from her.

The woman deserved him, she was sure, and Brandsley deserved her. Unprincipled wretches, both of them! But oh, how *could* he? Her unruly thoughts ran in despair. *How could he!*

When Lord Brandsley called again in Harley Street it was in company with his cousin. Damaris received him coolly, but he kept Mrs. Newington entranced with a commentary on his recent visit to Oatlands, where the Duke and Duchess of York had entertained a party of friends, and left her ecstatic with the promise of procuring an invitation for her and Lady Waring to the Grand Ball in honor of the Duke of Wellington, to be held at Carlton House on the twenty-first of July.

Damaris, more vexed than overjoyed at the prospect of this favor, contemplated the consequences of refusing to accept it. But since they included refusal of a royal command and bitter disappointment for her beloved aunt, that was clearly impossible. She resigned herself instead to the devising of as dazzling a gown as could be contrived this late in the season on her somewhat slender resources.

The Russian party had left England at the end of June, much to the relief of the Regent, but the hero of Toulouse, now elevated by a grateful sovereign to a dukedom, had arrived two days later, so that the celebrations continued unabated. The Duke of Wellington did not share the Regent's taste for pomp, and was more embarrassed than delighted by the honors paid to him, but at least he did not deliberately bait and humiliate the Prince. And the Regent was happily absorbed now in planning further dazzling entertainment for the populace, which was to culminate in August, when the victory celebrations would be combined with the marking of the centenary of Hanoverian rule in England.

The plans for his daughter's marriage to William of Orange were progressing less well, for the princess declared she would not have him, and on the twelfth of July she stormed out of her home, hired a common hackney in the street and fled to her mother's house. On her return she was packed off to Dorset, but there was no more talk of the marriage with William.

It was rumored that Charlotte, like many another young lady, had conceived a fancy for one of the Prussian princes. For her part, Damaris privately told Mrs. Newington, the princess was welcome to them. She had been vastly relieved to see the last of her own energetic and rather alarming admirer.

"A very well set-up young man," Mrs. Newington said consideringly. "But just a trifle—*overwhelming!*"

"Exactly, my dear aunt," Damaris laughed. "Oh, look at this gown in the *Ladies Magazine!* What would you say to a *Circassian* bodice to your gown, for the Grand Ball?"

Mrs. Newington looked very fine when dressed for the ball in a Circassian bodice over a gown with a Gothic trim, and with a turban on her hair adding the final elegant touch. Damaris was wearing pearl silk with an overdress of tulle trimmed with amber beads, and was glad that her appearance need cause her no shame. Other ladies might wear more jewelry or a richer trimming on their gowns, but she knew that she looked well and in high bloom, and just as fashionable as any of them.

She needed every ounce of confidence she could muster. Carlton House was already so lavishly decorated that foreign dignitaries received there were dazzled by its magnificence, comparing it with Versailles and St. Cloud. Tonight it was lit outside by flares and inside by thousands of lanterns and magnificent chandeliers. A brick polygon designed by Mr. Nash had been especially erected outside the Gothic conservatory, and made into a huge tented pavilion as big as Westminster Hall, by the addition of draped white muslin, interspersed with mirrors.

Indeed, Damaris thought she had never seen so many mirrors. Past the impressive entrance hall with its cornices flaunting Etruscan griffins, every one of the great rooms seemed to be hung with mirrors reflecting forests of Ionic columns, silvered capitals, splendid chandeliers and rich red curtains. It was easy to see why the Prince's guests had said that the decorations of Carlton House made their most extravagant clothes seem insignificant. And why Mr. Brummell, with a stroke of sartorial genius, had initiated the fashion for plain dark coats over immaculate white linen and quiet colored small-clothes. Only such stark contrast would have stood out in such splendor.

Mr. Brummell was not present, but Damaris was relieved to see one or two acquaintances among the crowd in the polygon, and pleased to catch a glimpse of the great soldier looking embarrassed when confronted with an enormous bust of himself commissioned by the Regent for the occasion.

When the musicians, hidden by a huge bank of flowers in the center of the floor, struck up, she did not lack for partners, and soon felt tolerably at ease, and able to look around at the victory transparencies that formed a part of the decoration along with a plethora of gilded "W's" in tribute to the guest of honor.

She found Lord Brandsley at her elbow and greeted him with what she hoped was tolerable composure and a nice blend of graciousness and distance, telling him that she and her aunt were greatly appreciative of his kindness in procuring them their invitation.

He took her onto the floor for a cotillion, and when

the dance ended suggested a stroll in the conservatory, overriding her hesitation with ruthless skill and bearing her off on his arm.

"Good heavens!" she could not help exclaiming as they entered the handsome portals. "It looks like a cathedral!"

Any resemblance to the modest apartment gracing Mrs. Rathbone's house was not to be thought of. Here were stained glass windows, intricately carved pillars, a marble floor and a ceiling that was a succession of graceful, fan-shaped traceries.

Lord Brandsley laughed. "Very apt," he said. "A temple to ostentation, perhaps."

"My aunt is quite speechless with awe and admiration," she told him. "Indeed, it was kind in you to think of us!"

He looked down at her. "You have already told me that, but this time you appear to be more sincere. Never mind that, I was not prompted entirely by kindness."

She looked at him a little warily, and he laughed again and said, "There is no better place to engage in a private conversation than in a large crowd of people, all too busy talking themselves to listen to what anyone else may be saying."

It was true that the high hum of conversation, and the strains of music floating into the open doors, made it possible for him to speak to her as privately as if they were alone, instead of threading their way through the hundreds of people admiring the Gothic vista of the conservatory. As he found a corner by a cluster of pillars that allowed them to stand still without being jostled, and smiled down at her, she said, "Am I to understand, Lord Brandsley, that you procured me an invitation, in order to speak privately with me?"

"In part," he said easily. "The other part was that I thought you might enjoy it. *Are* you enjoying it?"

"Yes," she said. "Because it is a great occasion, and I'm pleased to be sharing in it. But it is not an experience I should care to repeat. It is very hot, and crowded and noisy. Except for the sense of occasion, a quiet evening at home with friends might be preferred."

"Strangely, I had the same thought myself, not ten minutes past," he told her. "Have I told you that you are in great beauty tonight, Lady Waring?"

His eyes were on her gown, but he spoke almost absently, as though he was thinking of something else, and she responded with a hint of tartness in her tone, "Yes, you did—*twenty* minutes ago!"

"I'm touched," he said, his eyes laughing at her. "To think that you remember my poor compliment so exactly to the minute!"

Her eyes sparkled dangerously and he said, "No—forgive me! I should not tease you." Astonishingly, he took her hand, carrying it to his lips, but instead of kissing the back of it, he turned it at the last minute and put his lips briefly to the pulse spot of her wrist.

Startled, Damaris snatched her hand away, instinctively taking a backward step, and finding her way blocked by a solid set of pillars.

"You are quite safe here," he told her softly. "In any case, you stand in no danger from me, Lady Waring."

"Why did you wish to speak with me?" she asked him, her body taut, and her breathing constricted with a sudden, frightening awareness.

Something flickered in his eyes, he seemed to pause. Then he said lightly, "Must I have a particular reason? I enjoy your company. I find it pleasant to talk to you."

"Then you have done remarkably well without my company these past several weeks!" she said, without thinking.

His look was keen. Then he smiled. "I collect you have missed mine!"

"I did not say so," she said instantly. "I was merely remarking on your absence."

"How very ungracious of you," he said with mock reproach. "Do I really deserve such a set-down? I begin to think that you have missed me quite remarkably, you know!"

"You flatter yourself, sir!"

"Well, someone must," he replied. "For *you*, it seems, are quite determined on shattering my self-esteem."

Her teeth momentarily caught her underlip. When it had stopped quivering, she said frigidly, "I suspect that such a feat is quite beyond my power, Lord Brandsley!"

He laughed outright, and again she was obliged to catch her lip in her teeth. Then he sobered and said, "There was a reason for it, you know. I have been out of town . . ."

She raised her eyebrows at him, knowing that though he had left town for a short while, it did not encompass all the time he had kept away from Harley Street, and avoided her company.

He smiled and shook his head in ironical acknowledgement of her patent disbelief, and said quietly, "I cannot tell you the rest of it. Can you not take my word that there was a reason?"

Was, her mind echoed after him. For a few moments she had almost forgotten, but now a bitter rage flooded her being. How dared he? So he had tired of his *inamorata,* or she of him, and now he was prepared again to indulge in a little flirtation with Lady Waring.

But she must not show him how hurt and angry she was. Striving for calm, she said in a colorless voice, "But I know the reason, Lord Brandsley." At his sharp look she gave a little laugh and said, "Oh, I know that I should profess ignorance of such matters, but your opinion of my character has been so charmingly expressed, so delicately hinted at on several memorable occasions, that I don't fear to sink myself in *your* eyes. If I needed any confirmation of your feelings, you have just given it to me. For I am persuaded no man of *breeding* would expect a woman of *quality* to accept his advances within so short a time of having publicly expressed his regard for a woman of no reputation and no virtue!"

He had listened to her with a grave face and hard eyes. Now he said calmly, "So you heard that story."

"Yes, I heard it. A much more likely story than that

flimflam you tried to put about, regarding card games and dice."

A rather grim gleam of amusement briefly lightened the slate gray of his eyes. "You think so?" he said smoothly. "Your opinion of *my* character, Lady Waring, is hardly very high. *Do* I strike you as a man likely to take to the pursuit of high-flying birds of paradise?"

"I have no knowledge of your tastes in that direction," she said icily. "The propensities of gentlemen of the quality for such—such pursuits as you mention are a mystery to me."

"Well, you needn't sound so devilish straitlaced about it," he told her bluntly. "It was you who started this."

"Then I shall finish it now!" she flashed. "Please take me back to my aunt, Lord Brandsley."

"Permit me to tell you, Lady Waring, that you are a termagant!" he said, with some signs of exasperation.

"I *don't* permit you!" she said, as they turned and he began to make a ruthless passage for them through the throng.

He gave a crack of angry laughter, but did not reply. His mouth was hard with anger well controlled. Damaris held her head high, making a determined effort not to show her own feelings of chagrin, fury and despair.

As they neared her aunt, he stopped for a moment, checking her with an implacable hand on hers when she would have removed it from his arm.

"One moment," he said. "If you would allow yourself to find in my motives something other than malice toward you, it might occur to you to think a little more deeply about the stories you have heard."

"What do you mean?"

"I mean that I had thought you capable of working out for yourself how much importance to attach to a tale of a dubious nature concerning my supposed interest in another woman—I thought I had made it clear to you that my interest at the moment is in yourself."

127

"If that was so, my lord, it is an interest which appears to have waned—"

He made an exclamation of annoyance. "You seem determined not to understand! Did it never occur to you that one Banbury story might be used to cover another? That the only reason I could possibly have for calling out Haines was connected with a certain incident at your house?" Watching the astonished enlightenment dawn in her face, he said with a weary smile, "No. I see it did not. Or perhaps you preferred to believe that I was a loose screw. Here is your aunt, Lady Waring. I trust you will both continue to enjoy the evening."

Then, before she had recovered sufficiently from her shocked surprise to utter a word of apology or excuse, he had bowed to her with stiff punctiliousness, and moved away into the crowd.

chapter nine

Damaris and Mrs. Newington left the ball long before it ended at six o'clock in the morning. Damaris slept little, and when she did was beset by troubling dreams. After breakfast she hastily mended a pen and began the difficult task of writing a note to Lord Brandsley.

After several attempts, she dispatched with her footman a very brief missive requesting his lordship to call on her at his earliest convenience, for all her attempts to apologize by letter had seemed impossibly unsatisfactory.

She was on tenterhooks all day, but he did not come, and late in the afternoon a servant brought her a note from him. She tore open the seal and read that he had but this moment received hers, and would, if convenient, wait upon her the following day at four. He added that he hoped to speak privately with her.

Since that was her own earnest wish, she contrived to persuade her aunt to leave the house before the appointed hour, with the avowed intention of visiting Lackington Allen and Company in Finsbury Square, to inquire for a copy of Mr. Lewis's celebrated novel, *The Monk*. She had been privileged last night to meet the author himself. "And I don't know how it is," she said, "but I have never read it, although I have *often* heard it spoken of."

Damaris had dressed carefully in a pale lilac cambric morning dress done up to the neck and finished with a small self-ruffle at the throat. When Lord Brandsley was announced, she stood and waited for him, her hands clasped before her and her eyes fixed almost painfully on his face as he strode across the carpet to take her hand and salute it very correctly.

She sat on the velvet covered sofa while he took a nearby chair. Damaris clasped her hands in her lap and risked a quick glance at his face. The only expression she could see was one of polite inquiry.

"You sent for me," he said.

"Yes." She paused, trying to decide how to frame her apology.

"I regret I was not able to come yesterday," he said. "Some family business required my attention."

"Please—" she shook her head. "There is no need to apologize. In fact, I wanted to tell you—that I'm sorry for misjudging you. I did wonder if you fought Lord Alfred for my sake, at first. But when I heard the other story, I'm afraid I believed it. Please forgive me."

He stood up, suddenly, as though he must move, and strode to the window, only to turn when he reached it and face her across the room. Ruefully, he said, "This is heaping coals of fire, Lady Waring. If we are to talk of misjudgements, I suspect *I* have far more cause to ask for *your* forgiveness. I believe that I have been most damnably mistaken about you. *Why* in the name of heaven, have you allowed—even on occasion *encouraged* me to think that you were little better than an unprincipled adventuress?"

"I tried to explain to you at first," she said. "But you misunderstood. I despaired of making you believe me, whatever I said. Oh—it's true I did mislead you as to the bracelet, because—I suppose, because I was angry."

"I see. You were angry and wanted to hurt me."

"Hurt?" Her eyes flew to his face, for the first time recognizing the instinct which had prompted her to that foolish action. She said, a little unsteadily, "You didn't believe me, anyway."

"No. Have you ever been in love with my cousin?"

"Never."

"But he was in love with you. *Did* you make his mother think you would accept him, or did she make that up?"

"I'm afraid—I did hint at it," she admitted. "At the end."

"Are you going to tell me why?" As she hesitated, he said, "Was it because you thought you *might* accept him, even though you did not love him?"

"No!" She stood up, her hands still tightly clasped before her.

Brandsley moved towards her. "But you told *me* you meant to have him," he reminded her. "In fact, the only one you *don't* seem to have told is Edgely himself!"

"Because it wasn't true!" she said desperately. Her hands went up briefly to her heated cheeks. "I never *meant* to say it, only you were so very—"

"So very what?" he prompted her, as he stopped only two feet from her.

She bit her lip, and he said, "Well?"

"So very toplofty!" she said. "*Exactly* like your aunt!"

He frowned. "In what way?"

"In making it so very evident that you considered me vastly beneath Viscount Edgely's touch."

"I did *not* do that!"

"Oh, yes, you did. You made it very clear that I was not to think of marrying your cousin—"

"And that you might have thought of me!"

Damaris shook her head. "Against your better judgement," she said. "And I knew better than to take *that* seriously."

"Did you, indeed!"

"Of course. If your aunt had not made it clear that I would never be accepted by your lordship's family as a bride for Lord Edgely, I should still have been conscious of the unsuitability of it. I have already some experience of marrying out of my own order, you know. It is very uncomfortable to know that all one's relations-in-law have conceived an implacable dislike of one. Believe me, Lord Brandsley, I am fully sensible of all the objections to my marrying your cousin. And how much more forceful must those arguments be if, as you suggested, I should have looked even higher. *You* were implacably opposed to a match between Lord Edgely and myself—"

"Because of the age difference!" he interjected.

"Oh, no! That is not so very great, you know. If my station had been more near to his, I'm persuaded the match would not have been so disliked!"

He was silent, for a moment or two, frowning down at her. "For my part," he said, "I must always have objected. Was my aunt very rude to you?"

"Your aunt," she said, with a trace of bitterness, "is much too well-bred to be *rude*. She was just—"

"Stiff-rumped?" he suggested.

"Abominably! I beg your pardon—"

He grinned. "No, I should be begging yours. I begin to see how you felt." He paused, then asked abruptly, "Was your marriage very unpleasant?"

She looked up, about to answer, then flushed a little and said, with constraint, "I should not have spoken as I did. Pray don't regard it!"

"You said nothing improper. I collect you don't wish to speak of your marriage?"

She shook her head, turning away from him.

After a moment he said, "Then I shan't press you. But I *must* say to you something that has been in my mind. You told me once that you married of your own will, that your guardians did not press you. But why did your uncle allow it? Surely he could have prevented so unequal a match—"

"My uncle had died," she said. "My aunt—my poor aunt didn't know where to turn. And Sir Walter's offer was—it seemed a godsend."

"And you were—how old?"

"Sev–eighteen when I married him," she said.

The ormolu clock on the mantel ticked away several seconds. Then she heard him say, in a strange tone, "My poor darling!"

She was turning in surprise as his arms reached out, and the next moment he was holding her in a close embrace. Unnerved by the unexpected sympathy and warmth, she allowed two tears to fall on his immaculate lapel before she raised her head and made a movement of withdrawal which was checked at the outset. He raised a hand and wiped away the dampness on her cheeks with his fingers. She knew she should protest, but even as the words were on her lips, his mouth came down on hers with gentle firmness that drowned the protest in pleasure.

But when the gentleness changed to a hungry passion, she made an inarticulate sound and pushed strongly against him, until he raised his head and let her go.

"I beg your pardon," he said, but his eyes held a tender demand that caused a strange sensation in the region of her heart, and his mouth had a curve of humor.

He put out his hand to her, about to say something, when the sound of voices on the stairs stayed him. He made a sound of rueful exasperation and dropped his outstretched hand, and when Mrs. Rathbone and her daughter were announced by the butler, he was standing, aloof and composed, several yards from Damaris.

Charlotte, her cheeks flushed and her dark eyes dancing, entered the room before her mother, with an impetuousness that was uncharacteristic of her usual shy manner.

"Oh, Damaris!" she said. "We have something to tell you—*pray* wish me happy. For Lord Edgely has asked me to marry him!"

Standing behind and to the side of Damaris, the marquess could not see her face when she received the news. He saw the stillness of surprise, then the quick step forward as she embraced her young friend and said warmly, "Of course I do! With all my heart. That is famous news indeed."

Mrs. Rathbone, catching sight of him, gently reproved her daughter, who blushed and apologized as he added his felicitations.

"I knew, of course," he said. "And have already congratulated Lindo. A very fortunate young man."

"Oh, *thank* you, sir!" stammered Charlotte, but it was plain to see that she thought the good fortune all on her own side.

Damaris, begging her guests to seat themselves, thought that this must have been the family business that had detained the marquess yesterday. She had half-thought that he was making an excuse to punish her.

She was aware that his eyes rested on her often while he spoke quietly to Mrs. Rathbone. Charlotte talked to her excitedly of wedding clothes and engagement notices, and her awe of Lady Crawley, who had received her with gracious condescension this morning. Her own eyes she fixed resolutely on Charlotte's face, prettily flushed and bright eyed with happiness, and not at all plain, now.

Even when Lord Brandsley rose to go, she would not look directly at him, until he held her hand in his, tightening his fingers when she attempted to draw away. Then her eyes, half-indignant and half-shy, met his, to find them quizzically smiling at her.

She flushed, the polite words of farewell dying on her tongue, and looked helplessly back at him, until he took pity and released her fingers.

"I shall call again tomorrow," he said in a low voice. "And hope to find you alone."

Mrs. Newington returned from her errand in time to be regaled with Charlotte's news, which was of sufficient interest to divert her attention for the remainder of the day from her niece's air of abstractedness.

Damaris had much to think about, and her aunt's complacent remarks on Charlotte's good fortune, animated description of a feathered Oldenburg bonnet with a pleated satin lining and matching bow which she had glimpsed in a milliner's window on her way to Finsbury Square, and frequent reading aloud of particularly romantical and terrifying passages from Mr. Lewis's book, scarcely impinged on her consciousness.

Her mind was wholly taken up with the startling memory of Lord Brandsley's arms about her, his lips on hers, his voice with its gentle tones as he had spoken to her this afternoon.

Her feelings alternated between fear and hope. She could not but think that he must have been on the brink of a declaration when they had been interrupted. For surely he would not, otherwise, have kissed her *so*. She was astonished at herself for the degree of pleasurable feeling that kiss had wrung from her, and dimly she began to see that her aunt had been right, when she said that a loving and considerate husband might make the marriage relationship a different experience from the trials that Damaris had endured as the wife of Sir Walter Waring. It was true that as Lord Brandsley's passion increased, she had been a little alarmed, but he had let her go immediately and without impatience, and she had seen the concern in his face as he apologized. It seemed to her that he was capable of a patience and compassion that Sir Walter had never shown, for all his obvious generosity in material things, and his hearty air of kindness.

In short, her opposition to the idea of a second marriage was rapidly crumbling.

No sooner had she reached this conclusion than another alarm succeeded it. Lord Brandsley had not mentioned marriage, and it would have been proper to do so *before* he embraced her. If he had truly changed his opinion of her, the rather crude challenge he had made to her before could not now stand. But he had said he would call tomorrow and hope to find her alone. *Surely* that meant his kiss had been something much more than a sudden impulse, or an indulgence in an episode of idle dalliance?

When he called, rather early on the following day, to find her aunt with her, she managed to receive him with tolerable composure. He noted Mrs. Newington's presence with a slightly elevated eyebrow, but sat for some few minutes exchanging light conversation with both ladies before, his patience apparently at an end, he said bluntly, "I have something of a private nature to say to you, Lady Waring. Perhaps your aunt might excuse us—?"

Mrs. Newington, agog with curiosity and conjecture, assured him that by all means—only too happy—certainly, and pray not to trouble themselves to go into the breakfast parlor, for she had been just about to run up to her room to fetch some silks which she had forgotten to bring down—

Smiling kindly, Lord Brandsley bowed her out of the door and firmly closed it.

"Don't look so alarmed," he said to Damaris, who had risen to her feet. "I'm not going to kiss you again—just yet."

Her heart beating faster at the look in his eyes, Damaris said, "What did you wish to say to me, sir?"

"Can't you guess?" he asked, coming to her side and possessing himself of her hand. "Is it possible that you could forgive me the shocking things I have said to you, the unforgivable things I have believed of you?"

While he held her hand in his strong fingers, and looked at her with that particular rueful smile in his eyes, and a spark of something else...

"Very easily," she said, a tentative smile of her own dawning in her eyes.

"That is better than I deserve," he said. He kissed her fingers, and directed a searching look at her face. "But there is something further," he said. "Something even more presumptuous. Madam, will you do me the honor of becoming my wife?"

She held his eyes with a little effort, her face paling with emotion.

Then she gave a shaky little laugh and said, "Presumptuous! Sir, you are being absurd. The presumption must be on *my* side, surely, in marrying the Marquess of Brandsley!"

"Don't talk fustian!" he said sharply, his fingers crushing hers.

She drew in her breath quickly, her eyes wide, and he added more gently, his gaze fixed intently on her face, "You have not answered me, you know. Do you mean to refuse me?"

"*Refuse* you! Oh, no!" The color that had left her cheeks flooded back.

"Then let me hear you say yes," he suggested, a light in his eyes that made her feel strangely breathless.

She obeyed in a shaken voice, and he surveyed her a little longer with that disturbing look, then bent his head and, as he had once before, pressed his lips to the smooth skin of her inner wrist.

This time she did not pull away. Indeed, the fingers of her other hand hovered near his dark hair, tempted to touch it. But he raised his head and she dropped her hand quickly to her side.

Lord Brandsley looked at her rather searchingly. "Yesterday—" he said, "I think that I frightened you."

Avoiding his eyes, she admitted, "A little, perhaps."

He put both hands up to hold her face and make her look at him. Then after a moment he bent his head slowly and kissed her lips with great tenderness. His hands moved gently to her shoulders as she stood quietly in his embrace, and then he pulled her fully into his arms and kissed her more deeply, until she suddenly stiffened and broke away from his embrace, turning from him with her hands pressed to her cheeks.

"My dear!" he said. "I didn't mean to upset you. Forgive me!"

With an effort she regained some of her composure, turning to him with a smile on trembling lips, and her hands now clasped tightly on each other. "There is nothing to forgive," she assured him hastily. "On the contrary, it is *I* who—you must think me stupidly missish!"

"No!" He stood before her, lightly touching her arms with his fingers. "On the contrary, your modesty does you credit. I promise I shan't be so importunate again. I think that I hear your aunt returning. Shall we tell her our news?"

He smiled at her and turned to open the door to Mrs. Newington.

Damaris was grateful for his tact and restraint. Her emotions were in a turmoil, fear combining with feelings that were new to her, but not unpleasant. In a confused way, she was conscious that her fear itself had been not so much of the man and his passion, as of the unwonted sensations that passion had aroused in herself. Never before had she felt like this about a man, least of all the man who had for six years been her husband.

True to his word, Grenville kept his lovemaking during the days of their engagement well within the bounds of propriety. If, when he pressed her hand or brushed his lips lightly against her cheek as they met or parted, there was a gleam of rueful amusement in his eyes, he made it easy for her to ignore it. Once or twice he made her blush with a repetition of the intimate caress he liked to bestow on her inner wrist, but the smile of satisfaction with which he watched its effect was tempered by tenderness.

He had sent a notice to the gazette announcing his approaching nuptials, and managed to field the resultant quizzing of his friends and the barely concealed shock of certain of his relatives with an easy detachment. Except in the case of Lady Crawley, with whom he very nearly came to cuffs.

It was not to be expected that the countess would have received such surprising news with anything approaching complaisance. When, in courtesy, Lord Brandsley called on her to apprise her of it, she was for several moments rendered speechless. Unfortunately, as the marquess thought, she did not suffer long from this impediment, and in a very short time he was given to understand that he was not only more shatterbrained and far less up to snuff than she had ever before supposed, but quite possibly a candidate for Bedlam. "When I asked you to help my poor boy," she ended in shaking tones, "I little thought that *this* would be the result!"

"No more did I, ma'am," he said smilingly, quite unmoved by the opinion of his intelligence she had just delivered. "But if the object of your request to me was to prevent Lindo from marrying Lady Waring, you must admit that in that, at least, I would seem to have succeeded."

"*Don't* try to flummery me!" the countess said in awful accents. "Lindo's engagement to Miss Rathbone preceded yours by *days*, and you need not, in any case, expect me to believe that you were ever willing to sacrifice yourself in order to save him from That Woman!"

With a glint in his eyes, the marquess said, "No, indeed, though to my shame, something of the sort—still, that is neither here nor there. The fact is, Aunt, the engagement—*both* engagements—have taken place. And I must beg you *not* to refer to my chosen bride as That Woman!"

"I could," his aunt said wrathfully, "think of things a great deal worse—how you could allow yourself to be so taken in by such a *harpy*—"

"*Enough,* ma'am! I think that you forget yourself," he said brusquely.

The countess said bitterly, "I do not *forget*, Brandsley. I remember very clearly the way the—the way *Lady Waring* expressed herself to me on the subject of marriage. And it is of no use saying to me that she was speaking generally, for it was nothing of the sort. She meant then to have Lindo, and now she has found herself a bigger catch in you!"

Containing his temper with the knowledge that he had himself expressed similar views not so long ago, Brandsley replied with careful patience. "I think you were mistaken. It was you who first became particular on the subject, and patronized her. She has admitted to me that she allowed you to believe she might receive Lindo's addresses, only because she was angered by your attitude."

"Angered—by me! Well, if that don't pass everything! An uppish little country nobody, without name or rank or fortune, *angry* because I took exception to her luring *my son* into matrimony—"

"*That was not true,* ma'am. I think that you have said enough."

"Oho! You won't hear a word against her, I see! Well, she has *you* twisted about her finger, now. It really quite amazes me how men can be so besotted by a pretty face that they never suspect a take-in. I should have thought that *you* at least, would have learned from your previous mistake. Indeed, when I told dear Crawley I was at my wit's end to devise some means of preventing history from playing itself over, it was not with the thought that *you* would be the principal player once more!"

"You have a nice turn of phrase, Aunt, but I wish you will choose another theme. You are fair and far off, you know, and you can hardly expect me to listen with complaisance while you insult my affianced wife. I will *not* hear another word against her, if you please, and if you have any more to say on that head, I shall be obliged to take my leave."

His aunt conducted a visible struggle with her feelings, then said in a voice stiff with effort, "Very well. My lips are sealed henceforth. But I warn you, Brandsley, I will not receive her!"

"That is a pity," he said gently. "For if it is indeed the case, I regret I shall be obliged to cut my connection with you."

"Cut—!" Lady Crawley gasped. *"Brandsley,* you cannot mean it! Your own family—!"

"I do mean it. I should be sorry for it, believe me, but I will not allow *anyone* to slight *my wife,* ma'am. In any way," he added significantly.

"Oh, very well!" his aunt said crossly. "But I warn you, it goes against the pluck with me."

He looked at her consideringly. "I know. But recall I will not have her made uncomfortable," he said. "If you decide to receive us both, it must be done with real civility, not reluctant coldness."

"Brandsley!" the countess almost wailed. "You *cannot* expect me to be anything but reluctant, when you *know* my feelings on the matter!"

"I ask only that you take care not to show it. She has had enough of that nature to bear with already. I am determined that *my* name and consequence shall spare her that humiliation *this* time."

"Quite besotted!" murmured his aunt in failing tones. "How *could* you!"

The marquess allowed a flicker of irritation to cross

his face, and rose to take his leave. "I shall leave you, ma'am. Perhaps you would be good enough to inform me, when you feel able to receive Lady Waring with some measure of—warmth?"

"Never!" she said under her breath, and then, as he raised his brows, "Oh—very well!"

As his lordship left the premises, the countess called plaintively for her maid to be sent to her with a vinaigrette to soothe her lacerated nerves.

Viscount Edgely received the news with a good deal more pleasure than had his fond mamma. He wished his cousin happy and drank his health with the greatest good will.

Grenville eyed him with a little reserve. "My thanks," he said rather drily. "But I have to admit that until you announced your own engagement, I hardly expected you to be cock-a-hoop over this!"

A trifle flushed, Lindo replied, "Oh, *that* was over long ago!"

"So I—finally—have been brought to perceive! It has been over a good deal longer, I think, than you allowed me to know."

Lindo laughed. "Don't blame me too much, Gren! I own the temptation was too much. You were coming a little too much the older cousin, you know, and called me a *greenhead* as though I was scarce breeched! I meant no harm!"

"Well, I shan't apologize, because you have had more than your just revenge."

"What—a little private fun over your pangs of conscience at cutting me out? That's doing it rather brown, Gren."

"You don't know the half," his cousin said feelingly. After a pause, he said, "It *is* over for you, isn't it? You didn't transfer your attention to Miss Rathbone from some misguided sense of family feeling?"

Lindo first looked astonished, then burst into laughter that was too free not to be genuine. "Good God!" he said. "I'm not such a martyr. I don't deny that I was head over ears when I met Lady Waring, as who would not be? For though my Charlotte has the sweetest little phiz in all the world, there's no denying that Lady Waring is a regular diamond! But it was only calf love, after all. Tell you what, Gren, I'm vastly glad I *didn't* offer for her. She would only have turned me down, you know, and I should have been cast into the dismals. For although it wasn't a lasting passion, I don't mind telling you that it made me devilish uncomfortable at times."

A little askance, Grenville ventured, "You are sure, aren't you, that your feeling for Miss Rathbone is of a more lasting nature?"

"Perfectly sure," Lindo said simply. "I know you and mamma both think I'm a trifle young to be tying the knot, but I've agreed to a dashed long engagement, you know. The thing is, Charlotte is different—not only from Lady Waring, but all the other girls I've known. I know she is not what the world calls a *beauty*, but she has a great deal of countenance, once one gets to know her. And although her manners are retiring, among intimates she has a lively and cheerful disposition, in her quiet little way."

"And doesn't make you *devilish uncomfortable?*"

"No. Although I don't mind admitting I was a trifle put out when that army fellow was forever kicking his heels in the Rathbones' drawing room, and trying to impress her with tales of the Peninsula. But Charlotte is not a flirt."

Grenville refrained from pointing out that Charlotte lacked the usual equipment for flirting, not least of which was a modicum of vanity. She would, he thought, probably suit Lindo admirably.

Lindo said, "*You* may have your hands full, Gren."

At Grenville's look, he added hastily, "I don't mean to disparage Lady Waring, mind. Lord, you know how much *I* admire her. All those things I said about her, that evening when you told me you meant to offer for her, were sincerely meant, even though I wasn't any longer in love with her. But she can't help attracting admirers, you know, like bees about a honeypot."

"She may attract as many admirers as she likes," Grenville said equably. "They won't be married to her. *I* will."

Lindo looked a little thoughtful, but he said, "Well, I don't doubt *you* will manage the business with ease."

"Thank you. I shouldn't be marrying her if I didn't trust her, you know."

"Lord, Gren—I didn't mean *that!*" Lindo said anxiously. "It is only that—well, I don't mind telling you, I should soon be in the hips if a lot of frippery fellows were forever hanging about *my* wife! But I daresay you will know what to do about it."

"Certainly I shall." The marquess looked a little amused.

"By the bye, when *are* you getting riveted, Gren?"

The marquess gave his cousin a slightly pained grin. "Must you be so vulgar? We have not yet set a date for the nuptials. I shall inform all my relatives when it is certain."

"I imagine it will be quite soon though? There can be no cause for *you* to wait very long, and I believe Lady Waring has no relatives of her own?"

"I certainly hope not to wait too long," the marquess said calmly. "My betrothed, by the way, has agreed to accept a horse from me, to mark our engagement. Did you tell me that Heathrow was selling his stable?"

"Yes, some prime goers among them!" Lindo told him enthusiastically, the change of subject instantly accepted. Grenville watched him with a slightly abstracted smile, as he expatiated on Heathrow's horse-flesh.

It was true that he had hoped not to delay his wedding plans. But the mention of an early date had caused an unmistakable flash of panic in the sherry gold eyes of his betrothed.

He was not an obtuse man, and very little thought was needed for him to make a shrewd guess at the reason for his intended bride's fear and shyness with him. It was not hard to imagine the feelings of a young, untried girl married to a very much older and perhaps impatient man. It would take time for her to learn to respond to a different approach. The fact that she had accepted him, and did not shrink from his mild embraces, augured well, but there was clearly a case for a careful and not too hasty approach to marriage. He had, it seemed, been too sanguine in expecting the intimacies of the marriage bed to hold no terrors for a woman who had already some experience of them. On the contrary, it rather appeared that he was required to exercise more skill, judgement and self-control than if he had taken a virgin bride whom he might have initiated with a little care and very little trouble. A frightened, unwilling partner was the last thing he wanted.

So he set himself to woo her with patience and restraint until she could learn to trust him. He could only hope that the process would not be a lengthy one, and that his forbearance would be equal to the task.

chapter ten

Damaris accepted a very handsome emerald and diamond ring from the marquess, and allowed him to present her with a sweet-stepping, soft-mouthed mare
which enabled her to join him for morning rides in
Hyde Park, and an occasional gallop at Richmond.
Other gifts, except for an inexpensive reticule which
she admired in a shop window in Oxford Street, and a
copy of Lord Byron's latest poem, *The Corsair,* she
firmly refused, suggesting he should keep them until
they were married.

"Does it matter," he asked her, "whether you accept
them before or after our marriage? I don't have so great
a respect for the niceties of convention."

"No," she said. *"Your* place in society is secure. *My*
life could become most uncomfortable if I was known
to accept gifts that were outside the recognized bounds

of propriety. I am not perfectly sure I should have allowed you to give me my lovely mare."

"If my place is secure," he said shortly, "so will yours be, as my wife."

She glanced at him fleetingly and said, "Yes."

"And if anyone has dared to make you uncomfortable, I wish you will refer them to me. I'll soon set them to rights!"

With a hint of laughter, she said, "Oh no! As your *fiancée,* I refuse to countenance any more *liaisons* with opera dancers, my lord!"

For a moment he was surprised. Then he suppressed a smile and said, "I see what it is, you intend to keep me under the cat's foot when we are wed!"

Damaris gave a ripple of laughter at this unlikely picture. She could hardly imagine anything less likely than Brandsley submitting to his wife's domination. "You don't think anything of the kind!" she said. "For no one knows better than I that you wouldn't stand for it."

"No," he admitted. "I wouldn't. But that does not mean I shall be a tyrannical husband, you know," he added, with a hint of seriousness.

Damaris glanced up to find his eyes quizzically on her face. Her laugh a trifle forced, she said, "I assure you I have never thought so, sir."

She made to turn away from him, but with his hand on her wrist he said, *"Don't!* My love, don't be afraid to tell me what is in your mind!"

He saw the indecision in her eyes, and said, "I think I understand what troubles you. Believe me, you have nothing to fear from me."

She seemed about to answer him, when her aunt came into the room and the moment was lost. He released her hand and she took up her tambour frame from one of the buhl tables, and bent her head over the needlework.

Mrs. Newington having expressed a great desire to see the illuminations prepared in the Royal parks to celebrate the centenary, the marquess had got up a party of ladies and gentlemen to enjoy the festivities.

Some rain in the morning caused some anxious moments, not only to those responsible for organizing the entertainments, but to the would-be spectators. Mrs. Newington glanced out of the salon window and pronounced on the state of the weather every fifteen minutes, and Charlotte, who had driven to Harley Street with a young friend for a short visit, declared her mamma had implored her to leave the house, for she could not bear her daughter's fidgets any longer.

"Lord Brandsley will not cancel the party only for a little rain, will he?" she implored Damaris.

Thus applied to, Damaris laughed and said, "I'm sure he is not so chicken-hearted, but if it should be very wet, we must resign ourselves to staying home after all."

Fortunately the rain cleared in the afternoon, and by evening some half a million people were swarming in gay but orderly fashion through Green, Hyde and St. James's parks. Piccadilly, the Strand and Oxford Street were quite impassable for the crowds. The invasion was viewed with disfavor by the parks' cows, which refused for days afterwards to yield their milk, thus creating a shortage which was only relieved by the presence of several beer tents erected along the Serpentine for the occasion, the enterprising proprietors of which were so public spirited as to cause them to remain all the following week.

Brandsley's party arrived outside Buckingham House to see Mr. James Sadler, the celebrated aeronaut, make his balloon ascent and be rapidly wafted away by a westerly wind, dropping colored parachutes to mark his progress. The *Times* next day reported he had been borne over Essex to the North Sea coast, where, being obliged to cut the gasbag so as not to be carried out to sea, he had landed safely in the Mucking Marshes.

Lindo and Charlotte, being the youngest of the party, led the rest to the Serpentine, where mock battleships reenacted Trafalgar, and then over to Green Park, for the fireworks and the Storm of Badajos, fought over a canvas "Castle of Discord" one hundred and thirty feet high.

Brandsley shepherded his party to a vantage point

which gave them an excellent view of the castle, with its painted battlements manned by a small force of remarkably ferocious "Frenchmen" who tried, naturally without success, to repulse the attack of the gallant redcoats.

Charlotte hung on Lindo's arm with shining eyes, her lips parted slightly with excitement. Damaris watched them with a smile, noting the look in Lindo's eyes as he glanced down at his betrothed.

Grenville, too, had been watching them. He said, "You don't mind, do you?"

"Mind what?" Damaris looked up inquiringly.

"Seeing one of your cavaliers so patently in love with someone else."

"I should be very disappointed if he was not," she said. "I went to a great deal of trouble to throw them together. I always thought that, if Charlotte could ever overcome her shyness with him, they would *suit*."

"Did you indeed? I only wish you had confided in me!"

"Matchmakers never confide in anyone. It is fatal to a happy outcome!"

He laughed, and moved to stand by Lindo and Charlotte, but his hand held hers on his arm even as he chatted to them and admired the display, criticizing the battle tactics and arguing with Lindo in an amiable fashion on the strategy the redcoats should adopt. His thumb absently caressed the back of her hand, and even as she watched the raised bayonets of the soldiers glinting in the light of moon and the Japanese lanterns hung in the trees, she knew she felt more happy and secure than she had ever been since before her uncle's illness, so many years ago.

At midnight, on the stroke, to the accompanying of a terrifying explosion that made Charlotte shriek and bury her face in Lindo's green venetian coat, the canvas walls of the Castle of Discord were suddenly pulled away by a hidden mechanism, and a glittering vision was revealed. The Temple of Peace, illuminated by thousands of colored lamps, revolved majestically while fireworks burst about it, and some of Colonel Congreve's rockets, which the army had scorned during the actual war, lit the skies with a spectacular starburst of light, banging away in fine style. Fountains of water gushed from the jaws of carved lions into golden basins at the foot of the Temple, and on its roof a detachment of foot guards presented the royal standard.

When they had joined in the applause for the display, the marquess's party made for their carriages. The evening had been a delightful one, and fortunately they did not know that the elaborate illuminated pagoda that had been built on a Chinese bridge over the St. James's Park canal had burst into flames a few minutes after midnight, and fallen, killing two of the spectators who had imagined the fire to be one of the entertainments laid on for their delectation. When Damaris read about it later, and recalled her contentment that night, she wondered if it was a kind of omen.

Lady Crawley had been among the party who attended the jubilee celebrations, and under her nephew's warning eyes had greeted Damaris with cordiality. But beneath the determined civility, Damaris sensed the countess's antipathy. She was grateful that Grenville stayed by her side throughout their conversation, and made it easy for her to appear at ease.

Although unaware of Lord Brandsley's ultimatum, she was convinced that his aunt must view her with considerable disfavor, and had been grateful that the countess managed to hide her antipathy under a semblance of cordiality. Damaris knew that it must have gone much against her inclination, and considered her generous for her nephew's sake. Even to Mrs. Newington, also, Lady Crawley had unbent, going so far as to instruct her husband to offer his other arm to the lady when they were admiring the battleships on the Serpentine, and soliciting her opinion on the subject of the scandalous practice of ladies wearing pantaloons.

This latter piece of information Damaris learned the following day, for Mrs. Newington relayed the conversation in detail. "And only think, Damaris, Lady Crawley says the Princess Charlotte has a pair, and has *shown them off in public,* actually pulling up her skirt to do so."

"I don't think the princess sets herself up as a model of decorum, Aunt," Damaris commented with a faint smile.

"No, indeed. In fact, I believe that her language is peppered with all kinds of slang. I'm bound to say, if she was not a princess one would have to declare that she is not at all the thing!"

"Well, the higher one is in society, the more one is able to flout the conventions without fear of reprisal. And you would have to admit that she has had no good example from either of her parents. For a more rackety pair doesn't exist. I can't imagine why it is they are unable to live together. One would say that their way of life is so similar they would have suited admirably!"

"Indeed, they are both very shocking. But one would think the old queen must have some influence on her granddaughter."

"The girl seems very attached to her mamma. The story is that when the Regent forbade his daughter to visit his wife, they met in the park in their carriages, and embraced from the windows."

"Well, such affection is natural, of course, and Parliament, after all, did *not* find the Princess of Wales guilty of the dreadful charges that were brought against her. All the same, she *does* not seem a very proper person to have charge of an impressionable young girl. Lady Crawley told me that she had heard from a most reliable person, that Princess Caroline had positively *encouraged* her daughter to indulge in a most improper flirtation with Captain Hesse of the Dragoons, when she was at Kensington Palace last year."

"Good heavens! But isn't he supposed to be—"

"Exactly. The Duke of York's love-child. Which makes it *excessively* shocking."

"I should think so. It *cannot* be true!"

"Lady Crawley said—"

But Damaris was no longer attending. It had struck her quite forcibly that Lady Crawley had shown remarkable condescension to her aunt, and that Mrs. Newington was more than gratified by such attention. Perhaps the countess had repented of her supercilious treatment at their previous meeting, and tried to make amends. It did flit across her mind that Lady Crawley's attention to her aunt had prevented any necessity for her to engage in unnecessary conversation with Damaris herself, but no good would come of looking for ulterior motives where quite possibly none existed. She must be hopeful of being on good terms with Grenville's family, not only for her own sake, but his. She was aware that Lady Crawley was his only living aunt, and having lost his own mother he might be supposed to be close to her, although the tie was not one of blood.

Having determined to view the countess in the best possible light, Damaris began to feel uncomfortable about her own part in the regrettable lapse of taste and temper which had marked their first meeting.

From there it was only a short step to deciding that she must make her peace with the countess properly by apologizing and explaining herself.

At the end of the week, as the Regent's errant wife was embarking on the HMS *Jason* for an extended period abroad (during which her conduct moved the Privy Council to advise her husband that if she ever sought to return she was not to be admitted to the country), Damaris was calling on Lady Crawley.

She had come without her aunt, for she felt that what she must say was more easily conveyed without the presence of a third, and she was relieved to find, on being ushered into the countess's drawing room, that her hostess was alone.

The first civilities being exchanged, she begged pardon for calling uninvited, and was relieved to have her apologies graciously waved aside, although a certain stiffness of manner indicated that Lady Crawley, like herself, was finding the visit a little trying to the nerves.

A short silence ensued, the countess sitting ramrod-straight on a claw-footed sofa, and Damaris, with her hands nervously clenched on her reticule, trying to muster courage to say what she had come to say.

"Lady Crawley—" she began. "I am afraid that when we first met, you must have gained—I *allowed* you to gain a very false impression of my character. When we spoke of your son's—your son's affection—*possible* affections, if he should ever marry."

The countess's face had set in an icy mask, and Damaris felt her heart sink. *"Please,"* she said, "please let me try to explain. It was very bad of me—very foolish, and I know you thought that I—that I encouraged Lord Edgely to dangle after me. Believe me, it was *not* so. He was kind when I first came to London with my aunt, and I count him a friend. I know he was a little in love with me, for a time, but it was just a boy's fancy, and I would *not* have taken advantage of it, even if I had been—the kind of woman you evidently believed."

The countess deigned to raise her eyebrows interrogatively.

Damaris sighed. "Well, you *did* think so, didn't you?" she asked. "You see, *that* was what made me—made me—"

"Angry?" the countess inquired frostily.

"I'm afraid so," Damaris admitted meekly. "I should not have lost my temper, for you were only concerned for your son, which is very natural in a parent, and particularly so in Lord Edgely's case.

"I know he is your only child, and his sweetness of disposition is such that he would not recognize avarice, and might well be in danger from an unscrupulous woman such as you clearly believed me to be! I expect you had heard some tale brought you by a malicious person, too, for I have not been in town these several months without finding out there is always someone about, spreading the most shocking untruths about people."

"Very true," said the countess, as though reluctantly struck by this observation.

"Please say you will forgive me," Damaris begged eagerly. "If not for my own sake, then for the sake of the affection you bear your nephew."

"I find your conduct, Lady Waring, quite extraordinary," Lady Crawley said, but not with anger, rather with pained surprise.

"I know. But you see, I felt that you—that you might have told me what was in your mind, and I could have set it at ease at once. Oh, I *know* that my birth, my circumstances, made me a thoroughly ineligible match, quite apart from the fact that I am older. But—"

As she hesitated, Lady Crawley said, with the air of one making a discovery, "I hurt your feelings! Wounded your sensibilities!"

Damaris, recognizing that she was confronted with an aristocrat to whom the pride of those below her touch was incomprehensible, decided this was as close as the countess was likely to come to understanding what she had felt on the previous occasion. She said simply, "Yes, ma'am. You did. But even worse, I thought that you had wounded the sensibilities of my dear aunt, Mrs. Newington. I realize now, of course, that I was mistaken. You could not have meant to do any such thing, for your kindness to her at the jubilee celebration was not to be surpassed. Ever since she has talked of little else but your great goodness to her on that occasion, and the condescension you showed her. Do say you will forgive me."

Lady Crawley had the grace to blush. The suspicion Damaris had dismissed as unworthy had not been entirely unfounded, and the countess was aware that on that first occasion she had been less than courteous to both ladies. Well, it appeared she had been under a misapprehension. Dimly she saw that she had been unjust, and that Lady Waring had been constrained by that injustice to a course of conduct that had been, undoubtedly, reprehensible, but not entirely without cause. There was no denying the sincerity in her tone and manner now, and she well remembered the artificiality of both when she had discussed Lindo before.

Well, Grenville had hinted at this, but a fuller explanation from the young woman's own lips did seem to put a different complexion on the matter. She might still feel a little skeptical, but she could at least keep an open mind. Grenville was going to marry the girl, after all. Even if he discovered she was not what she *now* appeared to be, a gentleman could not cry off from an engagement once it was announced. And if she *was* an adventuress after all, certainly *she* would not break the tie.

So, the best thing, and the most comfortable, would

be to accept that a mistake had been made, and hope that the girl was genuine, after all, in her protestations of innocence and contrition.

Lady Crawley smiled and graciously held out her hand. "Come and sit by me, my dear. You have been very naughty, but I believe I understand. And you must forgive *me* if I was coming it a little too strong, that day. I own, I was very worried about my dear only boy!"

"Ma'am, you are too kind!" Damaris said warmly, accepting the invitation with relief. "Of course, I know that the inequality between myself and Lord Brandsley is too great for his relatives to accept *this* match with enthusiasm, but please believe me when I say I will do my best to make him happy!"

The countess was in agreement with the first part of this speech, but was too polite to say so. She merely patted the hand that Damaris had laid upon the sofa beside her, and said, "Well, marriages of attachment are very much in fashion nowadays, and I cannot say that I am sorry to see my own dear son affianced to a girl he appears to hold in the greatest affection. It was not so in *my* day of course, but I did become most sincerely attached to Lindo's father. It was a great blow to me when he died."

Damaris murmured appropriate words of sympathy. She was a good listener and, encouraged by her interested attention, Lady Crawley spent a most enjoyable quarter hour informing her of all the circumstances of her first marriage, her sad bereavement, her brave widowhood and her second, fortunately successful sally into marriage. At the end of this recital she was so much in charity with her niece-in-law to be, that she ventured the hope that Damaris, too, would find equal happiness in her second matrimonial venture, and issued a cordial invitation to Lady Waring and her dear aunt to attend a small, select party which she was holding the following Wednesday. "Just cards and a little music, you know," she said. "Quite informal. Such a pity Brandsley is not in town, to escort you. I shall ask Lindo to call for you."

Damaris, overwhelmed by so much attention, refused to put Lord Edgely to that trouble, and insisted that they could quite safely be conveyed in their own carriage, glad to be able to say that they had one.

The carriage was expensive to keep, but almost a necessity for two ladies living alone, and wishing to attend evening functions.

The party was just as select, although less small and informal than Damaris had been led to believe, and she was glad that she had worn a rather pretty white lace gown with an underskirt of champagne satin, and had twisted a strand of pearls into her coiffure. She had been at pains to look genteel as well as elegant, and was rewarded by the look of approval on Lady Crawley's face as she introduced her to the other guests. The countess was gracious to Mrs. Newington, also, and the two soon had their heads together discussing the Princess of Wales's latest start, and her declaration that if the English Court refused to accord her the dignities appropriate to her station, she was determined to remain "Caroline, a happy, merry soul!" What she would get up to on the continent was a subject for much enjoyable, if scandalized, conjecture.

When the marquess returned from his visit to his estate in Norfolk, and made for Harley Street without stopping to change out of his breeches and topboots, it was to find his betrothed entertaining his aunt, who seemed to be exhibiting every sign of being bosom-bows with Mrs. Newington.

Damaris greeted him with unaffected gladness, giving him both her hands, which he kissed one by one and then held, smiling down at her. His absence had not been entirely without calculation, for he had hoped she would miss him rather dreadfully. Certainly she seemed delighted at his return, but he saw no evidence that she had pined.

"You are in high bloom, my love," he said, drawing her apart when he had apologized for his informal attire, and exchanged civil greetings with the two aunts.

"Thank you," Damaris smiled. "Are your affairs in the country in hand?"

"My bailiff is coping well. But it is many years since I have been away so long from Louth."

Her eyes flickered and looked away. "Shall you stay with us for dinner?" she asked.

"I'm not dressed for it," he reminded her.

"We shan't care for that," she assured him. "There is only Aunt Tabby and myself." She looked up and laid her hand on his arm. "Please stay!"

The faint tightening about his mouth softened, and he put his hand over hers, and lifted it to kiss her wrist in the way he had.

Flushing, she whispered, "Oh, *pray* don't do that!"

His eyes gleamed a laughing challenge at her. "You are not going to tell me that you don't like it, are you? Because I shan't believe you!"

She cast him a glance of reproachful indignation, trying to withdraw her hand from his clasp. His grip tightened and he laughed.

"You are abominable!" she hissed.

"I daresay," he said carelessly. "No, don't be a scold, love. Only think, I have come all the way from Norfolk in such haste I've not even put off my traveling clothes, only to see you as soon as I reached town. How *can* you think of pulling caps with me?"

She looked up at the smile in his eyes, and reluctantly returned it. "Well, you *are* abominable," she said. "For you can't deny that you were teasing me. But you must be in want of some refreshment. I'll ring for a glass of wine and some cake."

"The sight of your face is refreshment enough."

Damaris laughed. "Very pretty, my lord. But I suspect you will make even prettier compliments on a full stomach than an empty one."

She moved away to pull at the bell rope, while her betrothed gave way to laughter, so that the two ladies with their heads together on the sofa turned to stare with approval at the young people whose gaiety, as Mrs. Newington whispered with satisfaction to Lady Crawley, pronounced them much in love.

Lady Crawley took her leave a short while later, and Mrs. Newington escorted her as far as the front door.

After bowing the two out of the room, Grenville strolled back to a chair beside Damaris, picked up his wine glass and said, cocking an eyebrow at her, "Well—

a-day! Now tell me what is happening between those two!"

Demurely, Damaris said, "Why, I believe they are bidding fair to become the fastest friends. Your aunt has been all kindness to us—"

Slightly startled, Grenville interrupted. "Is this true?"

"Certainly it is. Nothing could exceed her graciousness to us both. We are sincerely grateful."

He looked at her rather searchingly. "She does not patronize you?" he asked.

"Well—yes. A little. But that is just her way, you know; I expect she can't help it. Aunt Tabitha, I think, rather likes it. She feels a person of superior rank *should* show her superiority, I believe. And Lady Crawley has shown her a generosity that cannot but be pleasing. The fact is, they have been getting on famously together!"

Her eyes danced with laughter, and the marquess smiled with a faintly nonplussed expression, then laughed outright. "Good Lord!" he said. "Who would have thought it? But nothing could be better—"

"Nothing!" Damaris agreed.

After the jubilee day, London grew thin of company, as the great families left for their country estates or shooting boxes in time for the grouse season, and many of the gentility removed to Bath for the winter.

As he idly surveyed the cards on the mantel in her drawing room one day, Grenville remarked to Damaris, "The season is coming to an end. You have not half so many invitations as even a month ago."

Damaris, arranging a bouquet of flowers in a marble vase standing on a rosewood corner table, said absently, "No. Everyone seems to be leaving town. These flowers are a parting gift from Mr. Aslett."

"The devil they are!" He strolled over to her side, and looked critically at the blooms she was twitching into place. "What does the fellow mean by sending you flowers?"

She glanced up at him, and smiled. "Don't pretend

to be jealous of him," she said. "I know very well you never regarded Mr. Aslett as a serious rival."

"Where are *my* flowers?"

"The roses you sent yesterday? In my bedroom."

"Then I forgive you for paying more attention at the moment to Aslett's poor flowers than to me. Is he brokenhearted?"

Damaris laughed. "I doubt it. Don't you know he has taken to dangling after Miss Waterson? It's my belief he followed her to Bath."

He broke off the head of a bronze chrysanthemum and tucked it with negligent fingers into the front of her gown, enjoying the vivid flush that rose to her cheeks.

The fingers that touched the flower heads in the vase trembled a little. "At any rate," she said calmly, "they are beautiful."

"Yes," he said, looking down at her. "Very beautiful."

Her lip caught briefly in her teeth, and he reached for her, turning her into his arms. His eyes glinted as she looked up into his face. Then his arms tightened about her, crushing the flower in her bosom between them as his lips came down on hers, questioning, then seeking, then demanding an answer.

Damaris yielded to him, then stiffened in some slight alarm, and finally surrendered, allowing a clamor of feeling to overtake her senses, feeling she was being swept away on a flood-tide of emotion, but kept safe and sheltered by the strength and warmth of his arms and his love. Not yet able to match his passion, her response was tentative and unsure, but that it pleased him she had no doubt when he at last lifted his mouth from hers, his narrowed eyes blazing on her flushed face, his arms still keeping her close as his lips curved in a triumphant but tender smile.

"You see, my darling," he said. "There is nothing to be afraid of."

Damaris gave a strangely happy little sigh, and leaned her hot cheek against his shoulder.

He moved, tipping her chin up so that he could see her eyes. His fingertip brushed a stray curl from her temple. "You are not frightened of me, are you, Damaris?" he questioned.

She shook her head. "Forgive me. I've been very foolish, and you so patient—"

A rueful light entered his eyes. His hand still gently playing with her hair. "I am not a naturally patient man, my love. I want to marry you before the month is out, and take you home to Louth. I *will not* wait longer."

"Is that—an ultimatum?" Her eyes were wide and unafraid.

"Yes," he said, but he was smiling. "I'm afraid it is."

"Then—since I have no choice—" She smiled back at him, her eyes bemused with loving. "I shall marry you, my lord, whenever you choose."

The date of the wedding having been set, the two aunts reveled in the preparation. Since both Grenville and Damaris wanted only the simplest of ceremonies, it amazed and amused them both that Lady Crawley and Mrs. Newington threw up their hands in horror at the short time at their disposal to make the necessary arrangements.

Since Damaris had no male relative living, Mr. Rathbone was prevailed upon to stand in place of her father. Charlotte was to attend her, and Lindo to support the groom. Few friends were invited, and as there was to be no wedding journey it was not necessary to purchase a great many bride clothes. It was not possible, either, Damaris pointed out somewhat drily to her aunt, for she had very little money left over from their one London season, and she *would* not allow Lord Brandsley to frank her, even so close to the wedding.

He had promised her a trip to Paris the following spring to make up for the lack of a honeymoon. But she understood his wish to be at the Hall for the harvest, and felt, herself, that she would prefer to become used to his home before setting off on a journey to the Continent. In any case, although some intrepid travelers had crossed the Channel as soon as Napoleon was safely locked up on the tiny island of Elba, and the rightful French king installed in the midst of his subjects, Europe was still recovering from the ravages of the long years of war. A visit the following year would be far more pleasant.

Her bridal dress was of cream Brussels lace over satin, cut on simple lines with a satin ribbon under the bust, and a graceful demi-train. She would not wear a veil, but a tiny matching bonnet trimmed with satin roses had been devised by her dressmaker in collusion with a milliner, and she hoped that Grenville would be pleased with the result.

Four days before the wedding, the dress and bonnet were delivered to the house in Harley Street, and, Lady Crawley being present along with Charlotte and Mrs. Rathbone when the bandboxes containing the bride clothes were carried in by the footman, the ladies expressed a great curiosity to see them.

Carefully Damaris lifted them from the boxes to display them, and they were duly admired before she rang for her maid to put them carefully away.

Charlotte was helping her refold the dress, while Lady Crawley was expressing to Mrs. Newington and Mrs. Rathbone her satisfaction that her nephew was at last going to be wed. Damaris could hear her rather penetrating voice, although apparently meant to be lowered to a confidential note, quite clearly. She was not attending, listening rather to Charlotte's admiring comments on the wedding gown, and wistful daydreams about her own, but gradually the sense of Lady Crawley's remarks began to filter into her mind.

"—almost despaired of his ever finding a wife—" she heard. "—had quite buried himself in the country, you know. Of course, Lindo would have inherited, but a man—his own heir—And for all Grenville teased me about cutting out his cousin—when I told him he would soon be too old to attract—put the thought of marrying into his head, I believe—a legitimate heir—so important for a man—generations, you know, father to son—although Lindo is a Despard—not the same—no, I believe I made him see sense—thought he had plenty of time, I daresay—very fond of Lindo, of course, but a son of his own—I am not, I hope—have never let Lindo include Louth in his expectations—dear boy would

never—and every man must want sons—so natural—
Damaris—dear girl—her duty—and provide—well, of
course, but—Brandsley would never reproach—but one
must hope—a second marriage—in my own case, although—"

"Damaris!" Charlotte touched her arm, looking concerned. "Are you quite well? You look a little pale."

Damaris, smiling blindly said, "I—I expect it is excitement. That maid is taking a long time. I believe I
shall take these up myself. No—don't come, Charlotte,
I shall manage quite well on my own. I—I shan't be
long."

She met the maid on the stairs, but brushed her
aside with a quick, "Never mind, Hooton, I will put
them away."

But in her room she put the boxes on the bed, and
stood looking down at them with a dazed expression.
After a while she gazed about the room in an abstracted
fashion, and finally raised her fingers to her temples.
"What a *fool* I have been!" she whispered to herself in
anguished tones. "What a blind, stupid, selfish fool!"

Her gaze lit again on the boxes containing her beautiful wedding clothes. She winced and turned away,
making for the door. She must go back to her guests.
She must try to pretend that everything was normal,
that the wedding would take place as planned, in four
days time.

But could it?

As she descended the stairs she recalled Lady Crawley's whispered words—*Brandsley would never reproach*—

No, he would not reproach her. If she told him, he
would understand, he would not repudiate her.

He would not—he *could* not, in honor. He would hide
his disappointment and insist on the wedding going
forward.

No, she could never tell him. *But surely he must have
some inkling?*

From Lady Crawley's conversation, perhaps not.
Very likely not, it seemed. Perhaps he had not given
the matter sufficient thought, before he proposed. And
once she had accepted him, he would never withdraw.

She stood at the bottom of the stairs, thinking, *What shall I do? Oh, what can I do?*

But as she fixed a smile on her lips and moved toward the drawing room, her heart was leaden within her breast. For she knew what she had to do. The only thing, now, that could be done.

chapter eleven

Early the following morning a hired chaise left London and turned onto the Bath Road, heading, by stages, for Somerset.

Within the privacy of the carriage, Damaris sank thankfully back against the upholstery and gave way at last to racking tears which she had held back with great effort since yesterday. The postboy, who had thought when she hired the conveyance that she looked like a lady expecting imminent bereavement (her plum-colored pelisse and matching velvet bonnet indicating that the bereavement had not yet taken place), would have felt his suspicions confirmed by this display of grief, had he been privileged to see it.

Not only grief but also a misery of guilt weighed on his passenger's soul. She could not but feel that she was behaving dreadfully badly, and yet no other course of action, she was sure, would serve.

Creeping from the house in the early morning by the back stair, without even a maid to attend her, and with a minimum of clothing stuffed hastily into a small traveling bag, she had felt like a sneak-thief.

Her aunt would find a letter of explanation which Damaris had left in her own room, several hours hence, most probably. And the letter she had left for Lord Brandsley would be sent round to his house, to be read by him when he returned later in the day from Norfolk, where he had spent a few days overseeing the preparations for the reception of his bride in her new home....

At this thought a small, anguished moan escaped her, and she gulped and with a great effort dried her eyes and forced herself to a semblance of composure. It was useless to dwell on what might have been. She had done the only thing possible, and now—now she must learn to live with it.

Her aunt would be shocked, of course, and puzzled. Damaris wished she could have confided in Mrs. Newington, but it would not have done. If Brandsley took it into his head to question her, he would find the truth in no time at all. Damaris felt compunction at having left the older lady to deal with what remained to be done before the house in Harley Street was closed up, but that was all arranged for the end of the week, in any case. It would not now be possible, of course, for Mrs. Newington to spend some time with Lord and Lady Crawley at their country seat, as had been arranged for after the wedding which was not now going to take place. But Damaris had left enough money for her to follow her niece into Somerset with the remainder of their baggage.

She tried not to dwell on what Grenville's feelings must be when he discovered that he had been jilted. If he was angry, she was tolerably certain he would not vent his spleen on Mrs. Newington. If she could have been certain that his dominant feeling would be anger, she might have taken the less cowardly way of facing him with her sudden rejection rather than writing a letter and running away. But if—if he was hurt, if he pleaded and took her in his arms, *that* she might not be able to withstand.

No, this was the only way. He might be angry, he would probably despise her—in fact, it would be better if he did. But he could not make her change her mind. And if it was true, as it seemed to be, that the idea of marriage had taken hold of his mind, then there were many more worthy women to choose from, and *they* would more than likely be able to oblige him in the one thing in which *she* was so sadly deficient.

The horses had been changed twice before she felt able to descend from the chaise and take refreshment at one of the posting inns. She was not hungry, but drank a cup of tea, and tidied her person, being glad to note, in the mirror of the inn parlor, that the ravages of her tears were not too noticeable.

Later in the day she had a little boiled fowl and a syllabub, and felt slightly better, but her spirits were still very low, and the thought of what awaited her in Somerset did nothing to revive them. A small, dark house which had been closed for months, no servants to welcome her, and a reluctant cousin-in-law making it clear that he wished her anywhere but living on his doorstep, was a prospect hardly calculated to cheer her.

For a time she dozed lightly, and when she stirred again, dusk was beginning to fall. She would have to stop at the next inn for the night.

She heard the horses' hooves clattering on cobbles, and a flare of light passed the carriage windows as they drew to a restive halt. There was an exchange of voices outside, and as she prepared to alight, the door was thrown open and a tall figure, instead of stepping back to let her out, swung into the chaise beside her and shut the door.

Startled, she said, "Sir—I think a mistake—"

"There is no mistake," a hard voice answered her.

In the dimness she caught a glimpse of an implacable profile and gasped.

"Yes," said Lord Brandsley grimly, as the chaise jerked, and she automatically put a hand out to steady herself. It encountered the door handle and, driven by a blind instinct for flight, she made to open it.

"Oh, no!" said her companion. "I think not!"

His hand caught her wrist in a painful grip and forced her back into her seat, retaining his hold.

"I wish to get out," she said, trying to sound calm. "It is my intention to stay here for the night. If you have anything to say to me, sir—"

"I have a great deal to say to you, *madam!*" She had the impression he was speaking through clenched teeth. "And I am not going to say it in a public inn."

At that moment the chaise began to move. For a moment surprise held her still and silent. Then she tried to move again to call the postboy and tell him to stop, only to find herself roughly thrust against the leather back of the seat, her cry of angry protest cut off by a hard hand against her mouth. "It's of no use to scream," he said. "I told the postboy you are my wife, and have paid him well, in advance, to carry out my instructions, with the promise of more to come. I gave him the impression—without actually saying so—that you were a *runaway* wife, so he would be unsurprised, but distinctly unresponsive, if a few shrieks of protest should chance to catch his ears."

He removed his hand as the chaise picked up speed, and Damaris, fright and anger pushing misery and guilt into the background, said, *"How dare you!* Let me go this instant!"

He removed his hand from her wrist, saying, "But of course. You can hardly escape now."

The word *escape* conjured up alarming visions, but she forced herself to be calm. He was much more angry than she had ever seen him, and his violence had shown her a glimpse of something that she was dreadfully afraid she was unable to deal with. It had not occurred to her that he would come after her. She had thought his pride would have prevented it. Now she began to wonder with some trepidation just what it might drive him to.

"You—you had my letter, my lord," she said.

"Of course," he said shortly. "A pretty little farrago of lies and deceit, which I might have expected from you, if I had been less blinded by your undeniably lovely face, and the pretty fiction that you loved me!"

She turned her head away sharply at that, for his words stabbed unbearably, and he went on bitterly. "How did it go, now? You *begged my pardon* for being *foolishly tempted* by the prospect of marrying one far above your station, but you had *mistaken your own heart*. A nice touch, that last. I could have sworn, you know, that you don't have one—but then, if you have no heart, how could you be *mistaken* in it?"

Ignoring this, she said, "My aunt must have told you where I had gone. I hope, sir, you have not subjected her to the kind of Turkish manners you have just shown to *me!*"

Coldly, he said, "There was no need. She was only too pleased to tell me. She is convinced that you are suffering an attack of bridal nerves, and implored me to bring you back. She said she *knew that I could make you happy.*"

"She is—she is mistaken," Damaris said in a low voice.

"Oh, yes, to be sure!" he said sarcastically. "We are all of us mistaken. *You* have mistaken your heart, *I* have mistaken your character; your aunt, I fear, is vastly mistaken in your motives. I will tell you something, Lady Waring. You have been more mistaken than you know. When you thought you could make a May game of *me,* you made a mistake that is going to cost you dear!"

"It was not my intention," she said, "to—to make a May game of you. Indeed I am truly sorry—"

"At the moment you may well be sorry, because just now you are alone with me, and afraid, in spite of that veneer of calm you affect. But you will shortly be a great deal more sorry—and more afraid!"

Alerted to danger by the grimness in his tone, she tried in the darkness to make out his expression. "What do you intend to do with me?" she asked.

"Eventually—" he drawled, "take you back to London and marry you."

Brushing aside the implications of that first word, she said, "You can carry me back to London, I suppose, but you cannot *force* me to marry you! In any case, you surely don't really want an unwilling bride, and one, moreover, whose character, as you have made only too clear, fills you with—with disgust!"

"I congratulate you on a very accurate summing up of my feelings," he said, making her wince in the darkness. "I don't relish the thought of being leg-shackled to a lying, cheating little jade, but I like even less the prospect of allowing you such a shabby victory. I own that I was at fault in teasing you to try if you could attach my interest. Indeed, when I offered for you, I half expected that you would claim your triumph, and turn me down. It did not occur to me that such a private humiliation would not be enough for you. You wanted to see me brought low in public, didn't you? Wanted me made a, laughing stock again for the whole world. No wonder you teased and fought shy of me, and refused to set a wedding day. How you must have enjoyed seeing me dance to your tune! And then to cry off only days before the wedding—a master stroke, I admit, especially as I was out of town. But I arrived back quite early, you see, eager, as usual, to see my bride—only to find that she had fled me. You should have recalled that I travel a good deal faster than a post chaise."

Damaris, almost dazed by the diatribe he had directed at her, the dreadful things he thought, said, "I did not expect you to pursue me."

"Ah—! You thought you had thrown the last dice, and the game was won, did you? But the game is not yet done, and the next move, I think, is mine."

"But it is not true!" she said desperately. "I did *not* plan to jilt you for some paltry revenge. Please don't say such things!"

"Then why?" he demanded.

"I—told you, in my letter," she said unconvincingly.

"You *mistook your heart?*" he said derisively. "Come now, with your indubitable talent for lying, you must be able to do better than that!"

Her resolution wavered. If he really minded so much being jilted almost at the altar, perhaps, after all, it would be better to marry him.

But at that moment his temper, that he had held imperfectly in check, got the better of him. He seized her wrists, holding them in a cruel grip, and fitful moonlight showed her a countenance almost savage with fury. She cried out, and he pushed her roughly back into her corner, still retaining his hold on her, his face so close she could see the cold gleam of his eyes, hear the snap of his white teeth.

"Come, my darling," he said tauntingly. "What other Banbury tales can you think of to entertain me while we travel?"

Despairingly, she realized he was too angry to believe her. What was more, he never would believe her, and marriage now was impossible. He would never trust her again, and his violence terrified her.

"Please!" she cried. "Let me go—you are hurting!"

A moment longer he held her. Then he released her wrists and sat back in his seat. "Believe me," he said, "I could hurt you much more. And it would take very little to make me do it."

It was a few moments before she was able to speak. Then she said, shakenly, "Lord Brandsley, I beg of you, let me continue on my journey. I cannot—I *will* not marry you. There are reasons—I cannot speak of. Believe me, it will be better for *you*—as well as myself—" she added hastily. "I think that you exaggerate the—repercussions. Other people have admitted mistakes, broken engagements—and no one will hold *you* to blame."

"You are wasting your time," he told her. "The marriage will take place."

Angry at his stubbornness, overwrought with emotion, she cried, *"It will not!"* She took a deep breath, and decided to risk an explanation that he might be tempted to believe. "The truth is," she said, "I have a—particular aversion to the married state. I tried—I tried to overcome it because your great position and your fortune were offered to me, and the temptation was—I admit the temptation was considerable. The fact is, Lord Brandsley, I am not a suitable wife for any man. *You* must be aware that you are generally regarded as a handsome man, there are many women who would receive your attentions with pleasure. *I* cannot. I regret to tell you that I find your—your person, your touch—are repugnant to me!"

She heard a sharply indrawn breath, and clenched her hands tightly on each other, waiting for his reaction. When it came, his voice was harsh. "I am not unaware of your aversion to my touch," he said. "But your explanation is unconvincing. *That* circumstance existed from the beginning. But it is neither here nor there, now. I am not giving you a choice. You promised to marry me, and marry me you will!"

"You *cannot* force me!" she said fiercely.

"Perhaps not. But I think you will find the alternative even less agreeable."

He spoke almost carelessly, but she perceived very easily the veiled threat behind his words.

"What alternative?" she said, trying to keep her voice calm.

"I have a hunting box not ten miles from here. It is closed up at the moment, only the caretaker, a deaf old fellow, and his wife, will be there, but we could be tolerably comfortable for the next few days—and nights."

"Abduction?" she said, her voice sounding queer. Then, common sense asserting itself, she said, "It isn't true. We are on the London road."

"At the moment," he agreed. "But we shall shortly arrive at a crossroads, and the postboy has instructions to stop there and await my direction. Forward, to London—or, by another road, to my house. Of course, if we *did* spend the next few days there, your reputation would be—shall we say, sadly tarnished?"

"And I should be obliged to marry you to save it?" she said, trying to inject irony into her tones.

"If you do not," he said, "society will turn its back on you. You will never be accepted again in polite circles."

"I know," she admitted. But, rallying, she added, "I have done with London society, in any case, sir. I never intend to visit the metropolis again. And in Somerset—my real friends would never believe such a thing of me."

His silence encouraged her to add, "That threat will not induce me to marry you."

"A pity," he said at last. "But in the meantime, I

shall have enjoyed several days, at least, of your de-lightful—company."

He could not mean it, she thought, but a hollow feeling inside her told he that he was angry enough for anything. "You would not—" she whispered.

"Why not?" he asked. "You may find me repugnant, but in spite of my opinion of your character, I confess I find *your* person, and your somewhat reluctant kisses, delectable. Not that I would be willing to stop at kisses, of course, in the—circumstances we are discussing."

"No—" she said waveringly, shocked to find her voice sounding both pleading and horrified.

"Yes," he said flatly.

Damaris licked her dry lips. "Even if you mean it," she said, her brain racing, "you are not offering me a true choice. If I don't agree to marry you, you will carry out this detestable scheme; but if I do, I must submit to—to the same thing for the rest of my life."

"True," he said. "Then I will offer you a choice. You will come back with me to London. You will not breathe a word of this conversation to your aunt or anyone. You will say that you panicked needlessly, that my persuasion has convinced you of that, and you will marry me with every appearance of looking forward to a lifetime of happiness. And *I—*" he paused for a moment, then went on very deliberately. "I—having satisfied my honor, will be content with a *mariage blanc.* I give you my word that I will not, unless your—sentiments—change, require you to carry out your wifely duties to the full."

Damaris, her mind reeling, put her hands to her face. "But—"

"On the other hand," he continued ruthlessly, "if you refuse, I shall tell the postboy to turn the horses to the right when we reach the crossroads, and if you imagine I am too much the gentleman to take you by force, I should advise you not to be too confident of it. You will catch cold at that!"

Her continued silence seemed to infuriate him. He said suddenly, "I will give you a sample of what you can expect, to help you make up your mind!" Her bonnet was seized and flung impatiently on the floor.

She tried to move back, but in the confines of the chaise it was impossible. Her wrists were seized again, and, as she struggled, pinned behind her by one hard hand, while the other ungently pushed up her chin. He hauled her close to him so that she was quite unable to move, and kissed her forcefully and long, with a hard passion that was both insulting and terrifying. She was outraged and frightened, but even more painful than the rough, uncaring pressure of his lips and the hurtful grip on her wrists, was the memory that the last time he had kissed her had been so different....

"There!" he said implacably, still holding her. "No more gentlemanly hand-kissing, my lady. No soft words and pretty speeches. No gentleness. No more holding back, making allowances for your delicate sensibilities. Only this..."

He kissed her again, his hand sliding to the back of her neck, and holding her head, until her senses reeled and she thought she would faint. She whimpered a protest, and he raised his head again.

"Well?" he demanded, still so close to her that she felt the force of the word in his breath against her lips. "Which is it to be?"

She was conscious suddenly that the coach had stopped.

She heard the postboy call, "Milord? Which way?"

"Which way, Damaris?" Brandsley said, against her parted lips.

She tried to twist away, but he would not allow it.

"London," she gasped. "I'll go to London with you."

"Do I have your word you will go ahead with the marriage?"

"I—yes!" Sheer terror constricted her throat, making her words a mere whisper.

For a moment longer he stared down into the white blur of her face in the darkness. "Understand this," he said. "If you break it, I will still carry out the other plan. If you run away again, I shall find you, and do all that I threatened."

Then he abruptly let her go and leaned out to call, *"London!"*

As Damaris sank into her corner, trembling with

reaction, the chaise jerked forward. She suddenly felt very tired. The events which had taken place were like a nightmare. Her heart wept for the tender understanding that she had swept away by her actions. She had meant it for the best, for she had felt that she should free him. Now she had freed neither of them. The marriage would take place, after all, but it would not be the marriage that either of them had hoped for. All trust, all tenderness were gone, and in its place bitterness and suspicion and bleakness seemed all that remained. And fear.

She had thought Grenville a man of infinite compassion and understanding and rare patience. But she had never seen, until tonight, the full force and fury of his anger. Tonight he had bullied and threatened her, hurt her both physically and emotionally, and quite deliberately. She saw the dark shadow of her discarded hat on the floor and watched his booted foot move to kick it out of the way. She did not dare to stoop and pick it up. The man beside her who had insisted that she marry him to save him from the laughter of the *ton*, was a frightening stranger. He was to remain a stranger when she married him two days later.

As she covertly eyed his uncompromising profile, turning her gaze hastily away whenever he looked at her, she recalled the dark hours when she had, surprisingly, dozed, until at some time during the night she had felt herself lifted in strong arms, and, after a brief interval when the cold air chilled her face, deposited in what she realized was one of his private carriages. Of course, she thought sleepily, he had taken care that she should not be conveyed to her door by a curious postboy. When they arrived at Harley Street, he had hurried her into the house by a door Mrs. Newington had taken care to leave open, and instructed her to go straight up to her room. It seemed ironic that he, who had a few hours earlier threatened to wreck her reputation, was showing such great care for it now.

She had slept almost the entire day, and to Mrs. Newington's anxious queries when she emerged from her room, she returned a wan smile and a quiet admission that she had been foolish and overhasty, allowing muddleheaded fancies to take charge of her mind while Brandsley was away.

"I was sure it was nothing more," her aunt said. "And Lord Brandsley is so good—all patience, and showing nothing but concern for your welfare—and really dearest, it was not *the thing* to run away without seeing him—"

Damaris lifted her head and stared a moment, a faint color staining her pale cheeks. How well he must have managed to conceal his real feelings, until her aunt had given him the information he sought! It gave her a new insight into his character, that the fury he had unleashed at her had been at first so carefully hidden. And there had been the waiting carriage, too, coolly arranged before he had come after her. And the fact that he had caught up with her within such easy reach of his hunting box. She had a sudden chilling conviction that he might have found her much sooner, but had waited until she reached the place most convenient for his plan, before springing his trap.

The day before her wedding had passed in a kind of fatalistic dream. The future seemed threatening, but there was nothing to be done. She had given her word, and if she broke it, Brandsley's vengeance was certain and shocking.

Now, for better or worse, she was tied to this calculating, vengeful and terribly purposeful man who no longer loved her, if he ever had. Surely, she thought, if he had loved her with a genuine affection, he could not have accused her so bitterly, or used her so roughly. Even more, if his feelings for her had been deep and genuine, he would not so readily have offered to forgo the reality of their marriage in return for the face-saving outward form.

Strangely, she found that with rather humilating illogicality, she resented his rejection of her as a partner in love. The truth was that, far from finding his embraces abhorrent, she had lately begun positively to long for them. A growing confidence in her own ability to welcome and enjoy that side of marriage had been rudely shattered when he had so brutally demonstrated the fate that awaited her if she defied him, and she had been plunged into an abyss of panic and instinctive resistance. The burgeoning blossom of her hesitant response to his lovemaking had been cruelly crushed, and with a deliberation that filled her with forboding and misery, and yet there still remained buried deep within her aching heart, a wistful, barely breathing hope that some day he might again show her consideration and patience and tenderness.

None of those gentle qualities could be discerned in his face now, as he turned to her and asked with cold courtesy if she was in need of a rug or a hot brick.

Unaware that her thoughts had made her give a tiny shiver, she shook her head.

"If you mean to be in the sullens all the way to Louth, we will make a dull journey of it," he remarked.

"I am not in the sullens," she said. "I'm not cold, thank you."

He watched her for a few moments in silence, then shrugged and turned his head away once more.

She was glad when they alighted at an inn for a cold repast of salmon and a raised pie. The bustling atmosphere of the inn yard was welcome after the cold comfort of the chaise, and the task of getting through a meal that she did not especially want, at least partially disguised the lack of any but the most necessary courtesies between the newlyweds.

Brandsley had bespoken a private parlor and when they had finished their meal, he told her he would stroll out for an hour or so while she rested. Evidently he was not intending to travel at his own usual pace, and she might have been slightly cheered by his care for her wellbeing and comfort, had she not reflected that he must have planned it all before he arrived back in London to find her gone. Neither did his tone of voice encourage her to be sanguine in her hopes. He sounded bored and faintly impatient, as though he recognized that he must consider her, but would have preferred not to be obliged to travel in her company.

Although she had thought herself not hungry, and accepted the suggestion of a rest mainly because it would relieve her of the uncomfortable presence of her new husband for a time, both had their effect on the bride's spirits. She woke from a short nap feeling a good deal more herself than at any time these past few days. When Lord Brandsley returned and told her the horses were put to, requesting her with punctilious but still bored courtesy to be ready, if she would, to leave in a few minutes, she directed at him a sparkling glance which made him narrow his eyes, and kept him waiting a full ten minutes while she fussed with her hair and adjusted her silk bonnet to a nicety.

He did not complain, either then or when she began to take an interest in the passing scenery, demanding to know the names of the villages they passed through, and requesting information about every landmark. He answered her briefly but readily enough, and was eventually drawn into making comments of his own as they passed from forests of full-leaved great oaks and chestnuts, to hedgerows of elm and ash, and onto rolling countryside where the corn was high and straight in neatly ditched and hedged fields, and cattle and sheep grazed healthily on mown grass and clover over a landscape dotted with busy windmills and haystacks forty feet high.

A modicum of warmth entered his voice as he admired or criticized and took note of farming practices that he might try out at Louth. And Damaris passed gradually from a desire to tease him by making him talk to her to a genuine interest of her own in the subject that evidently had captured his enthusiasm.

The atmosphere was considerably less stiff by the time they bowled into another inn yard at Bishops Stortford and he told her they would rack up here for the night.

She could not forbear from a slight lift of her eyebrows, and he said drily, "I don't make a habit of traveling throughout the night," as he got out and let down the steps for her.

She had, she was relieved to find, a bedchamber to herself, the warmed sheets smelling pleasantly of lavender, and the service she enjoyed was excellent. She well knew *that* was due to her husband's air and consequence. No innkeeper and his staff had ever proved so anxious to please two gentlewomen of modest appearance and without a male escort, when she had traveled with her aunt.

The next two days passed in similar fashion, their pace leisurely, and their conversation pleasant but formal, as though they were two people who had just met, instead of husband and wife driving to their home for the first time.

He did not at once tell her when they entered on the Louth Hall estate, but something of eagerness in his manner made her ask him, "Are we there?"

The look he turned on her was slightly surprised, as though he had forgotten her, and she suffered a stab of piqued anger.

He said, "Yes. This is Louth." And then he turned to give a critical look at a field of ripened corn they were passing.

Feeling snubbed, Damaris bit her lip and clasped her hands on each other in a tight grip. Soon they were bowling up a handsome avenue of oaks, and she suppressed a quick sound of pleasure as the mellowed old building with its Norman gatetowers appeared before them, its bricks glowing in the light of a setting sun.

When he helped her to alight from the chaise, his eyes swept over her with an appraising air, as on the first occasion they had met, and she thought he was mentally gauging her fitness to be chatelaine of this ancestral pile that was his home and his heritage.

In one respect she knew with sudden desperate grief that she was sadly lacking. That he seemed now to have determined to cheat himself of an heir to all this grandeur in order to salvage his pride, was no real comfort to her. She had been at fault in the beginning; she could have avoided the whole heartbreaking disaster, if only she had *thought,* in time, instead of allowing herself to be dazzled by his proposal and by her longing for love, into forgetting the vital factor in the marriages of great families. It had been up to her to recognize that she was, *knew* herself to be, totally unfitted to be Brandsley's bride. When she had finally emerged from her bubble of happiness and self-deceit, it was far too late to untangle the knot she had made without drastically cutting the threads. And *that* Grenville had refused to allow.

He swept her into the hall, and she had a confused impression of a great coat of arms on a tapestry-hung wall, carved oaken chairs and a settle of apparent antiquity, and a beautiful Moorish patterned rug beneath her feet, before the row of servants that awaited them subsided into bows and curtsies.

Suddenly shy, she knew her smile was stiff as she acknowledged their respectful greetings, moving down the line at her husband's side. She wondered if she would ever remember all their names, for there seemed a great many of them, certainly at least a half-dozen more than she had been used to command in Sir Walter's household. And these, she realized, were only the house staff. She supposed at least a dozen gardeners must be employed to tend the extensive gardens outside the house, and many more to look after the park.

"Mrs. Bingham will show you to your bedchamber," Grenville said. "Dinner has been kept for us. Can you be ready in an hour?"

She said she could, and followed Mrs. Bingham up the stairs, the stone in the center worn smooth and hollowed out with centuries of use. The housekeeper's, she reminded herself, was one name she must remember. To that end, she kept it in her mind as they climbed the stairs and proceeded along a flagged gallery to a great brass bound door which, in the flickering light from the lamp, reminded her for a few tense moments of certain Gothic castles in the works of Mrs. Radcliffe and her numerous imitators.

But the chamber into which she was ushered dispelled the impression immediately. The apartment was spacious and, lit by the rays of the dying sun, seemed suffused with a warm golden light. The lamp, and candles which Mrs. Bingham lit for her at handsome wall sconces, further showed prettily papered walls instead of the somewhat overpowering tapestries that hung in the hall, a sturdy cedar wardrobe and light-colored marble washstand, a pretty toilette, and a small round table placed next to a comfortable chair drawn up by the fire, which was lit. The bed looked comfortable and the housekeeper promised it should be warmed directly and turned down for her ladyship. Everything was provided for her comfort, and she thanked the woman with genuine warmth in her smile that brought an answering softness to Mrs. Bingham's slightly forbidding countenance, before she left, promising to send her ladyship's own maid up directly, along with her trunks.

Later she dined with her husband in a room which felt much too large for two of them, and at a heavy oak table that seemed designed to keep them at a distance from each other. Before she went up to bed he told her that he would be occupied with his bailiff the following day, and that Mrs. Bingham would be at her service.

Taking that as a hint that she might occupy herself learning how to run this great house, Damaris nodded in acquiescence. For just a moment her heart sank a little, then she reminded herself that she was no novice at household management, after all, although not used to such a large establishment. And Mrs. Bingham seemed to be an admirable housekeeper. There was no dust on the furniture, and a faint odor of beeswax was discernible throughout the rooms. But the curtains in the dining room showed signs of fading, and one or two of the chairbacks looked worn. A particularly ugly silver epergne graced the middle of the dining table, and when Damaris dared to ask whether it was a family heirloom, Grenville glanced at it without interest and said he really didn't know. It had been there ever since he could remember.

About the whole house there was an air of the carelessness and the slight bareness of a bachelor establishment, the indefinable impression that comfort was taken for granted, but no very high standard of elegance was required. She would find enough to do.

One of the first things she did, after her extensive tour of the Hall in the wake of Mrs. Bingham, was to have the epergne removed and to replace it with a much smaller Staffordshire china vase. When Grenville sat down that evening to his dinner he glanced at it, seemed to note the roses and beech leaves with which she had filled it, and then addressed himself without comment to the soup that was set before him.

She asked him if his day with Mr. Hopley had been successful, and he said it had, but it was as well he was now able to give his time to the estate. They had reached the sweet course before she ventured to ask, "I hope you don't object to my having the epergne removed? It seemed a rather large piece, and although when there are only two of us to dine, we can have the covers laid at one end of the table, if we should have company, such a large center-piece makes conversation a trifle uncomfortable, I think."

"I daresay," he answered. "You may do just as you like, of course. Only if you cut up my comfort, my dear, I *shall* object."

He gave her an almost teasing smile with this speech, so that her spirits lifted a little, and she was able to smile back, a little doubtfully. "I shan't do *that*," she promised. "At least not intentionally. You must tell me if there is anything you dislike."

For some reason the smile on his face turned sardonic then, and she wondered sinkingly what she had said wrong. But he only said, "We *will* have company, of course. The bride-visits will begin as soon as my neighbors round about discover that we have arrived in the country. They will all be eager to felicitate the happy couple."

She could not have missed the sarcasm in that, but there was no retort she could have made in front of the silent servants. Perhaps he was sorry for it; in the drawing room when he joined her later, he took a chair close to hers and said, "You will miss London, but we are not devoid of a social life, here. No doubt you will soon be receiving invitations to the local soirées and parties. You need not be lonely."

She wondered if he was hinting that she should not expect a great deal of *his* company, but decided to act as though he had nothing but kindness in mind.

Quietly, she said, "I am used to country life, you know. You need not be afraid I shall grow bored."

She made herself too busy to be bored. And the local gentry called and left cards on her, and soon began sending invitations, which Brandsley told her to accept. They attended dinners and dances and card parties, and Damaris, with the double distinction of being a new bride and the wife of the most wellborn man in the neighborhood, learned to accept precedence over every other lady, a privilege that she found distinctly uncomfortable.

Inevitably there were those who were jealous, and although one or two showed signs that they would welcome a more close acquaintance than civility demanded, Damaris was wary of meeting their overtures to her. She was unsure in her new role, not certain she could distinguish the difference between a genuine desire for her friendship and unwelcome toadying to her husband's rank. She was, besides, unwilling to allow anyone to become close to her, for she had an almost morbid fear of their discovering the true nature of her relationship with her husband. In public he was all a man should be to his wife, solicitous of her comfort, showing her every proper attention, and in private....

The truth was that in private he was just the same, but, if anything, showed a little less warmth. Occasionally he would allow bitterness to color his voice when he spoke to her, a sarcastic remark to escape. She might have quarreled with him, but she quelled her own bitterness and told herself it was better to act with a certain dignity. But in the recesses of her mind she was haunted by the memory of his formidable temper when he had unleashed it in the post chaise on the Bath road. There were times when she suspected herself of cowardice.

If he had been less cold, she might have brought herself to confess the real reason behind her prewedding flight. Surely he would be more understanding, now that his first anger had cooled? But in spite of his aloof courtesy, she saw no sign of softness in his manner to her. That, and the brief glimpses of a resentment that still smouldered behind the hard facade, made her hold her own counsel. She felt that he had so completely lost his faith in her that he would again refuse to believe her. And when she thought about it, it seemed she had no right to expect him to. She had, after all, told him three different stories already, all of them admittedly false to some degree. He had believed none of them, but continued to hold fast to his bitter belief that she had accepted his suit and then rejected it out of pique and a desire for revenge. There could be no reason for supposing that when she finally confessed the truth he would find it any more acceptable than any of the spurious stories he had rejected.

chapter twelve

It was at one of the local parties—a dinner party for twenty persons—that Damaris was surprised to find a face very familiar to her from her days in Somerset.

She had been sitting with another lady, trying to affect a rapt interest in the various illnesses that had attacked the lady's apparently numerous and singularly unhealthy children, and the alarming range of cordials, elixirs and medicines with which they had consequently been dosed. Her attention wandering a little, her eyes strayed to her husband, and finding him smiling at a saucy young lady whose ostrich feather headdress almost tickled his chin, she quickly removed her gaze, trying to stifle the thought that he never smiled so at *her*. Then she found her wandering eyes caught in a meaningful way by a gentleman who had just entered the room and been greeted by their hosts. He bowed his head, and in answer to her sudden smile of recognition, crossed the room to her side, as the much-afflicted mother left it to join her spouse.

"Lady Waring!" he said, as she gave him her hand.

With a faint flush, she said, "Lady Brandsley, now, Mr. Westburne. I have recently married again."

He begged her pardon, with a deep flush coloring his own countenance. To put him at ease, she essayed a light laugh, saying, "Not at all, my dear sir! You were not to have known, how could you? But I did not expect to find such an old friend in this part of the world—do tell me how you have been going on?"

He sat down and began to do so, and it was several minutes before she again looked up, to find Grenville, not many yards away, regarding her and her companion with a hard curiosity.

He strolled over to her and she was obliged to perform the necessary introduction.

"Brandsley," she said, her voice a little nervous "This is Mr. Westburne, who was—Sir Walter's chaplain when I lived in Somerset."

She saw a faint ripple of some emotion that did not look pleasant, before Brandsley schooled his face to a polite mask and held out his hand. Mr. Westburne sprang to his feet and said "My lord!—honored!" with a fervor that brought a slightly contemptuous amusement to Grenville's eyes.

"Mr. Westburne is now the incumbent at a parish not far from here," Damaris said quickly. "He, too, is but recently come to reside in Norfolk."

Grenville said, "Have you been exchanging impressions of the country? What do you think of it, Westburne?"

Mr. Westburne thought the country very fine, the agriculture remarkable—Mr. Coke, the famed innovating landowner, was, he believed, only one of the great Norfolk gentlemen who were improving on the old methods—for he had heard that Lord Brandsley himself—

Here Mr. Westburne ran out of breath, and Brandsley said with negligent politeness, "If the subject interests you, come out to Louth sometime and get my bailiff to show you what we are doing there."

"Thank you, my Lord! Very kind! If I might have the honor of calling on her ladyship and yourself—"

"Certainly." Grenville cast an enigmatic look at Damaris, who said warmly, "We shall look forward to your visit, Mr. Westburne. You will tell me all the news from Somerset, I hope!"

"Delighted!" Mr. Westburne assured her. Then encountering Grenville's dismissive glance, he excused himself, bowed and moved away.

Sitting down beside his wife, Lord Brandsley observed with a brief laugh, "What a prosy fellow—something of a lickspittle, too, unless I'm mistaken." He cast her a sudden searching look, and added, "Do you *want* him to visit you?"

"Yes," she said. "I should be very glad to see him. He may not be up to your touch, my lord, but he and *I* have a great deal in common. Furthermore, I remember he had a great deal of nobility of character and kindness of heart which I have found singularly lacking in certain members of more exalted society!"

Her outburst was as unexpected to her as it evidently was to him. His careless and rather scornful dismissal of a man whom she knew to be inclined to babble a little out of shyness, and show an overdeveloped sense of the deference due to his superiors because of his consciousness of his own inferior station, had suddenly seemed of a piece with what she just now saw clearly as his abominable treatment of herself. Bowed by the weight of her own guilty conscience, she had borne with her husband's indifference and sometime ill temper with a semblance of fortitude. Now, hearing him negligently undervalue a man she knew to be good and kind, though neither brilliant nor highly thought of in society, and to whom she owed, moreover, a debt of gratitude, she became blazingly and disastrously angry.

Grenville's eyes, too, were glittering and narrowed with temper, as under his breath he said, *"Don't* rip up at *me,* you little shrew—!"

Then they were interrupted by another of the guests, and he was obliged to hide his anger under a mask of politeness.

Damaris, too, tried to conceal her emotions, and soon moved away to speak to her hostess. That lady, her eyes bright with curiosity, said immediately, "Lady Brandsley—I see you are acquainted with Mr. Westburne?"

Damaris said, "Yes. We are quite old friends."

"Indeed? He is quite a good-looking young man. I wonder that he is not married."

"Do you? Perhaps he may marry, now that he has a parish. He is a very good sort of man, and would make an excellent husband, I'm sure."

"Why, very good, Lady Brandsley. You and I must see what can be done about finding such an excellent young man a wife!"

Damaris, disenchanted at the present with the married state, smiled politely and changed the subject.

In the carriage on the way home, Grenville sat in brooding silence, but as they entered the Hall, he said quietly, "May I come up to your room? I wish to speak to you."

It was good of him, she supposed, to ask her permission. He had never been in her room since she had arrived, but she was conscious that it was his right to enter it whenever he chose.

She nodded, and preceded him up the stairs, and along the gallery. He closed the door behind them and as she turned to face him from the middle of the room, said inquiringly, "Your maid?"

"I told her not to wait up. I can manage on my own."

He smiled faintly and said, "Shall I help you?"

"No, thank you." She was thankful that there were few candles lit, and the shadows would hide her blush. "What is it you want to say to me, my lord?"

He hesitated for a moment or two, then said bluntly, "What was that fellow Westburne, to you?"

Put on her guard, she said with a faint hauteur, "He was my husband's chaplain. I have told you that."

He made a quick, impatient gesture and said, "Nothing more?"

"Certainly nothing more! Why should there be?"

Again there was a short pause. "You seemed extremely pleased to see him. And very quick to fly to his defense," he said deliberately.

With a stirring of her earlier anger, Damaris said, "Certainly I was pleased to see him. When one is among strangers, and unhappy, it is natural to welcome the presence of an old and kind friend."

"He was kind to you—in the past?"

"Extremely so! And now that I am in a position to repay that kindness in some measure, I intend to do so. I hope you will not object if I invite him to some of our parties, when we return the hospitality of your neighbors?"

He looked at the defiant set of her head and said shortly, "Have I reason to object?"

"No!"

"Very well. Invite him if you wish. When did he leave Sir Walter's employ?"

"He did not. He was still at Haver when my—when Sir Walter died."

"I see."

Damaris was about to turn away when his voice stayed her. "Do you know a man called Ibster?"

She stared in silence, wondering at the reason behind his question, and he said shortly, "Well?"

"Mr. Ibster was a friend of Sir Walter's."

"But no friend of yours." He took a few steps towards her, then halted.

"I—must confess I never liked him," Damaris said, warily.

"No more did I."

Her eyes widening with shock, she said, "You know him?"

"I met him in London. He was very willing to inform me of his view of the relationship between you and your—your late husband."

Damaris flushed angrily. "And I collect, my lord, that *you* were very willing to listen!"

Grimly, Grenville said, "Yes. I listened. I thought at the time he was an impartial observer. Since, it has occurred to me that his story was not without bias. Why should he want to hurt you, Damaris?"

She shook her head, avoiding his eyes. "I told you, he was a friend of Sir Walter's."

"Is that enough to make him your enemy?"

Damaris shrugged, and turned away, going to her dressing table and fiddling with the hairbrush that stood on its marble surface.

Grenville said, "He hinted at a liaison between you and the chaplain."

She turned then, her eyes blazing. "Then he lied! It was *he* who—"

She paused abruptly, clasped her hands tightly together and again turned her back to him, her gaze fixed on the dressing table.

"He who—what?" Grenville demanded.

"Nothing," she said. "I'm very tired, Brandsley. I would be obliged if you would leave me."

"No doubt. I shan't do so, however, until you tell me what you were about to say." He paused, and as she remained stubbornly silent, he said, "Were you going to say it was he who was your lover?"

She felt the words like a stab in the heart, an actual, tangible pain. Blindly she put a hand on the table before her to steady herself. Then she turned to him slowly, her eyes fixed on the elegant fall of his cravat, no higher. Quietly she said, "He was not my lover. I had no lovers. It was the one fault of which my husband—Sir Walter—never accused me. It has taken *you* to be as cruel and as insulting as that!"

"Damaris—!" His swift stride covered the distance between them, but she shrank from his outstretched hand, afraid that if he touched her she would not be able to conceal the bitter hurt he had caused.

"Don't touch me!" she gasped, turning her head away.

His hand was snatched back as though burnt. "I beg your pardon," he said stiffly.

"Please!" she whispered. "Please go."

For a few moments he remained standing close to her, but she would not meet his eyes. Then he let out a rough sigh and, turning on his heel, strode quickly from the room.

* * *

The harvest was over when Damaris received a letter from her aunt, franked by the Earl of Crawley, and full of ecstatic praise of his and his wife's kindness, and the splendors of their park, their acquaintance and their dazzling Palladian mansion. The earl had consulted Mr. Repton himself with a view to carrying out improvements on the property, and as a result had built an artificial hill which greatly improved the prospect of the house from the park....

Hurriedly Damaris skipped over the account of the numerous deer with which the park was stocked, and the peacocks which paraded on the lawns, and at the very last came upon the news which she hoped for and yet dreaded. Mrs. Newington had more than enjoyed her stay with the earl and countess, but did not wish any longer to impose on their hospitality. She might be looked for at Louth near the end of the following week.

Damaris waited until tea had been served in the drawing room after dinner, and she could be fairly certain of being uninterrupted, before imparting the news to her husband.

He received it without expression, merely inquiring how Mrs. Newington proposed to travel.

"She says that the earl has kindly insisted on sending her in his own chaise, and will provide outriders."

"Of course."

"They have been very good to my aunt—all kindness to her. Every courtesy has been shown her, she says." Damaris hesitated, looked up at Brandsley and said, nervously, "I hope—"

She stopped again, discouraged by the coldness of his eyes, the faintly arrogant, interrogative lift of his dark brows.

"Yes?" he said. "You hope—?"

"I hope that she will find as warm a welcome here," Damaris finished, almost defiantly, "as a member of your household."

He put down his cup and said with deliberation, "None of my guests, to my knowledge, have ever had reason to complain of *my* courtesy."

Damaris sank her teeth into her lower lip, almost

flinching as Brandsley suddenly stood up with a violent movement, and strode to the long window at one end of the room, turning there to face her.

"But perhaps," he said cuttingly, "as *my wife* you have a complaint against me? I will acknowledge that on one regrettable occasion prior to our nuptials, I allowed temper to get the better of me. But since I brought my unwilling bride to Louth, I have been at some pains, I thought, to treat you with a respect which I am only too well aware you do not—"

As he paused momentarily, she stood up herself, quivering with anger.

"—deserve?" she suggested. "If *that* remark is an instance of your courtesy, my lord—"

"You are too fast, madam!" he scythed into her words. "The word I was looking for was—*appreciate.*"

"*Appreciate?* I see. I am to be grateful, then, for your grudging courtesy, your appearance of civility before the servants, your pretense of studying my comfort when we are with friends? And I am to receive with pleasure, I suppose, your casual sarcasm, your veiled insults, your offensive suspicion?"

She thought he paled a little, but his cold expression did not alter. He said, "I have not meant to insult you. Unfortunately, I am no saint—I have only tried—God knows!—I have tried to accord to you all the courtesies you are entitled to expect as my wife. If I have sometimes failed in that, I must beg your pardon. As to the suspicion you speak of—I thought I had made it clear that I accept your word that neither Westburne nor Ibster was your lover. Good God—Westburne has been running tame here these last few weeks—do you think I would allow that if I thought there was anything in *that* story? But you will own that your demeanor, your very reticence on the subject, must have given me cause to wonder—"

"I own nothing of the kind. It seems to me, my lord, you need very little cause to *wonder—!*"

He stared a moment, then impatiently turned his back to her, jerking aside the brocade at the window to stare out into the night.

"Perhaps you are right," he said, his voice sounding

oddly muffled. "Ours is not a normal union, is it? I am more than normally jealous, it seems, of the rights which I have forfeited."

He suddenly swung round to face her, a queer smile playing about his lips. "Yes, I do wonder, Damaris. I wonder whenever I see you smile at another man, in a way you no longer smile at me. Would she shudder at *his* touch—would she cry out to *him*, not to come near her?"

"I'm—sorry!" she whispered.

"Are you?" He looked almost curiously at her.

Damaris looked away from his eyes, and he crossed the room toward her, but stopped carefully a few feet away. Almost gently he said, "You told me you are unhappy. Believe me, it was not my intention to make you so. Will it make you happier to have your aunt with you?"

"Perhaps," she said. "But—she will be disappointed if she perceives that we are—our marriage is not a harmonious one."

"Shall you tell her that?"

Damaris shook her head.

"Then rest assured, *I* shall not, either."

As she remained looking hesitant and worried, he added drily, "You think something more is required, perhaps? A fond word, a loving touch, now and then?"

"Is it too much to ask of you," she said, "that you should treat me with some—some semblance of fondness, for my aunt's sake?"

"Not at all," he answered, but his tone was hard. "But *you* will have to play your part, you know. You will need to learn not to flinch when I take your hand—" he continued, suiting the action to the word. "—and not to shrink from me when I touch you—"

He drew her to him by the hand that he held, tightening his fingers on the trembling of hers, and drawing an index finger lightly down the line of her cheek, until it came beneath her chin to lift her face.

With an effort she met his eyes, watched the flint gray darken and narrow, a spark of fire in the depths. She heard him draw in his breath sharply—and then she was abruptly released, as a servant opened the door and began to remove the tea cups.

The moment was shattered. Grenville returned to his musing at the window, and Damaris, disturbed and a little alarmed, fled to her own room.

Mrs. Newington arrived ready and willing to be vastly impressed by Louth Hall, which in every comparison with Lord Crawley's estate was pronounced, if not superior, at least equal. No peacocks paraded on the lawns, but the topiary was particularly fine, she thought, and the cypresses in the park were taller than any she had seen elsewhere. The dairy was a model of its kind, the cheese and butter it produced delicious, and the pineapples grown in Lord Brandsley's pinery even surpassed Lord Crawley's.

She admired the vast old hall, the salons, parlors and galleries, and the modern comfort of her own bedroom, with gratified awe. In fact the whole of the estate and house seemed to have so much taken hold of her mind, that Damaris seriously thought her own concern that her aunt should notice nothing amiss between the master of all this splendor and its new mistress, had been needless.

However, after two days spent admiring and exploring the beauties of the house, garden and park, Mrs. Newington did venture to inquire of her niece if she was perfectly happy.

Lightly, Damaris replied, "Who can claim *perfect* happiness, Aunt? Ask, rather, if I am as happy as I can be, and know that the answer is yes."

Her aunt was satisfied, for she had little guile herself and took the answer at its face value. Besides, her dearest wish was that Damaris should be happy, and in her, the wish was inclined to be mother of the conviction.

Grenville's behavior, too, had been exemplary. He had given every appearance of being glad to see his wife's aunt, and every attention to her comfort. To Damaris, too, he was unusually attentive, and there even seemed a new warmth in his eyes that brought to her breast a faint hope that he did not, after all, wholly despise her.

Grenville's scorching comment that Mr. Westburne had run tame at Louth was an exaggeration, but he had visited once or twice, and when he heard of Mrs. Newington's arrival made that an excuse for a courtesy call.

Damaris, whose expressed desire to hear all the gossip from Somerset had been more a politeness than a genuine desire to learn about a set of persons most of whom she would have preferred to forget, sat patiently by while Mr. Westburne repeated for her aunt's benefit all the news which he had previously relayed to herself. When Brandsley strolled into the room, the clergyman and the old lady were engaged in a comfortable conversation which they resumed almost at once, and he chose to sit beside his wife, speaking to her in a low voice.

"Your aunt, too, seems pleased to see Mr. Westburne. The young man has a charm for women which escapes the members of my sex, apparently."

"I know that you don't like him, but you will find few to share your prejudice, my lord."

Still keeping his voice low, but sounding a little nettled, he said, "I wish you would stop calling me that. It makes it difficult for me to playact the loving husband when you insist on being such a *formal* wife!"

She bowed her head over the needlework in her hands, stung by the reminder that he was only pretending to be loving.

He watched her in silence for a few moments. Then he said, "Shall we give a dinner party for our neighbors and introduce them to your aunt?"

"She would like that, I think. May I invite Mr. Westburne, too?"

"Of course." He rose from her side rather abruptly and moved away to address Mr. Westburne himself, and soon took the other man off to show him a lucerne field. Damaris, doubting whether Mr. Westburne's interest in agriculture was as great as politeness led him to pretend, wondered that her husband bothered to trouble himself with a man she felt he did not like. Perhaps it was simply his natural courtesy coming to the fore.

There were twelve couples for the dinner party. Damaris supervised the menu, which featured venison and game from their own preserves, as well as a saddle of mutton, turbot and several side dishes, followed by apple pie, custards and cheesecakes, and pineapple, strawberries and hothouse fruits of several varieties, and Mrs. Newington declared with fervor that never had she seen so fine a table set; the linen, the silver, the Sèvres dinner set, could not be rivaled.

Damaris was almost ready to go down, her maid adjusting the Grecian curls that brushed her neck from the fashionable high knot of her hair, when Grenville knocked and came into her room, carrying a small leather box.

He did not immediately speak, standing to one side as the maid fussed with the comb. Damaris sat still, keeping her head steady, but she knew he was watching intently.

When the girl stepped back, viewing her handiwork in the mirror, Grenville said quietly, "Have you finished?"

"Yes, sir."

"Then if your mistress does not require you, you may go."

The girl bobbed a respectful curtsey and quietly withdrew. Damaris sat straight and stiff, and her husband said, "Stand up."

She did so, turning slowly to face him. Her gown was a shimmering palest primrose silk, with a deep lace trim at the low neck that formed the only sleeves, just on the curve of her shoulders. His gaze slipped over her consideringly, and returned to the strand of pearls that encircled her throat. He stepped forward, laid the box he held on the dressing table and with his hands firmly on her shoulders, turned her so that she stood with her back to him.

She felt his fingers fumble with the clasp of the pearls, and automatically bent her head, but, guessing his intention, could not suppress a small protest. "What are you—please don't—"

But it was too late. She felt the cool slide of the pearls against her skin, then heard the faint rattling as they were placed on the dressing table. From the corner of her eye she saw his hand pick up the leather casket and flick it open. Quickly she closed her eyes, felt a coldness at her throat, his warm fingers again touching her nape as he fastened his gift.

She glanced in the mirror at the glitter of diamonds, and said stiffly, "Thank you, my lord. You are very generous."

"But it doesn't please you." His voice was flat, his mouth wry.

Impossible to explain to him. "Of course it pleases me," she said. "It's very beautiful. And very valuable."

"You scarcely wear the family pieces I gave you. I thought you might have liked this better."

"I shall wear it if it pleases you, my lord."

She knew that she had angered him. He stood rather rigidly, his face a cold, unreadable mask, but there was something deep in his gray eyes that frightened her.

"Our guests will be arriving," he said, and turned and opened the door for her. She had to quell an impulse to run as she passed him and went out of the room.

The dinner seemed interminable. Damaris made polite conversation with her guests and automatically kept an eye on the dishes as the footmen served them, checking that the sauces were smooth and creamy, the roasts not too underdone, the fruit washed and polished to perfection.

She caught the eyes of the ladies at last and led them to the drawing room, civilly begging one or two talented young misses to entertain them with a song or play a piece on the pianoforte. One of the girls was a very pretty brunette with a low, sweet singing voice, and as Damaris sat apparently attentive to her rendering of a Scottish lyric, her mind went back to a certain musical evening in London. She recalled the smile in Lord Brandsley's eyes as they had made lighthearted conversation, and he had made her laugh. Tonight she was far from laughter. She blamed herself for being ungracious, for angering him, perhaps even wounding him, with her offhanded acceptance of his gift. He was *not* like Sir Walter—he had made no move that suggested he expected a return for the money spent on jewels for her. And yet, oddly, although the unwilling memory of her first marriage had risen to haunt her at the sight of the case in Brandsley's hands, the glitter of the stones he fastened about her throat, she almost wished he *would* demand that crude payment. She told herself that was because she felt the guilt of being his wife only in name, felt the weight of the rights he had renounced. But another, deeper voice whispered that if only he would treat her with the consideration and patience he had shown her before the disastrous day that she had run away from him, she might not have found such an exaction of her duty so unwelcome, after all.

The gentlemen seemed a long time over their wine, the ladies showing signs of *ennui* before the masculine company arrived to enliven them.

Mr. Westburne, Damaris noticed, was flushed looking and more talkative than was usual with him in mixed company. She was surprised, a little later, to see Grenville take him aside and engage him in a low-voiced conversation. It was one thing for the marquess to feel obliged to do the civil when Mr. Westburne was the only male guest. It was quite another, Damaris felt, to single him out at a dinner gathering and hold him in conversation for quite twenty minutes. Without knowing precisely why, she felt herself uneasy.

When at last all the guests had called for their carriages and been driven off, the great oak doors closing for the final time, Mrs. Newington declared herself quite tired to death after *such* an agreeable party, and lost no time in taking her candle and retiring to bed.

Damaris gave the servants final instructions and went upstairs herself, finding Grenville climbing beside her. Instinctively, she quickened her pace, and as she reached the door of her room he gave a hard little laugh and leaned over to open it for her. She entered the room blindly, her breath coming fast, and hardly heard her maid exclaim at the beauty of the necklace. She was aware that Brandsley had followed her and having closed the door behind him, was still standing before it, but she would not look at him.

She went to her dressing table and bent her head to

remove the necklace, handing it to the girl to be put reverently away in the box which still stood there. "Find a safe place for that," Damaris said.

"Yes, my lady. Shall I take the pins out of your hair?"

"Please."

She felt the deft fingers undoing the knot, and the weight of her hair fell about her shoulders. Brandsley had not moved from his stance by the door, and when the maid began to unfasten her dress, Damaris said sharply, "Leave that! I shan't need you any more. Put away the necklace, then you may go to bed."

The girl obeyed quietly, dropping a curtsey as Grenville opened the door, sliding a sly sideways glance at them as she left the room.

Damaris, turning to face her husband, saw his lips twitch a little as he strolled over to her.

Jerkily, she said, "You wanted to speak to me, my lord?"

His mouth hardened. "I told you not to address me so!" he said.

"I beg your pardon," she said woodenly, wishing he had not stopped so close to her. She stood up, making to move away from him, but he caught her hand and held it, swinging it slightly as he watched her face, wryly noting her wary expression.

"We could deal better together than this, you know," he said gently. "You have not called me Grenville since you married me."

She was silent, feeling the strength of the fingers that held hers, the oddly comforting warmth of them.

Brandsley spoke again. "You did splendidly tonight. The party was very successful."

"Thank you," she said, still wary. "It was only a dinner party."

"Could you manage a house party at Christmas?" he asked. "I thought we might ask my aunt and Lord Crawley, with Lindo and Charlotte. Do you think Mrs. Rathbone would consider spending Christmas here with her family?"

"I'm not perfectly sure. But I'm certain she would not object to Charlotte's coming. She will be more than adequately chaperoned."

"By you and her future mother-in-law—yes."

"Lady Crawley alone would be sufficient, I imagine," Damaris said, with a sudden hint of laughter.

"Shall you mind *her* coming here?" he asked.

"No, of course not—my aunt will be in high gig at the prospect! Oh—! You are thinking that—that Lady Crawley did not approve of me, at first. But we are quite in accord now, you know!"

"Yes," he said slowly. "Would that *we* were—"

She held her breath, watching his face. His mouth was firm and set, but in his eyes there was a question. He lifted the hand he held, slowly, and still held her eyes as he set his lips to her wrist, watching her lips part with the sweet shock of it, her eyes darken with emotion.

"Damaris?" he whispered.

She swallowed, her eyes on his as though mesmerized.

"Damaris—" he said again, and reached out his other hand to encircle her waist with his arm and draw her closer. She was stiff, unsure of him and of herself, wanting to trust in his gentleness, but still a little afraid of him, nervous of what he might expect of her. She had thought she could not bear to have him kiss her, make love to her, while not loving her. Now it did not seem to matter. She felt his lips touch her cheek, brush gently across her mouth. Then he kissed her softly but with firmness, his fingers releasing hers and stealing gently up her arm to her shoulder, stroking the nervous rigidity of her back, tugging at the fastening of her dress.

Her eyes were closed, and she began to relax against him.

His lips left her mouth and he pressed small kisses on her temple, her cheek, and then her throat, and then she felt his fingertips, light as butterfly wings, trail down her neck to the base of her throat and rest there. "Why didn't you want my necklace?" he murmured in her ear.

At that moment it was beyond her to lie. "It reminded me—" she said in a confused whisper. "Sir Walter—he used to buy me necklaces, bracelets, brooches. But he always expected me to show my gratitude. He would always come to my room—after-wards—"

She felt him go still, his breath suddenly stopping in his throat. Then he straightened, and said quietly, "I see."

His arms fell from her, and she opened her eyes, blinking in bewilderment. His face was stony, in spite of the color that lay along his cheekbones, and the glitter that remained in his eyes. "You are tired," he said. "And I'm keeping you from your rest. Good night."

"Oh, no!" she cried softly when she understood. "I didn't mean it like that!"

But it was too late. He had already gone from the room, closing the door quietly behind him.

chapter thirteen

Damaris slept little that night, and in the morning was up before her maid came to waken her. Dressed for riding, with her hair hastily bundled into a careless knot, she went down to the stables and astonished one of the grooms by asking him to saddle her mare for her immediately.

A faint mist rose from the ground as she cantered across the park, the fresh morning air blowing from her mind the fuzziness of a late, stressful night and an inadequate rest.

She stopped at the brow of a low hill, and while the horse blew gentle clouds of steam from its nostrils, looked back at the Hall, its ancient towers softly golden in the morning sun, its tall dark windows lending mystery to the square outlines. A wisp of smoke rose from the kitchen chimneys, and from the stables another horse came trotting through the gateway to the park.

Even at this distance she recognized Grenville's easy, straightbacked seat, the confidence in his hands as he urged his horse into a full gallop.

Her own mare stamped impatiently, and she gathered up the reins in her hands, turning to make off down the other side of the slope. A shout stayed her. She debated whether to pretend she had not heard, for she did not feel ready, yet, to face her husband. But another call could not be ignored. She turned her head to watch him come thundering across the turf on his big, raking bay, and put the mare into her dainty walk, to go and meet him.

He pulled up close to her, gathering the reins into one hand to control the bay's tossing and snorting, the other resting on his thigh.

"Good morning, Damaris," he said, his eyes keen and searching. "You are up betimes, this morning, my lady wife—"

"It was such a beautiful morning," she said. "And—this little mare you gave me is such a beautiful mount..."

It was a clumsy attempt at making amends, but he cast a swift, narrow glance at her and said, "I remember you said once you liked to gallop. Shall we race?"

Suddenly lighthearted, she laughed. "A challenge? Very well—how far?"

He pointed out a solitary tree about a mile off, and before he had lowered his hand, she was off, her laughter floating back to him.

She pounded down the slope with him behind her, streaked across the flat meadow below as the bay's nose began to edge into her vision, and arrived at the tree breathless and still laughing as he drew level and then passed her. They pulled up and trotted side by side to a belt of woodland, turning gold and crimson but still in leaf, and as they reached its edge, Grenville leaned over to pull at her bridle, stopping his own mount and swinging himself to the ground.

He came round to her and held up his hands. Without hesitation she slid down into his arms, saw a spark kindle in his eyes as he looked down into her flushed face, and felt his lips brush lightly over hers before he released her to gather up the horses' reins and tether them to a branch.

He came back to her, walking slowly, smiling at her. She remembered how envious she had been lately of anyone he smiled at, any woman who could make him look kindly at her. She wanted to smile back, but her own face felt stiff, frozen by a sudden shyness.

A faint line appeared between his brows as he approached her. He said, "You look very grave. It was a very small kiss, after all...The winner's laurel, Damaris. Do you grudge me that?"

"No," she said. "But you were not the winner. We were neck and neck—"

"By a nose, I swear!" he said, a smile curving his lips again.

She shook her head. "A tie!"

"Stubborn creature! Very well, I concede a tie. Are you going to claim back your trophy?"

She shook her head and turned from him to hide her warm cheeks.

"A pity." The smile remained in his voice. He stood beside her, apparently admiring the sweep of the view before them, the distant slopes of blue-misted hills, the nearer folds of green rolling gently down to a long, flat sward broken by clumps of spreading old trees.

In a more sober tone, Grenville said, "Don't be afraid of me, I shan't kiss you again."

"I'm not afraid," she said, her eyes still on the distant hills. "Last night—I did not mean what you thought."

Rather carefully he said, "If you mean that you were willing to—oblige me from a sense of duty—"

Vehemently she shook her head. "No!"

"No?" He took her hands in his and turned her to face him, but she kept her head bowed. She had thought he would understand her words, but it was plain it did not, entirely. "Then tell me—"

"I did not mean to compare you with *him*," she said haltingly. "You are not like Sir Walter."

She broke away from him, unable to continue at that moment, flooded with old, remembered guilts and griefs, afraid of pouring into Grenville's ears the whole sad, sordid story of her first marriage, for he was kind this morning and too easy to confide in.

As though he could read her mind, he came to her side again, and said, "What *was* he like, then? Did he treat you badly?"

"Oh, no!" she exclaimed with a hint of bitter sorrow. "He was very kind—at first. Too generous—did not your friend Mr. Ibster tell you that?"

"Not my friend," Grenville objected. "What do you mean—*at first?*"

"Only that—at first he liked to spend his money on me, to buy me things. And later—later he implied that it was because I had demanded extravagant clothes and jewelry that he was short of money for the estate. I *had not* done so, I swear it! My aunt knows that I remonstrated with him—I never asked him to buy things for me—it was his own way of—of buying me—my affections. And I tried not to show that I found it impossible to return his regard—I *did* try! But he guessed at my repugnance, and it made him angry with me, and bad-tempered."

"Yes," Grenville murmured, and she realized that he might feel a certain sympathy with Sir Walter. She had told him, too, that she could not bear his touch.

"I should not discuss him with you," she said.

"Why not? The man is dead, nothing can hurt him, now."

She shook her head. "I was a bad wife to him when he was alive. I can at least honor his memory."

"Your sentiments do you honor," Grenville said. "But *I* am your husband now. Damaris—I know that your first marriage has left a mark on you. And I don't believe that you were a bad wife—merely a young one, with too little knowledge of life to know what you were doing when you accepted a man who should have known better than to offer for you."

"He was being kind," she said swiftly.

"Kind!" Grenville exclaimed. "You can say that?"

"You cannot understand," she said. "You have never been in need, as we were, and he was generous. I gave him poor payment for it."

"His generosity would have been more impressive

203

to *my* mind, if he had not attempted to exact repayment of that particular nature."

"Is that worse than the vengeance that *you* threatened me with, if I failed to marry you?"

"*Touché.* No, not worse. But perhaps more hypocritical."

They had begun walking along the edge of the wood, scuffing leaves with their feet. "Would you have carried out that threat?" she asked him in a low voice.

For a few moments he kept strolling beside her in silence. Then he said, "Perhaps. I was angry enough to threaten anything. When it came to the point—who knows?"

Damaris stopped, biting on her lip. Something about that dreadful night teased her brain. She had tried not to think about it since it happened, tried to block out the memory of Grenville's eyes blazing with anger, his face a mask of furious contempt.

He touched her arm and said gently, "It's over. Don't fret about it, now."

"Was it only to save your pride?" she asked him.

"No. Oh, I told myself that was the reason. I believed that was what you had planned—to see my pride dragged in the dust."

"It was not!" she denied vehemently. "It was *not* that!"

She knew he was waiting for her to explain her motives, but the implications still scared her. She was beginning to think that he was not convinced after all that she had planned all along to jilt him. But he had not declared what his feelings were, and she was groping for a way through the welter of suspicion, anger and misunderstanding that had divided them.

And still, in the recesses of her mind, lived a haunting memory of Sir Walter's sneering recriminations, his belittling of her because of her inadequacy, the bitter disappointment that he did not try to hide when she failed to provide him with the heir which in the afternoon of his life, he had decided was necessary to him. For years she had lived with his reproaches in her ears, reiterating her failure as a wife, as a woman, her inability to fulfill any of the functions expected of her.

She turned to hurry back to the horses, ignoring Grenville as he softly spoke her name.

She had to wait when she reached the mare for Grenville to help her onto its back, and when he came up she turned to him with a look of appeal that brought him up short. He stood looking at her for a second or two before placing his hands on her narrow waist and lifting her into the saddle. He gathered her reins up for her, but did not put them in her hands immediately. She looked down at his face and saw him smiling at her a little quizzically. "You won't always run away, Damaris," he said. "I made sure of that."

"What do you mean?"

"I mean that you are my wife," he said with deliberation, adding quickly as he saw the swift alarm in her face. "Don't look like that!"

He put the reins in her hands, closing his fingers over hers. "Trust me!" he said.

They rode back to the stables in silence that was filled with unspoken thoughts. Damaris knew that Grenville was trying to influence her, *willing* her to talk to him, to trust him with her confidence. But she was not yet ready. She had to think. She needed time, just a little more time.

As they dismounted, he said, "Will you ride with me tomorrow?"

Tomorrow. Was that time enough? she wondered. And if it was not, how long would he be willing to wait?

Again he seemed to have read her thoughts. As they entered the house, he took her hand, kissed her fingers lightly and said, putting a gentle finger on the small, worried frown on her brow, "Don't worry, there is plenty of time."

Apprised of the plan to have a house party for Christmas, Mrs. Newington was ecstatic. Nothing could have been more agreeable. Already her head was full of plans for a full program of delights. Damaris and Grenville, entering willynilly into these, found themselves smiling at each other in not unkind amusement, and Damaris, at least, had difficulty removing her gaze from his.

She had a half-frightening and half-delicious sense of impending crisis, a definite premonition of something coming to an inevitable climax. And Grenville, as though aware of her nervous state, spoke quietly to her, smiled often, and seemed determined to do all he could to reassure her.

As she sat with Mrs. Newington in the drawing room after dinner, her aunt said comfortably, "It's easy to see Lord Brandsley dotes on you, my dear. I knew you would be happy with him!"

"Dotes—?" she said faintly. "Oh, Aunt Tabby, no!"

"Of course he does. Don't tell me you don't know it—why, it's plainer than a pikestaff."

Damaris forced herself to remember that Aunt Tabitha saw what she wished to see, and reserve judgement. It seemed to her that Grenville did feel for her something warmer than he had allowed her to believe in the first weeks of their marriage. He seemed willing to believe that her reasons for trying to avoid the marriage had not been those he had hastily and bitterly assumed, and she was hopeful now—more than hopeful—that if she told the truth, he would believe her.

She must look at things calmly and rationally, not shy away from unpleasant thoughts as she had been doing, driven by fear and heartbreak. She had not been thinking rationally that night that Grenville had caught up with her and forced her to return with him to London. Now she would go back over that nightmare, with hope to sustain her, and try to make sense of it.

Grenville had, of course, been very angry. He had believed the worst possible construction he could have put on her flight, and yes, his pride had been flicked on the raw, making him angry and violent. But he had now admitted that pride was not the only reason he had wanted her back. He had *wanted* to marry her, enough to threaten to dishonor her if she refused, enough—yes—*enough to deprive himself of the opportunity of fathering an heir to his title and estate.*

There was the source of her hope. He had given her his word, and whatever else he had done to her, his word would remain sacred. Her mind went back to an earlier source of puzzlement, and now she told herself, *of course* he must have had some notion—he must have known, after all, how long she had been married to Sir Walter.... Perhaps, in spite of Sir Walter, in spite of Lady Crawley, Grenville would not consider his marriage fatally flawed if it did not produce an heir.

At the stables the following morning, he was before her, with the two horses saddled and waiting, and her heart leaped at the smile of greeting he bestowed on her before lifting her into the saddle.

For a while they rode silently, drinking in the morning, not fast but in perfect accord. Grenville led the way to the wood where they had walked the day before, but this time he took a narrow path between the trees, leading her to a quiet, leaf-strewn glade within the great old trees.

He took her down into his arms, and with his fingers resting lightly on her hips, said, "Well, my wife?"

"I must—ask you something," she said. "Will you tell me, please, what Mr. Ibster said to you about me?"

Grenville frowned. "Is that necessary?"

"I think so. If I know what he said, I can tell you whether or not it was true. I expect that some of it was true, and you will always wonder which parts you should believe—at least let me tell you myself—then you may decide."

"Very well." He took away his hands, and almost curtly said, "He told me that your husband had accused you of making him poor—you told me about that. That you had become cold to him when he stopped buying you every trinket you asked for, and refused him—"

"Refused—?"

"Refused to give him an heir." Grenville's voice had gone harsh. "I should not have believed him," he said. "Don't mind it—"

"But you did believe it, didn't you?" she asked painfully. "You did believe it, *then*."

"Yes—but not now, my darling! Not now."

But now it is too late, her mind said. At the same time, she heard herself speaking the words she knew Grenville was waiting for. "It is not true. None of it is true. He—Mr. Ibster—tried once to make love to me, in my husband's absence. Mr. Westburne intervened.

It was difficult for him, because he is a shy man, and Mr. Ibster tried to belittle him. Mr. Westburne stood his ground, and I have admired him since that time, and honored him. I think that since then Mr. Ibster has disliked us both. I am sure that he increased my husband's—Sir Walter's—resentment of me."

"Thank you for telling me," he said. "Although I already knew most of this."

"How did you know?"

"Mostly by guessing, but my guesses were confirmed by your inestimable Mr. Westburne." He smiled at her evident surprise. "Why do you imagine I have been cultivating that gentleman?"

She shook her head, bewildered.

"Damaris," he said, his hand reaching up to touch his fingers to her cheek. "Once before, you began to trust in me, I think. Do you recall the day that Aslett sent you flowers—the day you kissed me?"

Flushing, she nodded.

"Later," he said, "You told me you had attempted to *overcome your repugnance* to my touch. Were you pretending, that day?"

Faintly she shook her head. His hand came under her chin, lifting her face so that his eyes could look with a kind of tender ruthlessness into hers. *"No?"* he asked softly.

Damaris whispered, "No."

He took a quick, short breath, his hands moving until they cupped her head between them, his fingers still infinitely gentle. "But after that—" he said, and his face darkened with the memory, "—after that I frightened you. My God! I *deliberately* frightened you. I was so afraid of losing you, I was desperate, and there seemed no other way. I was a brute—*I*, who had sworn to be patient—I, who *knew* what your feelings were—none better! Can you ever forgive me for that?"

"Oh, please!" she cried, her hands going up to clasp at his and hold them, turning her cheek into his palm. "You were angry—too angry to realize what you were doing—"

"Oh, no!" Grenville said. "I knew—all too well—what I was doing. I was too angry to *care*—yes, that!

But not too angry to know! I have regretted it since—deeply, painfully!"

"And—the other?" she asked. "Did you regret your promise to me, also?"

The black self-accusation left his face, and was replaced by a rueful half-smile, with an odd trace of embarrassment lurking behind his eyes. "Must I be truthful?" he asked her.

She gave a faintly puzzled, hesitant smile back. "If you please," she said.

"You will think me a coxcomb," he said. "My darling, I have to confess that when I gave you my word not to insist on claiming my marital rights, *unless your sentiments changed,* I was confident that I could bring about that change. Even when I was furiously angry with you, I could not stop wanting you, needing you—and that in itself sometimes made me angry. I could not live with you and not want to make love to you."

"Then—" Damaris stirred, moved back from him. "Then, when you said it was to be a *mariage blanc,* you didn't mean it? You did not intend it to be so?"

"Not for long," he admitted. "But I swore to give you time, never to force you."

White-faced, she said, "An unconsummated marriage can be annulled, can't it?"

Blankly, he said, "Annulled?" Then he said harshly, "If you want to punish me, Damaris, try another tack."

She shook her head. "I don't want to punish you. Your pride need not suffer. I don't—I shall not object to confessing that I refused to consummate our marriage."

"You will do no such thing!"

"I will!" she cried. "It's best—"

"No!" He reached for her purposefully, and though she tried to evade him, she was soon pulled ruthlessly into his arms and held there.

"You promised—" she gasped. "You said you would not force me!"

"I will not force you." But his hand under her chin brought up her mouth to meet his, and his arms were a warm, tempting prison about her body. His kiss was at first carefully coaxing and gentle, but when her lips quivered into an unwilling response, his mouth became firm and passionate. She lay quiet in his arms when he stopped kissing her, and two tears escaped from her closed eyes. A finger flicked them away, and he said, "Now—no more talk of annulment, hmm?"

"You don't understand," she said, shaking her head in despair. "I'm barren! I cannot give you an heir to Louth Hall, I cannot give you children!"

There was a curiously blank quality in his silence. Then he said, "Does it matter? *So* much?"

As her eyes flew open, he said, "I'm sorry, my darling. I suppose it is important to a woman. You see, I *have* an heir—Lindo. Will you mind so much, if you don't give me a son to snatch the title from my cousin?"

"Do you mean—that *you* will not mind?" she asked blankly.

"I expect I should, but the fact is, I thought I should never marry, and that Lindo would inherit—he is a Despard, after all. I hardly gave the matter a thought—"

"But—Lady Crawley thought—she said—"

"What did she say? I'll wring her neck!"

"No—no, you must not blame her! It was not to *me,* but she spoke in my hearing, and she believed that something she had said to you had put the thought of marrying into your head, that you were determined to get an heir before it was too late."

"I *will* wring her neck!" Brandsley exclaimed wrathfully. "Of all the impertinent stupidities! And did it not occur to you, you absurd girl, that if I had been anxious to provide myself with heirs, I would have married some healthy, simpering miss with wide hips years ago, and fathered a tribe of strapping sons on her!"

"Grenville!"

He laughed. "My apologies, Lady Brandsley, but if I must shock you to make you call me by my name, I shall have to do it often. Must I tell you that the only thing that made me think of marriage was the thought of your marrying someone else—! *That* I could not have borne."

"Is that true?" she asked, still afraid to believe. "That you had not thought of marriage before?"

"Oh, once—a long time ago. I fancied myself in love in my greentime, and would have married her, if she had not run off with someone else. For which I give thanks daily."

She was looking at him gravely, and putting a finger to the twist at the corner of his mouth, she said, "She hurt you."

His hand caught at hers, his lips pressed into her palm. "Not as much as you did," he said. "I know I was a brute, when we first met, that I wronged you and insulted you—but what a revenge you took! Was it necessary to let me give you my heart, only to jilt me practically at the altar?"

Hurt, she pulled away from him. "You cannot still believe that! It was not planned like that—only after I heard Lady Crawley talking—don't you understand why I had to do it?"

He looked thunderstruck. "You mean because of this *nonsense* about giving me a son? But you let me accuse you—all those lies you told me—why not the truth?"

"I could not tell you the truth," she said. "You were too honorable a man to reproach me with cheating you, to repudiate the engagement."

"Rubbish!" he said forcefully. "Surely you must have realized that I loved you too much for it to matter?"

Damaris shook her head. "I was not certain of your heart," she confessed.

He frowned. "Even though I offered you marriage? Could you doubt me, after that?"

"I did not know," she said. "Do you recall that once you said you were not in love with me, but that you— you—"

"That I wanted you," he said calmly. "At the time, I also said I was not offering you marriage. I thought you would understand, when I did so, that my feelings had undergone a change."

"You—never said so."

"I must confess my pride balked at putting it into words. You see, I was very conscious of your victory, that you had accepted my challenge, and won. *I* had capitulated, thrown my heart at your feet. But you— I could never be sure if you had taken me at my word, accepted my title, my consequence, the comfort I could give you. I hoped to make you love me—but I could never be sure. And when you ran away—I thought I knew, then, that you had never loved me. It was the blackest day of my life."

"But I do love you—I do!"

He took her outstretched hands in his and pulled her close to him once more. "Yes," he said. "I believe you do, undeserving though I am. Were you miserable when you left me—?"

"Terribly!" she whispered against his shoulder.

"Little fool! How *could* you think that I cared more for nonexistent sons, than I did for you? How could you put me through such hell, for *that?*"

"I'm sorry! You see—" Incoherently, she tried to explain her own grief and confusion, the obtrusive memories from her first marriage, the terrible revival of all her feelings of inadequacy and uncertainty.

He let her pour it all out, stroking her hair, pressing his lips to her temple when she had finished, wiping the starting tears from her eyes with a softly whispered, "My poor darling! How could any man have used you so ill? I promise I will make it up to you."

"Will you?" She smiled at him mistily and with a hint of mischief. "It will take you a lifetime, sir, to atone for Sir Walter's sins as well as your own!"

"Is that to remind me not to throw the first stone?" he asked ruefully. "I'm afraid I deserve that. If you are to begin enumerating my sins—"

"I fear they are too numerous to mention—"

"Baggage!"

"How dare you, sir!" Damaris cried in mock indignation.

Grenville laughed, and suddenly bent and lifted her high into his arms.

"My beautiful baggage," he said, as she cried out softly, clutching his lapels. "I am about to shock you again."

In a few strides he had reached a small, mossy hollow under a canopy of leaves, and laid her down on its softness, reclining on his elbow beside her, his other hand still on her shoulder.

"My lord!" she said. "What are you doing?"

He smiled down at her. "Nothing you will not like, I promise! But I see that I shall have to be a little more drastic!"

He bent to kiss her, and then lifted his head to look inquiringly down into her face.

"Grenville—?" she said.

"Yes, my darling?"

"I—nothing." She looked back at him shyly, then suddenly lifted her hands to wind her arms about his neck. "Oh, Grenville!"

chapter fourteen

The Christmas festivities at Louth traditionally began with a party at the Hall for the farm workers and
their families. Damaris was a little anxious over the
preparations, but she need not have worried. The nov-
elty of having a mistress at the Hall would have more
than compensated for any deficiencies. Her presence
gave the party an added zest, and her husband's dependents went home filled with satisfaction as well as
dumplings and porter.

The Rathbones having accepted the invitation to
spend their Christmas in Norfolk, Charlotte and Lindo
enjoyed themselves immensely helping to decorate the
great hall and the dining room, even venturing out in
a light snowfall to assist in the dragging in of the Yule
log, which set up a merry blaze, warming the faded
tapestries into colorful life, and inviting the party to
congregate about its cheery heat.

On Christmas Day itself they dined on famed Norfolk turkeys and plum pudding and afterwards indulged in a noisy game of lottery, in which even Lady Crawley took part, unbending so far as to engage in a laughing contretemps with her host, over points.

The following day the whole party drove out in the afternoon, well wrapped against a cold wind, and in the evening a few neighborhood families joined them, six couples being mustered for dancing before a late supper, with Mrs. Rathbone playing lively country dances and waltzes for the enjoyment of the young people.

During an interval in their exertions, Grenville was standing by his wife, idly watching his cousin and Miss Rathbone as they argued amicably as to what music should next be requested. "Do you know, I believe that pair will do very well," he said. "I have sometimes wondered if they are too much alike, but Charlotte has brought out the best in Lindo. And she is in high bloom—much prettier than I have ever seen her."

"Charlotte tells me the wedding is set for May. You don't still think your cousin too young to marry?"

"Perhaps he is, a little. But he has found a girl who I think will make him happy. And could *I* advise anyone against entering into a state which has made me blissfully happy?"

His eyes teased her and she smiled at him. "I'm glad of that."

His hand closed over hers. "And you—? Have I made you happy, as I promised?"

"Need you ask me that?" As his hand tightened on her fingers, she said softly, "You have shown me a country I never knew existed. A place where love has cast out fear. I have been released from a dark prison, into a garden full of sunshine and flowers. How can you *ask* if I am happy?"

Lord Edgely and Charlotte took the floor, and the pianist began to play a lilting waltz. Grenville said, "Do you remember the first time we waltzed together, in London? You were cool and stiff with me..."

"And *you* were cold and suspicious!" she said.

He smiled down at her. "Do you think we might do better, now?"

He took her into the circle of his arm, and as they began the steps, he said, "You danced gracefully, even so. But I think it was when you laughed that I began to fall in love with you."

"Nonsense!" she teased. "You disliked me intensely!"

"Not at all. I only *wanted* to! Instead, I found myself in full accord with Lindo. He said you were the most beautiful woman in the room. He was right." He grinned. "So I decided to cut him out."

A shadow crossed her face, and he said swiftly, "I know I told you—told *myself*—that it was for another reason—a contemptible reason—that I pursued you, but the truth was, I couldn't help myself. Your attraction for me was so powerful it overcame even the dreadful suspicions I had of you. I know you have forgiven me them—but does the memory still have the power to hurt you?"

He looked concerned, and she smiled to reassure him. "No, of course not."

"It is all in the past, now."

"Yes," she said. But he had stirred up a faint memory of bitter hurt, and she said, keeping her voice light and teasing, "Well—I expect your betting friends would have been surprised that you went so far as actually to marry me, to save your cousin from the same fate."

"My—*betting* friends?" he repeated sharply.

Sorry that she had brought up a matter best forgotten, Damaris shook her head. "It's of no consequence now. I should not have mentioned it."

"I think you should," he said curtly. "Am I to understand that you think *I* made you the subject of a wager?"

She had not seen that look on his face for weeks. Nervously, she said, "Was it not so?"

"No!"

Damaris drooped a little with relief, and his arm about her tightened. In a fierce undertone he said, "Who told you such a thing?"

She shook her head. "He must have been mistaken."

"Who?"

"What does it matter?" she said. "It was untrue."

"But you believed it!" he said.

Thinking he was accusing her, she flared a little. "As *you* believed all the untruths you heard of *me!*" she reminded him. "Knowing what was your opinion of me, are you truly surprised at my believing it? I knew that it was true you were dangling after me only to stop me marrying Lindo. You told me so yourself—and was it not true that you—that you boasted of it at your club?"

"Certainly not!" he said coldly.

"Then how did it become common knowledge?" she demanded.

"It was *not* common knowledge!" he snapped.

The music stopped as she turned her head from him, biting on her lip. She murmured some excuse and walked away from him to speak briefly to a footman who had entered the room with a tray of lemonade, and shortly afterwards left the room.

Grenville was only stopped from following her by his duty as a host, and was relieved to see her return ten minutes later holding a pack of cards which apparently accounted for her absence, and looking quite calm and untroubled.

However, when the guests had gone and only the houseparty remained having a hot brandy cup before retiring for the night, she had begun to look a trifle pale and tired, and when he visited her room afterwards to find the maid just leaving, he was concerned at the shadows beneath her eyes.

"You have been tiring yourself!" he exclaimed. "If I had known how much work it would be for you, I should never have suggested this house party."

Damaris laughed, sounding a little strained. "That is nonsense, Brandsley! Mrs. Bingham has far more strain than I, and you have an army of servants. I'm only a little fagged, that is all—with dancing and too much enjoyment, if the truth is known. I shall have a good night's sleep and be as right as a trivet in the morning."

"Ah—a hint, I see!"

Damaris colored a little. "It was nothing of the sort, my lord."

"I *thought* you were offended with me. Now I'm sure of it."

"I am not offended—"

"Of course you are—and with reason, I'm afraid."

He caught her hands in his, and said, "I didn't mean to snap at you. I expect it was my own guilty conscience that made me do it, and I would rather bite out my tongue than hurt you by it. The fact is, I never *boasted* of my infamous scheme in company, but I did once say something to a friend which I realize now—too late— was foolishly indiscreet. It could perhaps have led to the story that you heard. I must own I was vexed that you had heard any such thing, more vexed that you believed it. But I cannot blame you."

"I should have known better than to believe it," she said. "And I should not have brought up the subject tonight. That was ill-judged of me. As you said, it is all in the past, and should be forgotten. I don't blame you any more, truly. It was only that—*that* did rankle, a little. I do feel better, knowing it was not true."

"And forgive me for my damnable temper?"

"You know I do. In any case, I believe I ripped up at you first, is that not so? I have been a naggy wife to you, of late."

"Have you? I had thought you sometimes a little *distraite,* but not *naggy,* my love! *Are* these guests and parties too much for you? Only tell me, and I'll send them all packing."

Damaris laughed. "No, you shall not! Your aunt, for one, would be mortally offended. How can you be so inhospitable?"

"Easily; I won't have your comfort cut up."

"Oh, Grenville!" she said, her eyes softening into tears.

"Goosecap!" he called her teasingly, as he kissed away the salty shimmer. "You *are* tired. Go to bed, and don't get out of it before nuncheon tomorrow! I will make your excuses to our guests."

She might have confided in him then, if she had not been afraid his concern for her would have led him to ruthlessly expel their visitors to insure her proper rest and care. As it was, she hugged her secret to her until the new year had begun, and Mrs. Newington and the physician had confirmed her own hopes.

He received the news so quietly that at first she was disappointed. Then she saw the deep glow in his gray eyes, and gave him her hands, wincing a little at the strength of his grip.

He apologized immediately and released them, and she gave a small laugh and flung herself against his chest, so that he was obliged to put his arms about her, so gently that she laughed again and said, "I shan't *break,* Grenville. I know it is proper to call it a *delicate condition,* but the truth is I never felt stronger in my life!"

He laughed a little unsteadily, and she looked into his face and said, "You *are* glad, aren't you, Grenville?"

"Yes. More glad than I ever thought I could be. But I'm terrified for you, too. You are going to have the very best of care, I promise you."

"Will Lindo mind?" she asked a little anxiously. "If it *is* a boy, an heir?"

"Lindo will not mind a bit. He will be almost as delighted as I am, and will tease me unmercifully about becoming a *family man.*"

"Then I hope," she said, "that it *is* a boy."

By the time her lying-in took place, the excitement of Napoleon's escape from Elba, the drama of the Hundred Days when he was at large again, and the glory and the bloodshed of Waterloo were all over. At Louth, in spite of the upheavals that shook the world outside, she had felt throughout her pregnancy that she and her child lived in a safe, impregnable cocoon where nothing could harm them. She had refused to go to London, watching with hope and happy peace the spring unfold about the Hall, the summer burgeon in the fields, and felt at one with Nature's world of abundance.

And now her child was born, the child she had once thought she could never have. She insisted on holding the tiny bundle in her arms when her husband was allowed into the room at last to see her.

When he stopped in the doorway, his face gaunt with

strain, his eyes, clouded with anxiety, meeting hers across the room, she said, holding out her hand, "You have been worried—and you must not! Your big-hipped, simpering miss could not have done better, Grenville!"

He smiled at that, and came over to her, gripping her hand tightly and saying nothing.

"They told you it is a daughter?" she asked, a little anxiously. "You don't mind—that it is not a boy?"

He shook his head. "It was you who hoped for a son," he said at last. "Are you disappointed?"

"No. Not if *you* are content. And there may be more—"

"I'm very content," he assured her. "And of course there will be more, if that is what you want." He looked down, and touched a finger to the baby's petal soft cheek. "I would be happy if they were all girls, and looked like their mother."

Damaris smiled. "A house full of women?" she asked. "Should you like that?"

"Why not—? I said, didn't I, that they should all be like you?"

"You always did have a pretty way with a compliment, my lord."

"And *you* always had a mighty provocative way of calling me *my lord*. You think yourself safe, now, no doubt. But when you are up and about again, we will see if you dare to tease me!"

"Oh, yes—you love to threaten me, I know! But do you know," she said softly, "I have the oddest conviction that so long as I am in your arms I am perfectly safe?"

His arms were gently encircling both her and their child, and he smiled down at her and laid his cheek against hers.

"You are," he said. "My own darling—you are perfectly safe in my heart."

ABOUT THE AUTHOR

Claire Lorel's ancestry on her mother's side can be traced as far back as the time of William the Conqueror. Later descendants of the Norman who accompanied William and fought at the Battle of Hastings became land owners in Norfolk, where the main branch of the family still occupies a magnificent moated manor house, parts of which date back to the 13th century. Various members of the family appear as minor figures in historical records, including one lady who was renowned both for her beauty and for her virtue at the glittering and licentious court of Charles II.

Always interested in history, Claire Lorel enjoyed writing from an early age, and her first short story was published in a woman's magazine when she was sixteen. Now married and with a teenage family, she spends most of her time writing full-length novels. She enjoys historical research, and also likes to read novels written in the eighteenth and nineteenth centuries, confessing that she often finds them more entertaining and satisfying than most modern fiction. She has a special love for Charlotte Brontë and her sister Emily, and acquired a "late but enduring" appreciation of Jane Austen after finding her "dull and boring" at school. She also reads widely in other fields, and likes to come home from the library with half-a-dozen books on as many different subjects.

Let COVENTRY Give You
A Little Old-Fashioned Romance

CURRENT BESTSELLERS
from POPULAR LIBRARY

GREAT ADVENTURES IN READING